PRAISE

The Wilderness Between Us

"There are some books that demand to be written, and from page one of *The Wilderness Between Us*, I recognized this groundbreaking novel as one of them. Penny Haw juxtaposes physical and psychological suspense in a riveting story, as we join the forest and its beautifully described flora and fauna in bearing witness to the transformation of the book's fully drawn cast of human characters. Haw's writing is crisp, unflinching, and ultimately a vehicle for opening the reader's heart to difficult realities we cannot afford to ignore. In her deft hands, anorexia is portrayed as a mental illness and not a 'human failing,' and the often oppressive nature of marriage is dealt with as an opportunity for healing and liberation. As one character reflects on finding the truth about her relationship with her husband: *How was it possible that putting the wilderness between them could bring such clarity?* The book answers that question and so much more. Highly recommended."

—**JOYCE YARROW,** author of *Zahara and the Lost Books of Light* and *Sandstorm*

"A thrilling read fraught with the tension of unravelling relationships, betrayal, broken bones, and callously revealed secrets . . . but is love enough for Derek, Faye, Geoffrey, Michelle, or Clare to save themselves and walk away from the churning waters, twisted undergrowth, and resigned grip of lifelong friendships? Will they seek to find each other, or will they choose to rather center themselves? You'll have to read to find out."

—**TRACY GOING**, award-winning television and news anchor, and author of *Brutal Legacy*

"In *The Wilderness Between Us*, Penny Haw transports the reader to the mountains of South Africa with vivid, engrossing descriptions. The novel is a gripping story about how two emotionally fragile women become separated from their hiking group and discover strength within themselves as they fight to survive. Fans of Cheryl Strayed's *Wild* should definitely add Haw's book to their TBR list."

—**DIANE BARNES,** author of *More Than*

"Penny Haw immerses us in the rugged wilderness on every level. I resonated with the landscape, as well as with the unfolding drama in the group of old friends. Haw's charming writing and deep connection with nature are coupled with an understanding of how humans tick. She skilfully intertwines the challenging physical journey with the inner worlds of her characters. Many demons are faced, and Haw does not shy away from confronting them. The unlikely friendship that develops between two of the women is deftly handled. Haw nudges truths to the surface and brings the sometimes-chilling wilderness right into our hearts."

—**GAIL GILBRIDE,** author of *Under the African Sun*

"*The Wilderness Between Us* is a well-crafted tale of friends stranded on a hiking trip by an unexpected storm. Set against the backdrop of a vibrant forest, Haw's protagonists shine. The novel alternates between the characters' current-day conflicts and the backstories that form them. *The Wilderness Between Us* includes the stories of domineering Derek; his wife, Faye, who grows to realize her inner strength; his ex-girlfriend Michelle; Michelle's husband, Geoffrey; and their daughter, Clare. Clare's journey with anorexia is wrought with honesty, empathy, and ultimately, optimism."

—**CAROL VAN DEN HENDE,** award-winning author of *Goodbye,* Orchid

"This interesting and highly readable drama centers around Clare, the daughter, who has anorexia, and Faye, the wife of Derek, whose own insecurities manifest themselves in the psychological abuse he bestows on Faye; he uses a version of the 'gaslighting' technique, lying to her about things she has said and done in order to make her doubt her own emotional stability. Clare's story is most compelling: how the anorexia began, the reasons behind it, the way in which it took hold, and the repercussions. Clare's self-awareness makes her likable, and I thought the whole subject was dealt with sensitively and intelligently, while still making for a good story in which I was totally engrossed."

—**TERRY TYLER**, author of twenty-two novels, including the dystopian Operation Galton trilogy

"Set during a trip into rough South African terrain, The *Wilderness Between Us* is a compelling story about the consequences of delusions, warped self-images, and egos gone awry. It's told with empathy and a great deal of suspense. Well worth your time."

—**B. LYNN GOODWIN**, owner of Writer Advice and author of *Talent* and *Never Too Late: From Wannabe to Wife at 62*

"Author Penny Haw has created a wonderful story with the South African outback as backdrop. Clare, who suffers from an eating disorder, is asked to take the place of her mother on a weeklong hike with her father and his close friends. During the trek, Clare confronts her demons with the help of her parents' friend Faye, who is dealing with her own difficulties. The story is wonderfully written, the reader feeling as if they are in the wilds of Africa. I was captivated from the first page, wanting to know more. Having a daughter with an eating disorder myself, I found a greater understanding of the sickness. I would recommend this book to anyone who loves a book filled with fast-paced prose, intrigue, and morality."

—**CHRISTOPHER BOWRON,** author of *Devil in the Grass* and *The Society of Necessities*

The Wilderness Between Us
by Penny Haw

Published by

◤köehlerbooks™

3705 Shore Drive
Virginia Beach, VA 23455
800-435-4811
www.koehlerbooks.com

The Wilderness Between Us

PENNY HAW

VIRGINIA BEACH
CAPE CHARLES

For Jan-Lucas, who never says,
"We're not going to talk about your book again, are we?"

Author's Note

Have we forgotten
that wilderness is not a place,
but a pattern of soul
where every tree, every bird and beast
is a soul maker?

"Wilderness" by Ian McCallum

None of the friends who hiked through the Tsitsikamma with me, not even she who awoke with a migraine, will recognise themselves in this story. They're not here. While the seed was planted as we walked, the tree grew up and out and into something unrecognisable. The trail exists, of course, and I urge you, if you have the chance, to tread its paths, raise your eyes and be elated. With its mountains, rivers, forests, flowers, birds and animals, the Tsitsikamma will soothe your soul—even if you had not yet registered its call to be calmed. You might note though, that the route and places I describe have been rearranged for the purpose of the story. This is not a guide book. Neither does it profess to offer medical counsel. The exploration of anorexia is loosely based on my own experience and, while I hope it throws some light on the pain and crushing shame that can accompany the condition, I am not a professional in the subject and make no claims as such. So indeed, this book is not a manual of any sort. It's a story about people and the wilderness, which "is not a place, but a pattern of soul."

—**Penny Haw**

Glossary

Aardvark—medium-sized, burrowing and nocturnal mammal native to Africa, the only living species of the prehistoric Tubulidentata order and its name is Afrikaans for "earth pig."

Bakkie—a light truck or pickup truck.

Bloukrans—blue cliff.

Boomslang—Afrikaans for "tree snake," a highly venomous, tree-living snake.

Braai—barbeque.

Buchu—a South African shrub with aromatic leaves.

CPR—cardiopulmonary resuscitation.

Caracal—medium-sized wild cat, native to Africa, with long, tufted ears.

Dagga—word used in parts of southern Africa to describe cannabis.

Donga—a gully formed by eroding action of water.

Duiker—small, brown antelope, native to sub-Saharan Africa.

Ericas—woody fynbos plants with small, narrow leaves and various flowers.

Fundi—expert, aficionado.

Fynbos—natural shrubs and vegetation occurring in Western and Eastern Cape in South Africa.

Genet—small, catlike African carnivore.

Goggas—South African term for any kind of small creature that crawls.

Grootkloof—big valley.

Heuningbos—honey bush.

Hadeda—Ibis bird native to sub-Saharan Africa and named for the loud calls it makes in flight.

Knysna loerie—a large turaco bird found in the forests of southern and eastern South Africa.

Lapa—communal cooking and entertainment area, typical of southern African camping and safari sites.

Lekker—South African word for good or pleasant.

Meneer—Afrikaans for "mister."

Naartjies—South African name for small, loose-skinned mandarin oranges.

Pelargonium—shrubby plant with fragrant leaves.

Poffertjes—small, fluffy pancakes popular in the Netherlands.

Protea—South African flowering plant.

Provita—savoury South African biscuit or cracker.

Quiver tree—a tall, branching species of succulent plant, indigenous to southern Africa, and also known as the Kokerboom.

Ratel—honey badger, a mammal native to Africa and Asia, which is named for a South African infantry fighting vehicle because of its tenacity.

Res—another way of saying residence, typically when referring to a university residence.

Restios—reed-like plant, which is considered part of South African fynbos.

Skink—a type of lizard.

Staffie—short for Staffordshire Bull Terrier, which is a short-haired terrier of medium size.

Tog bag—sports bag.

Tsitsikamma—comes from southern African Khoekhoe language: *tse-tsesa*, means "clear," and *gami*, means "water." This compound word refers to the clear water of the Tsitsikamma River, which runs through the Tsitsikamma National Park, a protected area on the Garden Route of South Africa.

Uni—short for university.

Varsity—another South African way of saying university.

Veld—open, uncultivated country or grassland in southern Africa.

Vygie—means "small fig" in Afrikaans and refers to a species of succulent flowering plants from southern Africa.

Wild Dagga—indigenous species of mint plant found in southern Africa, which typically has a bright orange flower and is known for its medicinal properties that are mildly psychoactive.

One

It was an unusually warm evening for that time of the year in the mountains, which might've been an omen if anyone had thought about it. For years, the friends had discussed the ideal season to do the hike. They'd finally settled on any six days that suited everyone's diary. Even then, they hadn't all been able to make it, which was how Clare came to be there.

With supper over, she sat on the stairs of the three-walled, thatch-roofed lapa, which, typical of southern African campsites, was the hub of the overnight campsite. Stacked on a counter behind her, eight stainless steel plates glistened in time to the coals flickering weakly in the firepit. Clare's aim was to stay out of the way of her father and his friends as they went about whatever it was older people did before bed.

The stone was cool against her legs and the air lightly scented with smoke, resin and damp forest floor. Pine needles hung motionless against the barely lit sky, which was flanked by two peaks rising east and west like tall, craggy sentinels. Bar the thrumming of the nearby stream, the distant *huoo-hoo-hoo* of a wood owl and the occasional crinkle of the cooling embers, the night was quiet.

The party of eight had left the rangers' offices for Heuningbos Hut shortly after ten that morning, trudging up a gravel track onto the mountainside for a few kilometres before following the path into a forest with towering trees and a disorderly understory. From there, the trail cut across large sections of mountain fynbos with plants Clare's father, Geoffrey, had taught her to identify years ago: ericas, restios, protea, daisies, legumes and vygies. The group had trekked through a marshy valley, crossed two rivers and finally climbed a steep hill to Heuningbos Hut. It was, said the information provided, the least strenuous day of the six-day hike and they'd arrived at their accommodation for the night just before the sun slid behind the trees.

"Peaceful, isn't it?"

Clare turned to see Faye looking up at her from the bottom of the stairs. Her dark hair, which had been flecked with grey and cropped in the same short style for as long as Clare remembered, was wet. She'd combed the fringe back, accentuating her heavy eyebrows and lashes, and the deep blue of her eyes.

Geoffrey liked to say that he and Clare's mother, Michelle, had been friends with Faye Mackenzie and her husband, Derek, and the other two couples in the group "since pa fell off the ox-wagon." Michelle, Diane and Derek were at school together and met Geoffrey, Bruce and Helen at university. Bev was most recent recruit and *she'd* been with Helen since Clare was a baby. The couples and their children had holidayed and partied together like family. Even so, it felt strange to Clare to be alone with one of the older generation.

"It is," she said, looking over the trees.

"Everything all right?"

Clare felt a prick of annoyance. "Yes. Thanks. And you?"

"Well, I'm looking forward to a good sleep." Faye laughed quietly. "Tomorrow's going to be a long one."

"I believe so," said Clare.

"Lucky you could come at such short notice."

"Yes."

"Your mom must've been so disappointed."

"She was."

"She and Diane have been trying to organise this trip for years."

Clare got to her feet. "Yes. Well, I'm going to get ready for bed, too. See you in the morning. Sleep well," she said, passing the older woman and making her way to the cabin.

Was her mother, a high court judge, upset about having to miss the hike when one of her cases was prolonged at the last minute? It seemed to Clare that work would always come first for Michelle. If anyone was disappointed it was her father, Geoffrey.

"Surely you can get a delay? I mean, really? We've been planning to do this together for years, decades even. All the organisation that's gone into it…" he'd said when Michelle delivered the news.

He and Clare had been in the kitchen, preparing supper. Clare wished her mother had waited to tell him when her parents were alone. Michelle walked out without replying.

"There's no chance of a delay," she said when she reappeared, heels exchanged for flip-flops, minutes later. She spoke as if she'd never left the room. "Clare can go in my place."

Her daughter and husband stared at her.

Michelle took a bottle of wine from the fridge and smiled at Clare. "Why not? Your interviews only begin the following week. It'll be good . . . fun."

Clare knew her mother had almost said, "good for you." She looked away.

Geoffrey handed Michelle a glass. "So you're certain?"

She bobbed her head. He blinked and turned to Clare. "Come with your old dad and his friends. We'll remind you how lucky you are to be young."

⟡

There was no one in the cabin when Clare slipped in to take a mattress from one of the bunk beds stacked against the walls. She dragged it onto the lawn, stopping mid-yard to look around.

The space that had been cleared for the lapa, hut and bathroom, all of which were fashioned from river stones, wasn't entirely level.

To her left, Clare saw an area buttressed by a short wall. The earth had been flattened as if someone planned to turn it into a flower bed but was beaten to it by the relentless tentacles of buffalo grass. The spot would do. Not only was it flat enough to sleep on without rolling or sliding off the bed, but it was also out of earshot of her father's snoring. Neither was it too close, she hoped, to the low bush on the edge of the forest to pique the curiosity of any creatures that might mosey by during the night. She hauled the mattress into position.

"What do you mean?" Geoffrey had asked when, during the long drive from Cape Town to the mountains, she told him that it was one thing to hike through the Tsitsikamma National Park with her parents' friends, but she wouldn't share the dormitory-style sleeping quarters with them. "That's how it is on these hikes. We'll be sleeping in the same room; not together. You know, like that."

Although Clare pretended not to notice, he was blushing. It began at his neck and swept over his balding crown where two clumps of grey-blonde hair perched like the ear tufts of an owl. Despite being flattened against his head by the Basson's Garden Services cap he wore whenever he was outdoors, the clumps sprung upwards like grass shoots after the first rains. Clare had often tugged them when she was younger. To her, the tufts symbolised who her father was: constant, unpretentious, decent, determined. And, although conversation between them nowadays wasn't as easy as it had been when she was younger, she understood his reticence. They were alike in that sense. Not everything benefitted from discussion. Sometimes it was better to be quiet and work things out on your own.

"I know," she said, thinking about how simultaneously exposed and restricted she'd feel in a shared hut, particularly (but not exclusively) with people twice her age. "I'd just rather be alone. Don't forget, you and Gran were the ones who taught me to enjoy sleeping outside."

"But what if the weather changes suddenly? It does that in the mountains."

"I'll go into the lapa."

Geoffrey grimaced. "I hope the others aren't offended."

She'd looked out of the car window, pulled a tress of hair from behind her ear and curled it around her finger. How could she have forgotten? Her father was concerned about what "the others" might think. She wondered whether her parents had updated their friends about her condition. Whether they, in turn, had speculated about how it would be to have her with them. Had Michelle warned them against watching her at mealtimes?

"They'll get over it," she said, trying to quash her discomfort. "You can tell them that I'm claustrophobic or something. I don't care."

"Or that you hate my snoring. At least that's the truth."

She sniggered.

He glanced at her. It reminded Clare how much her father liked to make her laugh. "The only problem is that then they'll *all* want to sleep elsewhere."

"Ja. True. It's probably best to say nothing."

As she stood at the outdoor tap brushing her teeth, Clare looked up and wished she'd paid more attention to what had, when she was a kid, seemed like never-ending discussions between her father and grandmother about the night sky. On camping trips, the conversations could have been lullabies, easing Clare and her younger siblings, Angus and Linda, to sleep. Almost everything she knew about the natural world, Clare had learned from her father and grandmother. They knew a lot. Especially Gran. If she'd been a more patient kid, Clare could've learned more.

During one of the final outings when the old woman accompanied the family, she described the differences between wilderness and city skies and how they affected the world. Then seven or eight years old, Clare had peevishly scuffed the sand with her bare toes as Gran rattled on about "human light pollution" and how sea turtles and dung beetles relied on "pristine night skies for navigation." Images of lumbering turtles and beetles were one thing, but when Gran started up about how the combination of the darkness and silence was a good time to "contemplate how immense the universe was," Clare had groaned out loud. She was certain that Angus and Linda would've guzzled all the marshmallows by the time she got back to the campfire. The moment Gran gazed upwards, still rambling on, Clare scampered away.

Now, at the tap, Clare tipped back her head as she rinsed her mouth. Was that the Southern Cross? She'd ask her father what had happened to his mother's astronomy books.

"Are you sure you want to sleep out here alone?"

Wearing running shorts and a t-shirt featuring a faded, eighties-style surfing logo, Derek wore no shoes, and his thin legs were pale.

"Yes," said Clare.

"You're not afraid?"

"Why would I be?"

He put his hands on his hips and leaned his long, narrow torso towards her. "Baboons," he whispered. She smelt toothpaste on his breath. "Didn't you hear them barking when we arrived?"

"I did, but they're unlikely to move around at night."

"Ah, because of the leopards," he said, continuing his cartoonish performance. Clare felt embarrassed on his behalf.

"That's a myth," she said. "Leopards rarely prey on baboons. They, the monkeys, move about in large groups and fight back viciously. Anyway, the baboons in this area are not habituated. They're unlikely to approach while we're here."

"Ha! Geoff taught you well."

She gave a half shrug and turned to go, not bothering to say that it was her grandmother, not her father, who had explained the habits of leopards and baboons to her. Derek walked with her.

"It's nice to have you along," he said. "We don't see much of you anymore now that you're all grown up."

Clare didn't respond as she closed her backpack.

He looked around. "You're right. It's lovely out here. Perhaps I'll bring my mattress outside, too."

"Derek?" It was Faye from the doorway of the hut. "Are you coming?"

He hesitated and opened his mouth as if to say something to his wife, but sighed instead.

"Sleep well," he said, walking away.

Clare slid into her sleeping bag and lay on her back, thinking about the day. The pace at which the group walked had surprised her. They were fitter than she'd imagined they'd be. When they stopped, which happened frequently, it wasn't to rest—not obviously, anyway—but rather to drink, snack or remove their boots and soak their feet in the rivers. Mostly though, her father and his friends paused to admire and discuss plants, trees, spoor and the views.

"Glad you came?" he'd asked that afternoon as he'd followed her across a plateau of restios that swayed lazily in the breeze.

"I am," she'd replied, without having to think about it. "I think I can manage six days of this."

Now though, as she sat up and rolled her sweatshirt into a makeshift pillow, Clare was uncertain. She wasn't afraid of sleeping outside but, ever since he had turned up on campus and insisted on taking her out to lunch, Derek unsettled her. She told herself he meant well and cared about her the way her parents cared about his and Faye's son, Zach. They'd all been friends for so long, they were practically family. There was nothing more to it. Even so, she was annoyed by Derek's attention, his comment about the baboons, and at herself for responding to his ridiculousness.

She got up, shone her torch into the cavernous opening of the lapa and followed the light around the raised fire-pit and the large stone and hardwood table, benches and counters. The fire iron stood against the wall alongside a row of tree stumps, which had been sawed and smoothed into simple seats. Ignoring how sooty the heavy rod made her hand, Clare took it, laid it alongside her mattress, climbed back into the bag and stared at the sky again.

She wanted to sleep and felt weary enough to do so, but her mind was restless. Her anxiety, she told herself, was unwarranted. Too bad.

It had taken hold. Clare willed herself to think about her grandmother again and recall something interesting, soothing, distracting that she had taught her. When that didn't work, she closed her eyes and tried to picture, section by section, the route the group had followed to reach the hut. But, as if harnessed to a powerful pulley somewhere else in her brain, her thoughts dragged up visions of the food she'd consumed that day instead.

A banana and yoghurt (low fat) for breakfast, half a cheese sandwich (buttered!) with black coffee at eleven (she couldn't bring herself to refuse her father with everyone else watching), roast chicken salad (no dressing) for lunch, and a sausage and baked potato for supper. Clare tallied the calories. After years of referencing calorie counters, it was easy. She totalled the hours walked and calculated the energy she'd expended. But even though the figures more or less balanced, she felt her heart speed up and her throat tighten. She slipped her hand into the sleeping bag and under her t-shirt, smoothing it over her stomach.

"There's nothing there, Clare. Nothing," she whispered.

But the pulley was more powerful and her fingers found a pinch of flesh.

"Fat," said her brain. "You're going to get fat. Get out of your sleeping bag and do some situps. It's okay. No one will see you."

"No. Stop it." She clenched her jaw. "You don't rule me."

"Just ten. Just to be sure."

Would the voice never go away? Would she ever really be in control again? Sometimes, more often recently, she thought she was. But then the balance shifted and she felt powerless again. Clare bent her knees and drew them upwards, as if to shield her stomach, and turned onto her side. That's when she heard a soft rustle.

The lower section of a bush on the edge of the lawn darkened as several of its leaves trembled. She could just make out the distinct thickset, low-slung form of a female honey badger. Then the animal stepped into full view on the lawn, where she paused, raised her head and looked around, nose twitching. Clare wondered if the badger could smell her and, if she did, what was going through the animal's mind. She looked so solid and, with her front legs slightly bowed, self-assured.

The badger's attitude made Clare think about how confident she had been when she was younger. She'd believed she could take on the world. She was regularly top of her class, often the centre of attention, a first-rate tennis player and captain of the hockey team, and there were few things she wasn't capable of. She had many friends, two of whom she'd known since she was a toddler. Clare was clever, funny, capable and loved. She hadn't imagined she'd ever be anything else. Had she been arrogant? Was that why things had changed? Had she needed a lesson in how to be humble?

The badger took several steps across the grass. The animal wasn't afraid, but she was cautious, pausing to consider her next move. Would she, Clare Basson, ever be as bold again, she wondered? Would she ever feel like old Clare did and walk into a room full of people without imagining what they thought about her? What they were saying? How they pitied her or judged her as weak? How they deliberated about what had happened to her and made her want to disappear? Would she ever be able to think about anything other than her shame?

The animal inched forward. Clare knew about the tenacity of the honey badger. The species was, said some, a "souped-up version of a weasel," which would take on an elephant or buffalo if cornered. But surely this one wouldn't approach her, would she?

Turning towards the lapa, the honey badger sniffed again and, with a decisive lurch, trotted forward. She smelt food. Clare breathed out as, tail now erect, the badger broke into a canter and disappeared into the shadows of the lapa.

"Are you asleep?"

"Oh, my God!"

There was a rattle of pots and the sound of claws on concrete as the honey badger fled.

"What was that?"

It was her father.

"Dad! Man! You scared me. What are doing? Creeping up on me like that?"

His eyes glistened in the dark. "Sorry. I didn't—"

"It was a ratel. I was watching her. She went into the kitchen."

"Cheeky creature." He gave in and laughed. "I'm sorry. I just wanted to see if you were okay."

"She wouldn't harm me, would she?"

"A sweet little ratel . . . honey badger?"

Clare didn't reply. He chuckled again.

"Do you want to come inside?" he asked.

"No."

"Shall I get my stuff? Sleep out here, too?"

"If you'd like to."

He nodded and walked towards the hut.

Clare remembered his snoring and wondered if she would get any sleep.

Two

Faye watched her husband stroll across the lawn towards her. For years, she had thought of him as tall but these days he seemed shorter, perhaps more so now with the mountain peaks looming high behind him. Was he slouching or were his vertebrae already flattening with age? She pushed her shoulders back and made a mental note to watch her posture. They were, as Zach had pointed out the last time he'd visited, middle-aged. It had somehow come as a surprise to Faye.

"What? Yes. I guess you're right. That's depressing. Thanks, Zach."

"Oh, for goodness' sake," said Derek, failing to notice her joking tone. "He's teasing. Must your hackles rise to everything?"

She'd winked at Zach and left the room, thinking about something she'd read recently. "Being a woman means being too young for everything until suddenly you are too old for everything, with at least ten years in between when you are simultaneously too young and too old."

Was she both too young and too old? Or had she already arrived at the categorically too-old stage?

Derek stopped in front of her, an arm's length away. "I thought you were already asleep."

She held up an empty mug. "I want some water. Will you come with me?"

He yawned but fell in step with her.

"What were you talking to Clare about?" she asked, regretting the question even as she spoke.

Faye had left home determined to unwind and enjoy herself. Perhaps Derek would see something desirable in her once more, and they'd remember why they were still together. She was already faltering. He'd inevitably interpret her question as insecure and suspicious.

She'd felt guilty about not being more disappointed when Derek told her Michelle wouldn't join them on the hike after all. It wasn't that Faye didn't like her, but it was easier to sustain a façade of self-assurance without their high-achieving friend around. Not only was Michelle a high court judge, but she also ran three-and-a-half-hour marathons, had her own column in a weekend newspaper and cooked like a Michelin chef. She'd barely pushed the pause button on her career to give birth to and raise three children, wore the same dress size as she had at university and, according to Derek, earned more than any of the others could ever dream about. It was hard for Faye not to feel as if she'd been assigned a minor role in the movie about her own life when Michelle was around.

She tried again. "I wondered if she—"

"I was just saying goodnight," he said.

Faye held the mug beneath the tap. "It's beautiful here, isn't it? Makes me realise how noisy the city is."

"Uh-huh."

"It'll be good to get going early tomorrow. Beat the heat and have time to swim in some of the rivers."

Derek looked up. "And beat the storm."

"Storm?"

"The woman in the office mentioned the possibility of storms inland when I signed the paperwork and fetched the maps this morning. Might reach us tomorrow."

Faye stared at him. "One of the rangers warned you?"

"Hmm. . . not really. Mentioned it in passing. Geoff checked his weather app. He would've said something if he thought it was a problem."

"When? When did Geoffrey check his app?"

"I don't know. A few days ago. No phones out here."

"A few days ago? But you didn't say anything to anyone else about what the ranger said?"

Derek shook his head. "I didn't want to create mass panic. I know how you women can be. We'll leave early and be at Grootkloof Cabin before the rain even starts."

"What about the rivers? Won't they flood if there's rain inland? Become difficult to cross?"

"You see," he said, throwing up his hands. "That's why I didn't say anything. Your default setting is panic."

Faye was silent.

Derek looked across the lawn. "She's better, isn't she? She looks better."

"Clare?" she asked, following his gaze to where she and the mattress created a small mound in the darkness.

He nodded.

She thought about the young woman, who, with her long hair, spindly limbs and narrow hips in tiny shorts as they hiked, could easily be mistaken for a carefree girl from a distance—but whose worried eyes and edgy energy suggested otherwise when she lingered long enough and stood close enough for anyone to notice. Faye had wondered if the others felt the same. Did they also want to tell Clare that, while they might not know exactly what she was going through, they had some idea of what lay ahead? And that, although they were certainly not always right, they had already more experience of being wrong than she? It made her feel old and unoriginal but the quote—were they the words of George Bernard Shaw?—"Youth is wasted on the young" came to mind.

"Well, she's been very ill. But Diane said Michelle is convinced she's recovered. Or at least, recovering," she said.

"Weird illness. I can't get my head around it."

"That's what it is; an illness."

"It doesn't make sense. I still think something must've triggered it," he said, peering across the yard.

"As I understand it—"

"I still believe she must've been attacked at university. Or something else odd happened during first-year. All those parties. The drinking perhaps."

"Attacked? Why—"

Derek ignore her. "But Michelle insists that's not the case. Says it's about control, self-esteem and that kind of stuff."

"You spoke to Michelle about Clare?"

"Briefly. A while ago . . . can't remember the exact occasion." He looked away and gestured towards Clare. "Still, she looks good. God knows we're all carrying too much weight."

Faye swallowed.

"Really, Derek? 'Good'? There's nothing to her. Did you notice how little she eats?"

He stared at his wife, his mouth set in a line. Faye braced herself for rebuke or scorn, or a bit of both. Instead, Derek exhaled through pouting lips and said, "Let's go to bed, shall we? I'm bushed."

She took a sip of water. "To be honest, I'm surprised Geoffrey and Michelle suggested she come. Do you think they mean us to look after her?"

"Of course not. She seems fine. And Geoff's here."

"Is that why you came outside to check on her?"

Derek glared at her again. Faye looked down. She'd done it again.

"I mean, she's outside and—" she said.

But Derek was already walking towards the cabin.

Faye watched him go. She was tired and longed to crawl into bed, to sleep and try again tomorrow. But she'd wait before following Derek, give him a chance to nod off. She didn't want to make their friends uncomfortable. Or perhaps they'd dismiss Faye's silence as Derek usually did: as yet another of her ill-humoured, gratuitous over-reactions to his "unique sense of humour." It was, after all, how she'd defended Derek's sarcasm in the early days.

An exchange with her mother, when the two of them met for lunch shortly after Faye and Derek announced their engagement, came to mind.

"What do you mean, 'his comments can be biting'?" asked Faye. "It's his wit; he's sharp, as in clever. It's what makes him interesting."

Veronica laid down her cutlery and replied, with a tiny smile, "You know what they say about the thing that you most admire in a person when you first meet them becoming the thing that most annoys you over time, don't you?"

Faye couldn't remember how the conversation concluded. Just as she did not reveal her frustrations about her marriage to her friends, she never admitted to her mother that she'd been right about Derek. With Veronica dead for more than a year now, Faye wished she had mentioned it to her years previously. It might have helped to confide in her mother. It might have made her braver.

The light went off in the hut and Faye heard muffled murmurings as her friends and husband bade one another goodnight. She felt in her pocket for her torch. Had the others noticed she wasn't there? Did Derek tell them she probably had her torch with her? Would he have bothered?

❦

Despite the glittering stars, smear of the Milky Way, splinter of moon and the dim glow of the sun behind a mountain range in the distance, the night was darker than Faye was accustomed to. It was entirely black where the massifs met the trees.

With darkness came the clatter of frogs rising above the sound of the stream. The rattling reminded Faye of the noise she and the other six- or seven-year-olds had made as they scampered across a wooden floor to begin tap lessons. Back then, the sound of her tap shoes legitimised her as a dancer, despite how her tapping typically lagged everyone else's. She'd told Derek about the lessons when she was still giddy with young love.

"I wish I'd known you then," he'd said, rearranging a stray lock of hair that had escaped from behind her ear. "I'd have watched you dance through the window."

How she'd loved him for the thought.

Faye sat on the lawn and looked towards the forest. The idea of being in the trees in the dark frightened her. She didn't know what she might encounter there. It was different by day. It had been a long time since she'd experienced the peace she'd felt as they'd hiked through the forest earlier. The enormity and density of the trees made her feel insignificant and yet, alive. While Derek complained that he felt confined and stifled by their nearness, Faye felt strangely at home. As if answering an ancient craving, her genetic material responded to the tall, woody plants. She slid her hands across their rough bark and lay her ear against their trunks as if listening for a heartbeat.

It was odd because, while she felt soothed by the trees, Faye wasn't at ease with being in the wilderness in general. She was city-born and -bred, and had largely holidayed at the seaside as a child. While she'd undertaken several camping trips into the mountains and alongside rivers with Derek, Zach and their friends, she'd never felt safe in the outdoors, waking regularly at night, frightened by the silence or the unfamiliar sounds of nature. But in the trees during the day, it was a different story.

"Oh, God, you and your trees," said Derek when she'd leaned against a giant yellowwood shortly after they followed the path into the forest.

He'd stopped and turned to face the others. Faye recognised the look on his face; her husband had come up with something to amuse his friends. Helen was familiar with the stance, too.

"Guys! Derek demands our attention," she joked, draping an arm over Bev's shoulders.

Derek picked up a stick and raised it in a posture that made Faye think of an illustration of Moses addressing the Israelites in a children's bible her aunt had given her for her eighth birthday. She'd loved the pictures.

With everyone's eyes on him, Derek said, in a loud (Moses-like?) voice, "If dating apps existed when we were young, Faye could've snared a lumberjack instead of me by—wait for it—signing up with Timber!"

There was laughter, more polite than Derek would no doubt have hoped for.

"Anyone for water?" asked Bruce.

Faye smiled. "No, thanks," she said, unintentionally stroking the tree as if apologising for her husband's silly pun.

When had Derek's teasing changed from humorous to hurtful? Or was it the way she perceived it that had changed? He still raked in the laughs from his friends. Perhaps because they were seldom the target of his ribbing. That was Faye's hardship.

In the early days, it had felt good to be the focus of Derek's attention. He was top dog in the group and, she had to concede, her ticket in.

Zach was a toddler when Faye first tried to tell Derek how hurtful his teasing could be. They'd spent a weekend camping on the coast with their friends. His relentless gags about Faye's poor mothering abilities—she'd forgotten to put the bag she'd packed for Zach in the car and they'd had to go into a nearby village to buy new stuff—wore thin after the first day. Derek didn't notice.

"Look," he said, pointing to Diane as she smeared two-year-old Alice with sunscreen. "Ali is wearing the same swimsuit she wore last week. What's that, Di? Oh, you didn't think she needed a full set of new clothing for the weekend? Ha-ha."

When they had pulled in to the garage at home that night, Zach's bag lay on the floor near the wall. Faye suddenly recalled Derek putting it there after he'd insisted on rearranging things and had taken it out of the trunk where she'd placed it. She'd wondered if he remembered too, but said nothing.

"We should do that more often," he said, as they prepared for bed later.

She didn't respond.

"Go away with the gang, I mean," continued Derek. "We don't see enough of them. It was like old times. Well . . . except for all the rugrats."

He chuckled. Still, Faye said nothing.

"What? You don't agree? You didn't enjoy the weekend?"

"I did," she said, avoiding his eyes as she fluffed her pillow. "It's just—"

"Don't tell me you still feel like an outsider. Please Faye, not after all this time."

"What? No, of course not."

"What then?"

"It's just that when we're with other people you seem to enjoy making fun of me."

"Making *fun* of you?"

"Yes, the teasing, it . . . it was a bit much this weekend."

He leaned towards her. "Teasing?"

"About leaving Zach's bag. Did you see it—"

"Oh, for heaven's sake, don't be so sensitive. I was joking. You must know that?"

"The thing is, it's always at my expense."

"That's nonsense. I kid everyone. What's wrong with you? Are you . . . . You're not—?"

Faye climbed into bed and picked up her book. "No. Don't worry about it. Forget I said anything."

"Sure. Okay. It's just . . . well, it's as if my wife just doesn't get me all of a sudden," he muttered as he headed into the bathroom.

More like your wife *finally* gets you, thought Faye.

The weekend came up again a few weeks later when, at Diane and Bruce's home for Sunday lunch, the women were alone in the kitchen.

"Did you ever find Zach's bag?" asked Diane.

Faye looked around. Derek was outside with Bruce and she'd had a glass of wine. "It was in the garage. Where he," she jerked her head towards the garden, "dumped it. I'd put it in the car, he took it out to re-organise things and didn't put it back."

"What? Really?" said Diane. "What did he say to that?"

Faye wrinkled her nose and shook her head but said nothing.

"He didn't apologise? After his endless jokes all weekend?"

She regretted having said anything. "Don't mention it. Please, Diane. I don't want to remind him about it."

Her friend frowned at her across the counter. Faye smiled at her. "It'll just start him up again. I . . . We've heard enough of that one."

"I won't say a word," said Diane. "Not that he's likely to put on his best performance without Michelle around anyway."

"What do you mean?"

"Ah. You know how he is. How they all are. Always trying to impress Michelle. It's how it has always been. Come. Let's get the food on the table."

Now, Faye lay on her back and looked at the sky. It was pretty but she couldn't imagine relaxing enough to sleep outside. She closed her eyes and pictured the night seeping into her head, saturating her brain like a blotting paper soaking up ink, until there was no room for thoughts, just peace. It worked. She felt calm, which was unusual for her, particularly when she was alone. Her life had been at the behest of Derek and Zach for so long, she wasn't sure what to do when they weren't around. In the past, the idea of being alone had agitated her. But perhaps she'd changed. Maybe middle-aged Faye would be okay on her own. The thought surprised her. Where had it come from? Was this what a dark night in the wilderness did to a person?

The creaking of floorboards disrupted her thoughts. Faye turned towards the sound. A silhouetted figure briefly filled the doorway of the cabin before disappearing into the dark in the direction of Clare.

Three

With a bank of cumulonimbi shrouding the sun and much of the sky, it was cooler than the day before. Billowing grey at the base and white at the top, the clouds embellished what was already a fine view of the mountains and forests. It was, thought Faye, as if an inebriated artist had taken a brush to a completed artwork, impetuously adding drama to what had been a calm landscape painting.

Diane, Bruce and Geoffrey huddled in the lapa. Heads bent over their mugs and a thin plume of white smoke rising up between them from the firepit, they appeared to be conferring over something serious. Oblivious to Faye's approach, Geoffrey put his cup down and walked in the other direction.

Bruce spotted her first. "Morning. Sleep okay?" As ever, he was the consummate host. No matter where the friends were, the role was always his. "Coffee? The water has just boiled."

Derek's bed had been empty and his sleeping bag rolled when Faye awoke. As she scanned the yard for her husband, she saw Geoffrey crouching alongside the unmoving form of Clare.

"She's got a migraine," said Diane, following her gaze. "Feeling awful apparently. Vomiting since the early hours."

"Oh dear. Michelle seemed to think the headaches had stopped, but clearly not. Poor girl."

"She insists we go on," said Bruce. "Says she'll hitch a ride to Grootkloof with the rangers when they come to transfer our stuff. Good thing we decided on the slack-packing option."

Faye stared at him. "Is that a good idea? I mean, leaving her here on—"

"Worried me too, but Geoffrey says the migraines pass within a few hours. There's nothing much any of us can do for her. She's dosed herself and wants to lie still. Says she'll be fine to continue tomorrow," he said.

"But leaving her alone? Do we know what time the rangers will come?"

Diane shook her head. "Not exactly. There's no way of contacting them."

"The info sheet indicates sometime after lunch," said Bruce.

"I don't—"

Bruce poured water into Faye's mug. "It also says if anyone decides not to hike on any particular day, they should wait at the huts for the rangers to transport them to the next overnight stop."

"But what if she's still feeling unwell when they arrive? Wouldn't she like company?"

"Apparently not," said Diane.

"Geoffrey says she always insists on being left alone when she's like this. He'll help her into the cabin before we leave." Bruce rinsed his mug. "We should eat breakfast and get ready to go. We've quite a distance to cover today."

It was true, thought Faye, thinking about the route map she'd briefly perused at home. The second day of the hike included a long descent down a steep ravine and a major river crossing just before they reached the overnight stop at Grootkloof Cabin. She remembered Derek's comment the previous night about the weather, and looked up. The clouds were lower and stonier than when she'd left the cabin.

Or did they seem that way because she was looking at them from a different angle? But what if, as the ranger suggested it might, it had rained heavily inland and the river was already swollen? Should she risk the wrath of her husband and warn her friends? When she turned to Diane, Faye spotted him approaching with Helen and Bev. They were laughing at something Derek had said. As if the mirth was too much to bear, Helen leaned forward to briefly rest her forehead on her wife's shoulder. Bev put her arm around Helen as, still giggling, they climbed the stairs into the lapa. Derek beamed. He was proud of his wit, as was Faye when it wasn't laced with sarcasm or ridicule.

"We should get a move on," he said, patting Diane's shoulder in matey kind of way—or as one might chivvy on an animal.

"Hills to climb, rivers to ford and," he turned and winked at Faye, "trees to hug."

She smiled without meaning to. Pavlovian conditioning, she thought, her neck and cheeks growing warm.

"Just as I was saying," said Bruce. "Let's eat, pack and go. Anyone else for coffee?"

❧

Faye was placing her bag near the cabin door when Geoffrey and Clare appeared. Head lowered and shielding her eyes with one hand while clutching her father's elbow with the other, the young woman shuffled in and lowered herself onto a bed. Geoffrey unrolled the sleeping bag and helped her into it. Clare's eyes were closed and her movements laboured.

"I'll put your bag under the bed, shall I?" said Geoffrey quietly.

"Thanks. And a bucket." She barely moved her mouth as if the effort and the sound of her words were unbearable.

Faye tiptoed closer. "Shall I close the curtains? Get some water?"

"Yes. Thanks." Geoffrey took a flask from Clare's pack and handed it over.

When she returned, she met him at the door where he placed his bag alongside hers. He took the flask to where Clare lay, sleeping bag pulled over her head, put the water down and patted her shoulder lightly.

"Hope it passes soon, sweetie. See you this evening."

"Bye, Dad." Her words were scarcely audible.

Faye took her daypack and followed Geoffrey from the cabin. He waved at the others who were waiting at the edge of the yard.

"Geoffrey," she called.

He stopped and turned to her with a smile.

"Should I close the door?" She gestured towards the cabin.

"Um . . ." Geoffrey adjusted his cap as if it might clarify his thinking. "No, don't. She'd prefer it open. Leave it open."

"Are you sure this is a good idea?" asked Faye.

She knew it wasn't, but also anticipated his response. Wasn't this what people do? Express their concern in times of uncertainty, as if doing so might exempt them from blame if things go wrong?

He fiddled with his cap again. "She insists. The tablets knock her out. She'll sleep and, by the time the rangers arrive, she'll have more or less recovered. You'll see. She'll be herself by the time we see her this evening."

"But—"

"Come on, you two," shouted Derek. "Let's get going!"

Geoffrey gave Faye the kind of placating smile one gives children when the ice-cream shop turns out to be closed after you've promised them a treat, and turned to join the others. She shouldered her backpack and followed, glancing heavenwards again.

Gone were the patches of blue that had dotted the sky earlier. The green of the vegetation popped, vivid against the metal grey of the clouds, and the mountains seemed taller as if rising to meet them. This time the view reminded Faye of the childishly exaggerated proportions and colours of Zach's primary school drawings.

As she neared the group, she heard Bev's voice. "We've all packed rain jackets, I hope?"

There was murmured confirmation. Derek said nothing as he strode ahead towards the small wooden bridge. Already trailing, Faye paused as she crossed, leaning lightly on the rail and looking down onto the stream. She and Bev had been there the previous afternoon. They'd wanted to swim but changed their minds when they saw how small the brook was. Now though, the water was flowing strongly, swirling between the boulders, pooling in a large, dark pond and lapping hungrily at the banks. Clearly, rain had fallen somewhere in the catchment area. Faye pictured the map, trying to recall whether the stream fed into the Bloukrans River, which could make crossing it difficult in a few hours. She couldn't remember and looked up, wanting to ask one of the others. Or say something, at least. But the group had moved on.

❧

A steep, lung-burning hill led them away from the water. Eventually the trail spilled onto a plateau that stretched into nothingness to the north until it met the mountains. Less than a hundred metres to the south, the earth fell away abruptly into a deep gorge. Carved by the elements over millennia, the ravine culminated in the snaking, watery chasm that was the Bloukrans River.

Once on flat terrain, the hikers picked up their pace and, although she had almost closed the gap on the incline, Faye lagged again. She was still fifty metres or so behind when, little over an hour later, the trees rose up from the earth ahead like a legion of leafy warriors. Faye was breathless and hoped the group would stop for a moment. They didn't. Instead, they slid under the trees, single-file behind Derek. She followed into the shade but, hot and irritated, stopped a few metres in, slid her bag from her shoulders and took her sweatshirt off.

Instead of the calm she'd experienced among the trees the previous day, Faye was tense. Surely the others were curious about Derek's pace? His militant marching? Or had he disclosed the ranger's warning by now? That might explain their collaborative haste.

She looked around, hoping to find something to distract and soothe her. Her eyes fell on the bark of a large yellowwood tree, peeling and flaking in dark purplish-brown chunks to expose its lighter and younger red-brown under-bark. A butterfly with black dots on its orange wings flitted through a grove of tangled climbers and then flew out of the forest as if it had taken a wrong turn and arrived there by mistake. Like brollies on a fairy beach, a cluster of cream-coloured toadstools grew in a sandy patch of soil. It was a pretty place, but Faye's prickliness prevailed.

She looked through the trees to where the others were shrinking in the distance and was about to follow when she heard a barking sound.

"*Kow-kow-kow-kow.*"

A pair of medium-sized green and blue birds bounded from branch to branch in the canopy. She watched as, with a flash of crimson, the Knysna loeries spread their wings and launched themselves into the air, mewling like uptight tomcats at full moon. Faye tried to track their flight but they disappeared together.

Together.

That was why she was bothered. It wasn't just that she was having trouble keeping up with today's advanced pace. It was also because they should not have left Clare alone. They were breaking the first rule of hiking—stay together—and it bothered her.

It didn't matter that Clare was in the cabin rather than on the trail. Or that the rangers would transport her to the overnight stop in their vehicle. *What if she didn't feel better?* Illness doesn't follow the same pattern time and again. *What if something happened to the rangers and she wasn't collected? What if they arrived, took the bags and supplies from the lapa and didn't notice Clare sleeping on the bed? What if they, too, left her alone?*

"Faye!"

It was Diane, returning to round up the straggler. Faye watched as her friend drew near. Robust in hiking leggings and a pale blue, sleeveless puffer jacket, Diane sported an aluminium walking pole in each hand. Her cheeks were rosy and the damp strands of hair escaping her wide-brimmed hat were the colour of harvest-ready wheat. Diane had switched between being a fun-loving blonde and spirited redhead for as long as Faye had known her. Recently though, she'd settled on blonde, insisting that the milder colouring drew less attention to the lines on her face.

"Are you okay? Come on."

Faye shook her head. "I'm going back," she said.

"Is something wrong?" Diane came closer. "I know we're hurtling at a ridiculous pace. Derek says a *Getaway* article recommended arriving at the Grootkloof Cabin early because it's so gorgeous. But I could walk slower with you if you prefer?"

"Hmm? Really . . . *Getaway*? I see."

Her friend shrugged.

"No. I'm fine, but I don't like the idea of Clare being on her own. I'll go back and wait for the rangers with her." She tied her sweatshirt around her waist.

"But . . ." Diane glanced over her shoulder towards the others. "She insisted. So did Geoffrey."

"I know, but what if it was Zach? Or Alice? Wouldn't you want one of us to be with her?"

"I guess so. Sure. But in that case, Geoffrey should go. I'll run and call him."

"No. Leave him," said Faye. "I'll go back."

"But—"

"Really. I want to. Let's leave it at that."

"Do you want me to come with you?" asked Diane, not bothering to disguise a sigh.

Faye recognised the reaction. It was classic Diane. Even as she extended an offer of help, it was clear she hoped it would be declined. Faye had seen it many times, including when Diane "offered" to babysit Zach, fetch Derek from the airport when Faye's mother was in hospital and take on an additional school run when Faye was feeling unwell. It wasn't that she was a terrible friend; Diane simply hated being inconvenienced.

"No, seriously. It's fine. Thank you but you go ahead and tell the others. I'll see you this evening. Go! Before they leave you behind, too."

As she watched Diane walk-trot away, Faye took a few steps off the path and rested against a large, mossy trunk. It was damp and would probably stain her shorts but she liked the soft, cold feel of it against her body. It cooled her down and made her feel connected to the world, to the forest.

When the sound of Diane's footsteps had faded, the forest was quiet, save for the gentle rustling of the leaves in the upper boughs. Faye looked up, wondering if the loeries would return if she remained still. Their re-appearance was more likely than Derek returning for her.

four

There were benefits to walking fast, thought Geoffrey as he followed Derek on the single-track through the trees. It involved more puffing and less chatting. He knew his friends meant well, but he'd had enough of their questions about Clare. He was unsettled enough by letting her convince him to leave her at Heuningbos, and didn't need their prompting.

"How long does she typically sleep?" Bruce had asked.

"Did she get migraines before she got so thin?" enquired Helen.

"Poor thing. Remember you went through a patch when we thought you were getting them, Hel?" said Bev. "Turned out they were hormonal, treatable. I'm sure she's had that checked out, hasn't she, Geoffrey?"

He shrugged, nodded, "Yes, yes," and picked up his pace, grateful to Derek for striding ahead and creating distance between the hikers. The space helped magnify the intensity of the wilderness and Geoffrey took it in, frame by frame. The grassy burst of francolins startled by the thump of his boots. The sweet rose and citrus aroma of the pelargonium carried by a light breeze. The placid cooing of doves rendered invisible by the foliage. The dampening of his footsteps as the trail was enveloped by trees.

The energy and rhythm reminded Geoffrey of gardening and

why he loved it. Clients were surprised to see him working shoulder to shoulder with his employees as they composted flower beds, trimmed branches, mowed lawns and dug trenches. They were more familiar with proprietors of such businesses doing little more than sunning their elbows as they piloted their bakkies around the suburbs. Typically, these men stayed seated, shouting instructions to their workers as they off-loaded equipment before driving away, and then cruising back when the work was done.

But that wasn't why Geoffrey started Basson's Garden Services. If his ambition had been to issue directives, he would have stayed with the bank. He liked the action and exercise of gardening almost as much as he enjoyed being outdoors all day and seeing his landscape plans take shape, his workers mastering new skills and the plants they sowed flourishing. Geoffrey thrived on the tangible nature of horticulture, the dirt, sweat and beauty of it. The haziness of financial services, where numbers were the only things that (sometimes) grew and clients were rarely more than names on statements, could not compare.

In the early days of the business, Basson's clients were equally disbelieving when they spotted a baby seat, which, at first glance, appeared to have been forsaken in the shade in their gardens. They'd crane their necks, creep closer and discover that it contained pink-faced Clare, drooling as she slept. When they lifted their heads to look around, Geoffrey, mowing, digging or clipping in the vicinity, would smile and wave indifferently, as if caring for babies was something all nurserymen did. With Michelle back at work a few weeks after giving birth, Geoffrey took care of the baby during the day. Clare slept through the screeching of chainsaws, clattering of lawn mowers and thrashing of weedeaters. She lolled in the sweaty crook of her father's arm as he sat sideways on the bakkie seat, legs stretched out in front of him, and bottle-fed her. She took her first steps into the arms of Geoffrey's right-hand man, Vincent, in the muddiest section of Mrs Vermeulen's bed of Angel Face Floribunda roses, and her first word was "mulch."

Clare. His adored firstborn.

Geoffrey glanced over his shoulder to check that he and Derek weren't too far ahead of the others. Helen and Bev rounded the corner, closely followed by Bruce. Diane and Faye, together at the back, no doubt, were nowhere to be seen. He walked on, unable to stop thinking about Clare. His stomach churned like it used to when, still a boy, he'd wait to run onto the rugby field for a game. Now though, it was all anxiety and no anticipation.

He hoped that his daughter's nausea would have passed by now, allowing her to sleep soundly. He thought again about how he'd tried to persuade her that he should stay at the cabin with her, but Clare insisted he go. She didn't want to be fussed over under any circumstances and was adamant her headache should not upset the others' plans. Even after Bruce and Derek had assured him that leaving her to be collected by the rangers was not only acceptable, but advisable, Geoffrey briefly considered pretending to leave, but actually lying low in the lapa until his daughter awoke. He knew, however, how that would infuriate her. She wasn't a child. He had to respect her wishes. Stop watching her. Trust her. It was the only way of getting things back to what they had been between them.

Geoffrey thought of Michelle's words when they first saw how bad things were. He'd pleaded with his wife to help him persuade Clare not to go back to university.

"We can't force her, Geoffrey. She's an adult. I know she's ill, but if we don't allow her to make her own decisions, she'll push us away. We have to support her by giving her space."

He'd cried when he realised how out of control she was. He and Michelle argued for days about the best way of handling Clare's condition. Geoffrey couldn't sleep. He had no appetite and no will to work. He gave Vincent the keys to his bakkie and, for a fortnight, sat at his computer, barely rallying the energy to respond to emails or send invoices. For the first time in eighteen years, his fingernails were clean and the calluses on his hands shrivelled.

When he overheard Angus tell Linda not to bother telling their father about her hockey match because "all he worries about is Clare," Geoffrey called his doctor and asked her to refer him to a therapist. If Clare wouldn't seek help, he would. It might help him be a better father.

He wasn't sure it made any difference to Clare, but Geoffrey felt better. The sessions gave him a glimpse at what she might be going through, though he wasn't sure he'd ever truly understand. He was able to talk to Michelle, Angus and Linda about Clare's illness and how it made him feel, without breaking down. The sessions gave him the chance to express his guilt and helplessness and to ask some of the questions that bombarded him in the early hours. *How could he have allowed this to happen to Clare? What had he missed? What kind of father couldn't make his daughter well?* Geoffrey's therapist helped him see what he could control and what he couldn't. The heaviness in his heart lifted slightly and he could once more see beyond Clare. He went shopping for a new hockey stick with Linda, practised with her and watched all her games. He played touch rugby with Angus and helped him fix his bike, and reserved a weekend away for him and Michelle.

Vincent returned his bakkie keys, relieved.

"You might not be able to lift as many bags of soil as me, Geoffrey, but I don't have as many answers for the clients as you do," he said.

Clare hugged him when she said goodbye before returning to university and, as he tried not to focus on how fragile she felt in his arms, he heard her whisper, "I'm so sorry, Dad."

Geoffrey had stepped back and looked into her eyes, wanting to tell her it was okay, it would be okay if she was okay, but he felt his eyes brim and couldn't speak. She patted his shoulder and left. It was still so hard.

❧

When he looked up again, Geoffrey saw that Derek had stopped in the middle of the path and was peering behind him at the others.

"Let's give them a moment," he said, as Geoffrey paused alongside him.

Geoffrey looked into the forest. Dappled light fell onto a grove of large ferns, their fronds angling outwards like the raised arms of a charismatic choir as they sang. The undergrowth was made up of greens of every hue.

He wished Clare was there to see it, to enjoy the cool, mottled peace. As much as he enjoyed the wordlessness of the walk, he would have happily exchanged the quiet to be with her and talk, as they had the previous day. About the plants and creatures they saw. How comfortable their boots were. The sweet taste of the water in the streams. How steep the trail was and how their muscles ached.

They had spoken about everything except how they felt for one another and whether those feelings had changed during the past three years. Geoffrey was determined that, before the six days were over, he would tell his daughter that, no matter how she felt and how things might've changed for her, his love for her hadn't.

"There. Coming around the corner," said Derek. "Let's go or they'll think we're taking a break."

"Why don't we? It'll give us a chance to regroup."

"Tired, Geoff? Why don't you hang back with the women?" Derek chuckled and glanced at the sky. "There'll be time to regroup at the river."

five

Faye pulled her bottle from her pack and squirted some water into her mouth. With the others out of sight, she was suddenly eager to leave the forest. There was a gloominess to it now, the dark sky and towering trees shielding the daylight. The vegetation was too close. The air too thick. Even the silence seemed threatening.

She pictured Clare, a small, solitary mound on her mattress in the yard the previous night, and tried to imagine what it was like to be so fearless. Had she ever been courageous? Before the stresses of motherhood, worries about the failing health and eventual deaths of her parents, and the weight of continually disappointing her husband had made her anxious? There'd been a time, in her teens, when Faye would disappear alone into the plantation near her parents' home for an entire Saturday. Except she wasn't alone. She had Dingo Rue and Wallis Simpson trotting at her heels. Perhaps that was the difference. She didn't have any superpowers, but the dogs did. She wished she had a dog with her in the forest now.

As she slid the bottle back into its pouch, Faye had the tingling sense of being watched. Her shoulders and neck stiffened. She shook her head gently, straightened her back and looked around.

Thick with trees, bushes and ferns, the forest was a shady tousle of vegetation, practically impenetrable beyond the path. Several giant trees, like the one she rested against, lay dead and decaying where they'd fallen years ago, creating fertile surfaces for other life. A caravan of ants, each insect hauling a tiny piece of plant, trickled past her boots and disappeared, one by one, beneath a chunk of bark.

The air was musty with mould and decomposing plants but there was something else too, another smell. Faye lifted her head and sniffed. She couldn't place it. The fustiness reminded her of the odour in her car when she fetched Zach and his friends from the athletics track. Yes. That was it. The forest reeked like perspiring young sportsmen wearing kit that was saturated with sweat. It was the kind of grime that had accumulated over time and which no amount of washing would ever eradicate. Only the smell in the forest was much worse. Was it a plant? A dead animal? Were the odour and feeling of being watched related?

Faye rubbed her hands together. Her palms were wet. She took two deep breaths to calm herself. That didn't help. *Forget the mysterious smell, it's time to go,* she thought, glancing at her bag on the floor. She was about to lift it when the sharp crack of a branch and scuffling of leaves behind her cut through the quiet. She turned slowly.

A few metres away, three bush pigs stared down their long, bristly snouts at her over a leafy branch.

"Oh, my," she whispered.

The pigs' small eyes glistened, unblinking. The largest was the height of a big Labrador retriever, but much broader. His spiky stubble and whiskers protruded at all angles along his jaw and above his nostrils in an even unrulier version of Zach's messiest morning hair. He flicked a fuzzy ear towards her. *Was it a sign? Would they charge her? Were wild pigs carnivorous? Why wouldn't they be?*

Faye remembered how horrified she'd been when a school friend told her that domestic sows sometimes ate their newborn piglets. She searched her mind for something else she might know about pigs and their behaviour. All she could come up with was the image of the cover of George Orwell's *Animal Farm* featuring an illustration of the porcine antagonist, Napoleon. His little eyes were red and there was blood on his trotters. Faye remembered how the boar had commanded the dogs he'd raised to chase Snowball from the farm, and how he'd allowed Boxer to die without calling the vet.

There was no doubt about it; pigs could be monsters.

She had to get out of the forest. Right away. Put some distance between herself and Napoleon before her imagination imploded. But she was afraid to take her eyes off the trio and remained fixed to the spot. What if they were like some dogs, who, while a cat stood her ground, wouldn't chase her, but the moment the feline bolted, would pursue her with ardour?

As she stared at Napoleon, Faye noticed the leaves of the arum lilies behind him shudder. The pale, prickly manes of at least two more pigs flickered against the green foliage as they slid between the plants. What were they doing? Rooting about in the undergrowth or sharpening their tusks? She gasped. Did pigs do that? Was it something her pig-wise school friend told her? Why would she think it otherwise? How many more were there? Was she surrounded by the creatures? If so, she'd have to carefully plan her escape route.

Only a few metres lay between her and the path. But if there were more pigs behind her, she'd have to find a detour. That might pose the additional risk of getting lost. She must stay on the path. She breathed in and looked around, eyes straining to spot any further movement in the shrubbery. If there were any more pigs in the plants, they were well hidden.

Faye turned back to face the gawking hogs. They hadn't moved. Napoleon's ear twitched again.

"Right," she whispered. "Here goes."

In a single movement, she leaned over, snatched the handles of her backpack and, crashing through the scrub and leaping over logs and branches, scarpered towards the path. Behind her, the pigs snorted and squealed in alarm and, in a flurry of hairy bodies and thwacking trotters, smashed the undergrowth as they fled in the opposite direction.

Even when she realised that the animals were as terrified as she was, Faye continued running until she had left the forest and was back in the open. Out of breath, her legs trembling, she couldn't recall when last she'd sprinted like that. In fact, she didn't realise she still had it in her. She stopped and rested her hands on her knees to recover, half laughing and half sobbing.

After she'd turned and checked once more that the pigs had definitely bolted, she looked across the veld. With swathes of restios bending under the weight of their seeds and the flowers of the wild dagga plant rising upwards like naartjies pinned on skewers as far as the eye could see, the plateau calmed her. In the distance, the purple hue of the ericas faded into the faraway foothills. There were no dark shadows to mislead her here and the vegetation didn't crowd her. Even the clouds, with their dense, darker bottoms, were no longer unsettling.

The vastness made Faye aware of her solitude. Her husband and friends were walking in the other direction. It would take almost two hours before she got back to Heuningbos Hut. How small she was out here. How alone. Yet, as she walked on, breathing in the soft air, glancing at the tiny tubular flowers that lined the path, and listening to the sharp *chee-chee-chee* of the sunbirds as they flew, quick and erratic, between the proteas, Faye was at peace. She felt connected. To what, she couldn't be sure.

Composed again, she felt a pang of regret that she hadn't had the courage to enjoy the forest while she was alone. Perhaps there'd be other opportunities during the next four days. She thought about the pigs and wondered if the others had seen them. Perhaps they'd see more during the hike. It was ridiculous for her to have panicked and imagined that the animals might attack her. She was glad there hadn't been anyone else around to witness it and chided herself for not having read up on the wildlife in the area. It could've prevented her imagination from spinning into the far corners of absurdity. She might've been calm enough to photograph the animals. What a picture the three peering at her over the leaves would have made.

She would have captioned it "Napoleon, Josephine and Maria," she thought, even though it would have made no sense to anyone but her.

Faye regularly cursed her predisposition to be fearful. How and why had she become afraid of so many things? It annoyed Derek because it added to her inclination to, as he put it, "consistently overreact" and "always anticipate the worst possible scenario." He was right, wasn't he? It's why she was returning to the hut, wasn't it? Because she feared something terrible might happen to Clare.

Fear was why Faye hadn't resumed her career despite, when she left to give birth, agreeing with Derek that she would go back to work the year Zach began school. By then though, after being at home for six years, she felt petrified by the notion she wouldn't be able to adapt to the changes in the medical equipment industry. She was afraid she no longer had the aptitude and confidence to understand and sell highly technical products, and was sure she'd mess up and fail. She wasn't, she told herself, familiar with the computerisation, digitisation and whatever other technological advancements had been introduced at so rapid a rate in recent years. She worried she was too far behind to catch up.

"Fair enough," said Derek with a shrug, when she told him of her concerns. "You're not the quickest adopter of new technology and systems. In fact, you're more of a technophobe."

"Really? I didn't realise I was that—"

"Well, think about how long it took you to learn Excel," he said.

As she recalled, she'd picked it up reasonably quickly and was even called on to help colleagues who found the software difficult to master. But she said nothing to Derek. Perhaps she was wrong. Maybe she had battled with it initially and had said as much to him. It was a long time ago. Motherhood must have dulled her memory.

Most of all though, Faye feared that no one would employ her after her prolonged absence from the workplace. They'd judge her for staying away so long and find her wanting. Derek didn't try to dispel her self-doubts. Neither did he suggest that she look for employment in another field, one she might find less daunting. In fact, he didn't expend any time or energy at all encouraging her or trying to persuade her to change her mind. To the contrary, he quickly convinced her that staying at home was the right decision.

"It's okay, actually, you not working. Don't worry about it," he said at dinner one evening. "I made a spreadsheet to calculate how much you'd have to earn, after tax, to cover a housekeeper, au pair and additional costs for things like commuting, car maintenance and work outfits. Given that you'd probably work on commission and it would take you several months to build up a client base and truly start selling, it works out better if you stay at home."

Faye didn't ask for further explanation. Neither did she point out how much effort went into looking after a home and family. She was relieved, but only briefly. It wasn't just about the money. There was something about having a career that had completed her. She felt guilty at the thought, but being a mother wasn't the same. Although she never complained about it, she was bored, particularly when Zach was at school. In addition, she realised that having made the decision not to contribute financially meant she had to account to Derek for every cent of "his" income she spent. It wasn't that he was patently closefisted, but neither did he ever suggest it was unnecessary for her to itemise every purchase she made.

She'd thought about it often over the years, but only raised the idea of finding a job once more. Even then, it was just an oblique reference to the notion.

Zach was at high school and Faye had been co-opted to work on a fund-raising project for the school with several other parents, including Diane. One evening, after the committee had met to finalise details for an event, Diane and Faye walked together to the carpark.

"Have you ever thought of going into project management?" asked Diane.

Faye looked at her, amused. "No. Goodness. Why would I? I barely know what it is."

"Google it," said Diane, nudging her with her elbow. "You're a natural. Honestly. And I think you'd enjoy it."

"Really? Thanks—I think."

They were quiet for a moment. Then Diane asked, "Would you like to work again? I mean, you were fabulously successful before Zach. Did you not want to go back? I've always wondered. Or was it Derek's choice?"

Faye felt herself redden and was glad it was twilight. "I was going to. The original plan was that I would. Once Zach started school. But then so much time had passed and things had changed, I didn't feel I'd be up to it. Derek and I—"

"That's nonsense," said Diane, stopping and turning to face her. "I've seen you in action at home for years and here, over the past few weeks. You have tons to offer. Your organisational and delegating skills are off the charts and you're super diplomatic, which gets everyone behind you. Pfft! 'Not up to it', my arse."

Faye tittered, not sure what to say.

"I'll leave it at that," continued Diane, picking up on Faye's discomfit. "It's just that if you wanted to get out and go back to work, you should. I mean, I know he's your spouse and we like to keep the peace, but don't let Derek stop you from looking for a job if you want to work. It's hardly as if you'd inconvenience him. It's your life. And you certainly shouldn't doubt your competency."

"Who would employ someone who has been out of the loop for as long as I have?"

"You might be surprised," said Diane, waving as she headed to her car.

Derek was watching television when Faye arrived home. She made tea and, handing him a cup, said, "Diane thinks I'd make a good project manager."

"Why on earth would she think that?" he asked, not taking his eyes off the screen.

She never again mentioned her conversation with Diane or the idea of working.

Six

Clare woke to the sound of rain clattering on the corrugated iron roof, the noise amplified by the cabin's lack of a ceiling. Her chemically induced sleep had been dense and dreamless. She was disorientated until the smooth sensation of the sleeping bag against her neck towed her back to the place and time.

Buffeted by the wind, the door swung to and fro as it bumped one of seven canvas bags lined up in the flooded entrance. Clare got up, pulled the carriers, several of which were thoroughly soaked, into the room and closed the door. She pictured the unhappy faces of the hikers when they removed their wet clothing later, and wondered who among them had decided to leave the door open.

Although her head was thick with sleep and the aftermath of painkillers, and her mouth dry and fuzzy, Clare's migraine and nausea were gone. She looked out of the window as she drank from her flask.

The trees and mountains were hidden behind a heavy curtain of rain, driven at an angle by the wind. The precipitation was wall-like and isolating. Clare imagined her father somewhere on the other side, out of sight and out of reach. She hoped it wasn't raining wherever he was. The vaporous cover gave her the sense of being truly alone. Cut off. Separated. It didn't scare her. Quite the opposite. She enjoyed the seclusion. It made her think about her grandmother again.

"We come into the world alone. We leave alone. Sure, while we're here, we get to know other people, some better than others. But if you're not okay on your own, not self-sufficient and calm, happy, in fact, in your own company, you'll forever be afraid, dreading the inevitable moment you are alone, and nervous about how you'll cope. Remember that. Get used to being alone. Enjoy your solitude," she'd said.

While her grandmother spoke, Clare had noticed Michelle rolling her eyes. Later, as Geoffrey drove the family home, her mother glanced in the review mirror and said, "Kids, don't pay too much attention to your grandmother's morbid take on life today. She was probably just a little lonely and low. Perhaps feeling sad, as she does sometimes, about grandpa dying at so young an age."

"Hmm. Not necessarily," said Geoffrey. "She's always believed that about being alone. I don't think she was low at all. Just her normal matter-of-fact self."

Michelle looked at him. "Really? Oh. Okay. She's *your* mother. Seemed to me she was a little morose."

"No," said Geoffrey, putting an end to the conversation.

Clare hadn't properly understood Gran's thinking at the time. Nor had she thought much about it. But recently she had, and it made sense. Clare had grown accustomed to being alone. Mostly, she liked it. It was easier. She was in control of things and didn't have to worry about who was watching and what they thought. She could pretend she was the same as she'd always been. Or at least, that she was getting there.

She swiped her fingers across the window pane, clearing the condensation for a better view. The path to the cabin was flooded and several gullies of water bounced down towards the stream. It was nearly midday and had clearly been raining for some time. She'd slept for more than four hours, which explained why she felt so much better. The combination of sleep and analgesics was the only thing that relieved her migraines. She knew, having suffered them a few times a year since puberty.

The rangers, her father had said, would arrive at Heuningbos sometime after lunch. She'd brush her teeth and dash to the lapa to make coffee. Food, she thought, ignoring the rumble of her stomach, would be unnecessary since she wouldn't be hiking today. Also, she'd have to eat this evening with her father and his friends on watch.

The coals were almost ready for the small pot of water she'd prepared when Clare heard footsteps splashing across the lawn and thumping up the lapa stairs. She expected to see a ranger, but it was Faye. Puffing heavily, she ran under cover, pushed the hood off her head and dumped her daypack on the table.

"My God! I'm wet through," she said, wiping the water from her face.

Clare peered into the haze behind her, expecting the others to follow.

"No, just me," said Faye, shaking the water from her limbs. "What a downpour! I could barely see my hand in front of my face. You should see the stream. It's really flooding now."

"What happened?"

Faye didn't look at her. "I . . . I decided to turn back."

"Because of the rain?"

"No. It hadn't started raining yet. I . . . uh . . . thought I'd come and wait with you."

Clare felt herself grow warm. There it was, the uninvited concern. Her dad had wanted to stay with her. Derek had offered, too. But she'd insisted they go. It was bad enough being the youngster on the hike. Not to mention the one with "the problem." She didn't want to be babysat. Could she have made herself any clearer?

She held the pot up to Faye. "I was about to make coffee. Would you like some?"

"Love some. Thanks. Your migraine is gone then?"

"Yes. It has. Thank you," she said. "I'll get more water."

"Let me go. You stay dry," said Faye, pulling the hood over her head and taking the container to the outside tap.

She returned, dripping once more, and placed the pot on the fire. "I'm going to the cabin to change. The rangers won't want me in their car like this."

"Sure." Clare pushed the coals around the pot with a piece of firewood. "A warning, though. When I woke up, it was already raining and some of the bags got wet. I hope yours wasn't among them."

Faye wrinkled her nose and ran back into the rain.

Clare thought about Faye's description of the stream. If it was already flooded, there was a good chance the other rivers were, too. She pictured the two they'd crossed on the trail the previous day and wondered if the track the rangers had to follow to get to them would traverse the same rivers. Given the route, it made sense. What if the flooding made it impossible for them to reach Heuningbos? Or if the dirt track was washed so badly it became impassable?

Faye returned wearing trousers and a sweatshirt.

"I was one of the lucky ones," she said.

Clare was silent.

"I don't want to be a worry-wart, but if this rain doesn't let up soon, I wonder if the rangers will reach us," continued Faye.

Clare gestured towards the four utility boxes and three cooler boxes lined up along the far wall. "What about these?" she said. "If they can't get to us, will the rangers be able to get some other supplies to my father and the others?"

"I don't know. I hope they've crossed the river by now."

"The others?"

"Yes."

They were quiet as Clare made coffee. Faye added wood to the fire. It had grown cool and the women stood close to the coals as they drank. Clare wondered why her father hadn't persuaded Faye not to return to Heuningbos.

"I'm going to eat my lunch," said Faye, putting her coffee down and digging in her backpack. "Would you like a sandwich?"

"No," said Clare. "Thanks."

The other woman tipped her head towards the boxes. "There are some rusks in our box. Would you like one of those?"

"No!" She hadn't meant to speak so loudly. She took a deep breath and said, quieter now, "I don't want anything to eat, thank you."

Faye unwrapped her sandwich, eyes down.

Clare rubbed her forehead. She should be used to people forcing food on her by now. They couldn't help themselves. Or perhaps they didn't realise they were doing it. Would Faye have offered to share her lunch if Clare was someone else? Probably. She was a kind woman. But sometimes Clare wondered if people felt challenged by her resistance and wanted to be the ones who broke through to her. She glanced at Faye, now chewing quietly as she stared out into the rain. She didn't look like a woman who wanted to prove anything to anyone. Clare was embarrassed by her own behaviour.

"It's just that . . . sorry. I don't feel that well after all. I think I'm going to go and lie down again."

She held her mug under the water pouring off the roof, rinsed it and put it in her father's box of supplies before pulling on her jacket.

"See you later," said Faye, as Clare trotted down the stairs.

She flopped onto the bed, slotting her rolled-up sleeping bag under her head. It wasn't that she was sleepy. A second cup of coffee would've been preferable, but she'd messed up too badly to hang around in the lapa. Clare winced at the thought of what Faye must think of her. How rude she was. How unhinged. Again, she wished the woman hadn't come back. If only people understood it was better to leave her alone. She was fine on her own. But how could her parents' friends know that? The Clare they'd known had been sociable, fun, easy-going. She closed her eyes. How could they know what she was like when they hadn't seen that she'd become another Clare, one not even she knew.

It started shortly before she'd left for university. Clare had always been lean, sporty and, as Michelle said, "a late developer." While her friends began wearing bras in their early teens, Clare was flat-chested and fine with it. Her mother chuckled and said that it must come from her father's side of the family since she'd been busty at twelve.

Then, in Clare's final year of school, things changed. At first, she thought she was simply gaining weight because she wasn't as active as usual while studying for final exams. But then she saw she finally had breasts. Not only that, but her hips and buttocks were rounding out, too. It was okay until she stopped in at the Mackenzie's house to borrow some notes from Zach.

She and Zach were sitting in the kitchen, drinking Coke and discussing the tedium of studying, when Derek arrived home from work. Clare had meant to leave earlier but lost track of time.

"I was just on my way," she said, standing up after she and Derek had greeted one another. She felt his eyes on her and was suddenly aware of how tight her t-shirt and jeans were. She pulled her t-shirt over her stomach.

"You're looking good, Clare. Quite the young lady," said Derek.

Zach coloured and jumped to his feet. "Don't forget the book," he said, leading her out of the room.

When she got home, she examined herself in the mirror. "Quite the young lady" meant she had breasts. And a bum, waist and hips. What did that mean? She thought of Zach's uncomfortable reaction to Derek's comment. She hadn't experienced anything like it before. She wasn't sure what it implied but felt unprepared for whatever it might be.

The next day, Clare went running. Michelle was pleased, convinced that spending too much time at her desk wasn't healthy for her daughter. By the end of the month, Clare was running eight to ten kilometres a day and had lost almost four kilograms. Her new bra was baggy.

Two months later, Clare left home to attend university. If she was anxious about moving away from her family to a new town, making new friends and experiencing new things, she reassured herself she was strong and in control. After all, if she was able to reduce her intake to less than eight hundred calories (which generally meant below six hundred) and run up to ten kilometres a day, she could handle anything, couldn't she? It wasn't as if, at that point, managing her eating and exercise was easy. It required vigilance. She thought about food constantly, working out what she could and couldn't eat, and writing down everything in a tiny notebook. She bought a *Guide to Calories* from a second-hand book shop, but it didn't take long to memorise the nutritional value of the few things she ate.

At first, she ran in the morning before breakfast. Once at university, she added an evening run to her schedule, too. When one of her friends commented on her twice-a-day habit, she decided to wake up earlier and run before it was light. After a while, her evening runs grew so long that it was dark by the time she returned.

It wasn't that Clare was never hungry. Initially, she was always hungry. She pictured the roast dinners followed by dessert that Michelle prepared, and remembered how the family would groan happily after over-indulging. But the thrill of denying her hunger and not responding to it was more satisfying than giving in. After a while, she became so accustomed to hunger she stopped noticing it, with the exception of during her runs, when being hungry added to the euphoria. In fact, the combination of hunger and exercise provided such positive feelings of self-control that, between runs, she grew impatient to experience them again. Was running addictive? If it was, was that a bad thing?

She settled in at university quickly. The town was smaller than she was accustomed to but, given that most of the students came from other parts of the country, friendships formed quickly. Within a few weeks, Clare was dating kind and funny Will, who was a member of a large circle of friends that formed during the students' first week on campus.

Life was good. She loved the place and the people. Lectures were interesting, as was her social life. She continued to run and was selected for the university hockey team. It was after a match when she first realised others had noticed.

"Clare? A minute?"

Coach Gordan had just finished debriefing the team after an exciting two-one win against one of the university's chief rivals. Clare stood while the others headed for the changeroom. She and the coach exchanged smiles.

"Nice game, Clare. But I noticed you ran out of steam in the second half. Everything okay?"

Clare swallowed. It was true. Her stamina hadn't held out, despite her pushing herself as hard as she could.

"Yes. I'm fine. It was a fast game. I guess I just wasn't up to the pace. I'll step up my training and—"

The coach shook her head and cut her off. "You're thinner every week. Is that intentional?"

Clare gave an embarrassed snort. "No. I guess, it's just that I'm doing a lot."

"Debbie says you've gone vegetarian?"

"Yes."

"That's new?"

"Yes."

"Hmm. Is it possible you're not getting enough protein?"

"I hadn't thought of that," said Clare, which was a lie. The reason she'd stopped eating meat was to reduce her calorie intake. For a while, it had stopped her friends from commenting on how little she put on her plate in the dining room.

She left the hockey field having assured coach Gordan she'd improve her diet. The next week, she quit the team. She never spoke to the coach or Debbie again.

It was Will who made her face the truth. He also bore the brunt of the fallout. They were walking together to lectures one morning. Will took her hand.

"You're quiet today," he said.

"A bit tired," she replied. "It's been a busy week."

"Perhaps you should sleep in over the weekend. You don't have to wake up at five to run every morning, you know."

Clare stopped, pulled her hand out of his and looked at him. "How do you know I run at five every morning? Do you spy on the women's residence?"

He laughed. "No! Lynne told me."

Lynne lived in the room across the passage from Clare. "Is *she* spying on me?"

Will frowned. "No. I mean, I don't think so. She hears you go out, I guess."

"Why do people care about when I run and how much I eat? What is it with you?"

"What? Clare, be reasonable. You're thin and you're getting thinner. We care about you. That's why."

"God! Not you, too. I am not thin. I might be slight, but that's because I run. Runners are typically slight. Or hadn't you noticed?"

"It's not just the running," mumbled Will. This clearly wasn't easy for him.

"What? I eat."

"Do you? No one sees you doing it. Not me. Not your friends at res. A boiled egg for breakfast? An apple for lunch? Salad for supper, setting aside the feta cheese? That's not eating."

"You take notes? All of you?"

Will scuffed the gravel, his trainers growing dusty. "We care. That's all."

"Well, I can't bear it," she said, her eyes brimming. "I can't bear the watching and the questions and the judging. It's stifling. Just give me . . . give me some space. All of you." She turned and walked away, head down, tears hot on her cheeks.

She avoided Will and her other friends for the rest of the morning, slipping into lectures at the last minute and sitting alone in the back row. She told herself she was angry, which was a way of quelling the waves of humiliation that swept over her when she thought about people talking about her eating and running habits. They clearly thought there was something wrong with her, probably out of envy because *they* had no self-control. Particularly Debbie, who was forever stuffing her face. Clare winced, ashamed of her thoughts. It was unlike her to be mean.

As she walked towards her residence at lunchtime, head down to avoid seeing anyone she knew, Clare realised what she needed to do. She needed to eat. She'd put her books in her room, go to the dining room, queue with her friends, stack her plate as they did theirs, sit with them and eat. She'd chat to them as she cleaned her plate and after lunch, she'd find Will and apologise.

It was at that moment she realised she was no longer in control.

The trembling began below her ribs, and ran up her torso and down her legs simultaneously. She leaned against a wall. Her lungs were heaving but she couldn't get enough oxygen into her system. Her head spun.

"Are you okay?" asked a girl walking by.

"Yes, thanks," said Clare, staggering off the path and plonking herself on a bench where she pretended to examine a book.

The shaking had intensified. What was happening? Why did she feel so panicky? All she had to do was get to the dining room and eat. But she couldn't. The thought of filling a plate with food and eating, without calculating the calories for every mouthful to be certain she could run far enough to burn them off, terrified her. She had never been so afraid of anything in her life. There was no way Clare was going to eat like everyone else. She couldn't. *Why?* The word seemed to echo in her head. *Why? Why? Why?*

Because you'll get fat, came the answer, *and being fat is the worst thing that could ever happen to you because it means you have no self-control.*

There it was. Clare was petrified of gaining weight, not because she'd previously considered herself overweight but because of what ratcheting up kilograms would say about her: that she had no control.

But it didn't make sense.

Of course she was in control. Wasn't that what she'd proved over the months? She thought about how proud she was when she paged through her notebook, looking at how she'd reduced her intake week-by-week. She remembered the jolt of joy she felt when the scale registered a kilogram less at her Monday morning weigh-in. What, if not control, had made that possible? Now all she needed to do was to use that same control to propel her to the dining room to eat a plate of food. Why couldn't she? What had happened ? Why was she so weak? Who was in control if it wasn't her? What had taken over?

She sat while the other students filed past her. When the path was empty, she stood and walked to her room, flung herself on her bed and cried. She'd never felt such shame. She was out of control. People were watching, talking and pitying her.

Clare broke up with Will that afternoon and stopped doing things and going places with her friends.

"Too much work," she said, when they knocked on her door to invite her out.

"Too much work," she said, when her parents asked her if she'd come home during the holidays.

When she wasn't in lectures or running, Clare was at the library or working in her room. She finished top of the class in most of her subjects in her first year—fuelled by then on less than five hundred calories and at least two runs per day.

After she'd run, she'd examine her naked body in her mirror. She'd pinch the flesh on her stomach between her fingers and whisper, "Still fat, Clare." A hundred sit-ups were meted out as punishment.

When she left her room, she'd wear layers, finishing with an oversized man's shirt, regardless of the weather. Only once again that year did she catch Will's eye. He was sitting on a low wall in a quad outside the library with his hand on Jenny from Ecology One's knee. A glance was all it took to reveal the pity he felt for Clare. It was, she thought, as she adjusted the sleeping bag under her neck and looked out at the sheets of rain pouring past the window, the same look Faye had given her when Clare had lashed out at her in the lapa earlier.

Seven

Derek was unusually laconic as he led the way. Even his response when Diane announced that Faye had returned to Heuningbos Hut was economical.

"I'm not chasing after her to argue, if that's what she's hoping for," he said, gazing at the sky.

Geoffrey removed his cap and rubbed his ears. "Clare will be annoyed. She was clear she didn't want to inconvenience anyone. Honestly, all she wants is to be alone when the migraines hit. There's nothing anyone can do for her."

"It might be for the best," said Derek. "Faye was lagging. Come. We should move on."

"What about a quick tea break?" said Diane, tired after having had to walk-jog to catch up.

"Not a good idea. Eat and drink on the go. We don't want to risk getting caught in the rain."

He tried to keep his voice casual, not wanting to let on how worried he was about the heavy skies, and reluctant to reveal the ranger's warning so late in the day. He'd noticed earlier the clouds seemed to come from inland, which suggested the rain she had warned him about might've fallen elsewhere. But, he'd reasoned to himself when they left the cabin, the rain seemed far off and if they left early and moved fast, they'd be okay. Now, with the clouds drawing nearer and the wind picking up, he wondered if he'd made the right decision.

"It's better not to leave Heuningbos if you have any doubt about the weather," the ranger had said the previous day after telling him about the forecast. "If there's heavy rain, meneer, you do not want to try and cross the Bloukrans," she'd advised.

"But heavy rain? At this time of year?" said Derek. He'd been impatient to join the others outside the park office so they could get going.

"Ja. It would be unusual," said the woman, stamping his permit with a thump. "But it does happen. We're in the mountains. Not far from the sea. The weather is unpredictable."

"Your route guide says there's a rope crossing."

"Yes, but it doesn't help if the river is flooded." She gave him a tight smile. "I'm just saying, meneer, again: stay at Heuningbos and do not risk the Bloukrans River if there is any doubt. It can take days before the river subsides enough for us to reach you. That can be a big deal. Crossing any river in flood is very dangerous. And if you succeed, and we can't get your supplies to you at Grootkloof, it could spoil an otherwise lekker hike."

"What about the escape routes? We could use one of those, couldn't we?"

The ranger shook her head and chuckled without looking at him. "Meneer, maybe you could just accept what I have to say. If it rains, don't try and cross the Bloukrans. Just stay at Heuningbos. Okay?"

As the terrain evened out after the steep descent down the ravine, and the hikers approached the dense wall of reeds and bushes that grew along the river, Derek heard the loud rushing of water. He stopped and fished out the map from the pocket of his shorts and unfolded it. Bruce stood at his shoulder, squinting at the document.

"Here," said Derek, jabbing a finger at the paper. "We're here.

The crossing point is two or three hundred metres away. It should be sign-posted."

The others gathered around. "This is the rope crossing, right?" asked Helen.

Derek nodded.

"The river sounds terribly full," she said.

"That's why the ropes are there," said Derek, annoyed to feel his pulse quickening.

As if on cue, a light prickle of rain settled on his arm. Hoping the others didn't notice it, he folded the map, shoved it back into his pocket and walked on quickly.

A hand-painted arrow on a wooden sign pointed to the crossing spot, directing the hikers along a short path through tall reeds to the edge of Bloukrans River. They stood, staring at the fast-moving water, which was unusually ruddy for a mountain river. As he suspected others in the group might too, Derek recognised the mud as indication of flooding upstream. He said nothing.

"Here we go," said Geoffrey, pointing slightly upstream to where two thick ropes were loosely strung across the river, one above the other about a metre apart.

Derek walked to where the cables were tied around the base of a large boulder and, further back, again around the trunk of a tree.

"Looks safe," he called.

He noticed Bev and Helen hanging back as the others made their way through the sand and over the boulders towards him. The friends joked that Bev was a worrier while Helen was a warrior, which made them the perfect pair.

"Are you okay?" asked Helen, placing her hand on her wife's arm.

"I don't think it's a good idea."

"What do you mean?"

"What if something, like a log or a pile of sticks and stuff, is washed down the river while we're crossing and knocks into us? We could lose our grip. I mean, Hel, look how fast the water is flowing."

Derek pretended he hadn't heard the exchange, but Helen called to the group, "Guys! Maybe we should look for another spot to cross? Where the water spreads over a wider area and isn't as deep?"

"I don't think that's a good idea," shouted Bruce. "We need to stay on the trail."

Diane chimed in, "Also, it's starting to rain. We shouldn't waste time."

Derek was relieved that his friends had spoken up against Helen's suggestion. The reeds and steep banks would make it too difficult to navigate the river bank to find a better spot to cross and, with the rain pelting ever harder, time was against them. Helen's idea, he thought, was the kind of highly-strung, over-analytical proposal Faye might've made. Derek was accustomed to setting his wife right, but didn't want to argue with his friends. For one thing, there wasn't time.

"Are you going, Geoff?" he asked, pulling his hood up. "Or shall I lead the way?"

Geoffrey looked into the river. "The idea is to hang on to the bottom rope and walk through the water, right? I'm not meant to attempt a tightrope technique, am I?"

"I think the top rope is for those who carry their supplies with them. They'd tie the bags above them to keep everything dry."

"Right," he said, sounding anything but sure as he placed a hand on the lower rope.

"Wait," shouted Bev, who had followed Helen to where the others were.

Everyone turned to look at her, Derek with a frown. Surely she wasn't going to insist that they follow her wife's suggestion after all.

"Go on the upper side of the rope. So that it's between you and being washed away," she said.

"Good point," said Derek.

It was a slow process and, with the water flowing knee-high and the rain coming down harder, the hikers were saturated when Geoffrey, Bruce, Helen and Bev reached the other side. While Geoffrey helped his friends out of the river and up the bank, Derek had taken up the position of helping them find their footing as they began crossing. It allowed him to urge them on.

"Okay, Di, your turn," he said, once Helen and Bev, melded together like frightened children for the entire crossing, were out of the water.

Holding onto Derek with one hand and the rope with the other, Diane stepped into the water. She'd watched her friends totter across, gasping as the cold water soaked their clothing, and hoped she'd worked out where the wobbly boulders and potholes were.

"Thanks," she said, releasing Derek's hand so that she could clutch the rope with both hands.

She was almost midway across the river when they heard it. The water grew louder. At first it seemed to roar, but then the thunderous rolling was accompanied by cracking and crashing sounds. Diane, head down as she concentrated on placing one foot ahead of the other, didn't look up. The flood advanced like an ocean wave, surging to the shore with no sign of breaking. It swept with it debris from upstream, a weighty, tangled mass of branches, reeds and uprooted plants. Diane was oblivious and didn't notice anything until it reached her.

The muddy water and saturated wreckage hit her hard, flinging her body around so that she was facing it. Branches walloped her as they sped by. The force against her body and the ropes made her convulse as if electrified. Diane screamed and clasped the rope with both hands, her back pinned against the thick cable. The water and its woody contents rose around her legs.

Geoffrey leapt backwards to avoid a waterborne tree, which— with its branches caught up in the rope—swung around towards him. Bruce, Helen and Bev looked on, aghast, from the bank.

"Oh, my God! Diane!" yelled Bev. "Hold on!"

On the other side of the river, Derek hung onto the rope, ignoring how it burned his hands. The rain came down in sheets and the river, already nudging the cuffs of his shorts, continued to rise. First, he felt numb. *Why the hell hadn't Di moved faster and got out of the way?*

Was she deaf? Surely she'd heard the wave approaching. Then he grew impatient. *Why didn't she get out of the river now? What was she doing, staying there like a trapped frog? Why didn't she fight her way across?*

The rope jerked again as a large log slammed into it, swaying briefly in the water between Derek and Diane before being swept on. The debris was going to keep coming and the water was rising. Derek knew he had to do something.

"Don't let go! I'm coming," he shouted.

Diane looked at him, her face stricken. She was crying and Derek noticed blood seeping through her blouse and across her chest. Beyond her, Geoffrey and Bruce wrestled to untangle the tree that formed a barrier between them and Diane. Bev turned to Helen, tears flowing freely. Helen wrapped her arms around her wife.

"It's okay. It's okay," she said, patting Bev on the back. "Let me think. Let me think."

By the time Derek reached Diane, the water had risen to her thighs. She was no longer crying but her breathing was laboured.

"My arm," she groaned, glancing to her right to where any blood not immediately washed away by the hissing rain seeped through the cotton of her shirt, dripped into the water and was quickly carried away. "I can't hold on much longer."

Derek stood in front of her, shielding her from the water. "Hold on with your injured arm," he said. "Let the other one go, turn and face the others and grab the rope again in that direction. I've got you."

She stared at him, afraid.

"Come on, Di! You have no choice! We'll both drown if you don't move."

But before Diane could release her hand to turn, Derek was flung forward, crashing into her as if lifted and thrown. His chin smacked into the top of her head, momentarily stunning them both. They swayed, welded together for several seconds until Diane pushed her head back and looked up at him. Derek's eyes were closed.

"Are you okay?"

"Argh—my back," he moaned. "My back."

"Oh, God," she whispered. "What are we—"

Derek's Adam's apple slowly crawled up and down his throat as he swallowed deeply. "Give me a moment . . . a moment."

Geoffrey and Bruce had freed the tree and Bruce was inching towards his wife. Geoffrey stepped into the water, too.

"No," said Bruce. "Stay there. Keep your strength to help us out."

Geoffrey hesitated and stepped backwards out of the water. Bev sobbed loudly.

By the time Bruce reached Diane and Derek, the pair had recovered enough for Diane to turn and hold the rope with both hands. Derek didn't have the strength to prevent his body from pressing tightly up against Diane's, but they were able to inch their way towards Bruce. With her husband and their friend huddled close around her, Diane stopped crying and, teeth chattering, pulled herself towards the bank. The trio made their way to Geoffrey, who helped them out of the water one at a time. Helen and Bev tugged them up the slippery path and onto the bank, Bev still sobbing.

Diane sat, Helen kneeling alongside her, as Bruce unbuttoned her shirt so that Bev could examine her wounds. Geoffrey held his head in his hands, his cap saturated and glued to his skull. Derek limped a short distance from the group, pain shooting up his spine with every step. When his knees gave way, he sank to the ground and rolled onto his back, silent and spent.

Eight

Faye was restless. She wished she'd brought her book to the lapa when she changed her clothes in the cabin earlier. It would be awkward to go back after Clare had clearly gone there to escape her. The girl might think she was checking up on her, or coming to make amends. It would only add to the tension between them.

She looked around, fidgety and unaccustomed to not being busy. If she was at home, she'd have been cleaning something, sorting out cupboards, gardening or baking. The wind had calmed a little but the rain was relentless. As it poured off the roof in the curtains across the open section of the lapa, Faye imagined she was sheltering in a waterfall. With the earth drenched, several channels of water flowed fast towards the stream. A pair of hadedas hid beneath a bush on the edge of the lawn, drawing their long, curved beaks towards their puffed-out chests and looking into the rain like two disapproving, double-chinned authoritarians.

As soon as the rain let up, Faye would, she decided, go to the bridge to see how the water-course had changed. She wondered again about the others. If they'd been unable to cross the river and had to retrace their steps, they would have appeared by now. They must be safe, though without supplies, at Grootkloof Cabin.

While she knew that it was probably the upshot of boredom,

Faye decided she was hungry and looked at the boxes of supplies lined up against the wall. She'd packed ample food to satisfy herself and Derek. Even with the fresh items for the rest of the hike labelled and stored in the refrigerator in the rangers' office for delivery to the relevant cabins each day, there were plenty of options on hand. It would soon be dark and it was clear that the rangers wouldn't fetch them today. She and Clare weren't going anywhere. Cooking would help pass the time.

Faye lifted the lids of the utility container and cooler box she'd packed. Eggs, pasta, olive oil, mayonnaise, tuna, beans, peanut butter, onions, garlic, pesto, bacon, potatoes, feta, cheddar, cream cheese, butter, cream, milk salt, pepper, tea, coffee, wine and a small bottle of dried mixed herbs. What should she make? What would Michelle do? What gourmet camping dish would her friend whip up over the fire single-handedly? Faye felt a flash of annoyance. Why did she always compare herself to Michelle when she knew she'd always judge herself to be inferior? Wasn't there anything that she was proud of? Was there nothing that she had achieved that Michelle hadn't? It wasn't as if she was useless at everything she did.

Faye had found a job as a junior accountant at GNS Medical Supplies less than a week after her final university exam. Her parents had explained years earlier that they would pay for the three years it should take her to get her bachelor's degree in accounting. After that, she'd be on her own, even if she failed and was required to re-sit her exams. (She didn't.) There was no money to fund further studies or to support a break between studying and working. That Derek, Diane, Bruce and Helen would spend several weeks in Diane's parents' holiday home on the West Coast during the summer holidays while Faye learned the ropes at GNS Medical Supplies neither surprised nor troubled her. She might've momentarily wished she could be with them, and certainly she missed Derek, but Faye was pragmatic.

She hadn't been born to money like her friends.

It didn't take her long to settle at GNS. The work was largely procedural. Her boss, Ellen, was serious and fair and her colleagues were welcoming and friendly. Although Faye didn't complain— accountancy was her chosen field, after all—her day-to-day work involving things like accounts payable and receivable, inventory, payroll, fixed assets and the like was pretty dry. The products sold by GNS Medical Supplies, on the other hand, fascinated her. She pored over the company's catalogues and, whenever she had the chance, quizzed her colleagues in the tech, marketing and sales departments about the surgical instruments, the latest developments in medical rehabilitation apparatus and what was new in hospital furniture. It was after a discussion she'd had with someone in the canteen about a new range of paramedic equipment that George Hallman, head of sales, fell into step with her as she walked down the passage.

"Faye, is it?"

"Yes."

"George, from sales," he said, shaking her hand.

She smiled, hoping he wasn't going to ask her out. She'd already turned down Frank from warehousing and had hoped her response, "Thank you, but I have a boyfriend," would get around so she wouldn't have the displeasure of rejecting others. Not that she imagined they were lining up to ask her out, but there were many more men at the company than women. To her relief, George wasn't interested in her. Not in *that* way, at least.

"I overheard you talking to Cynthia about our new range. She mentioned previously how clued up you are," he said.

"Clued up?"

"Would you be interested in a job in sales?"

"Sales? No, I don't—"

"The thing is, our best salespeople are those who are genuinely interested in what they're selling. If they're excited by the product, clients get excited, too."

"But I don't—"

"We'd start you as an assistant. Teach you everything you need to know before you go out into the field. Think about it. I need to build my team and I think you might have what it takes. If you're interested, I'll have a word with Ellen. It'll all be aboveboard. If it doesn't work out for you, I'm pretty sure she'll take you back in accounts. She speaks highly of you."

Faye blushed. "Oh. Okay. Thanks."

George nodded and began walking away. Then he stopped and turned back. "By the way, the package is more than you'll make in accounts. And once you're in the field, there'll be commission, too. It's pretty good. Ask Cynthia."

Faye didn't ask Cynthia. In fact, she didn't mention her conversation with George to anyone. It was Ellen who brought it up a week later when they were alone in the office.

"George is wondering why you haven't gotten back to him about his offer," she said.

Faye emitted an embarrassed chuckle. "I didn't think it was an offer. I mean, a serious one."

Ellen leaned against the partition that separated Faye's desk from her colleague's. "I don't want to lose you, but I think he's right; you'd make an excellent salesperson."

She hadn't expected this. Faye thought of salespeople as self-assured, garrulous types, people who enjoyed talking and always had a joke on hand. People like Derek.

"Really? But I don't think I have the . . . the—"

Ellen raised her brows. "The confidence? Ego?"

Faye sniggered but said nothing.

"It's different in this industry because of the nature of the products and the clientele." Ellen waited a beat. "Do you want to know why George and I think that you would make an excellent salesperson?"

She nodded.

"You're a hard worker and you learn quickly. But more than that, you're genuinely interested in the company and its products, and you're resourceful." She looked around and continued more quietly.

"I wouldn't say this if anyone else was around and I will deny it if you ever quote me on it, but you're wasted here, Faye."

Within three months, Faye was visiting clients with George. By the end of the year, when George was booked off for knee surgery, Faye was making her own appointments and calling on hospitals, pharmacies, doctors and dentists alone.

George and Ellen were right; she was an excellent salesperson. But only, she reasoned modestly when anyone commented on it, because she was observant and paid attention when her clients told her about their experiences and trends they noticed in their fields. She made notes, kept lists, read up on innovations elsewhere and looked for answers when her clients pointed out problems or when she noticed there might be better ways of doing things. But it wasn't just that she was good at selling medical equipment; she loved it. Her knowledge and interest was so well-regarded that she was soon co-opted to planning meetings by GNS's buying department.

Shortly after that, one of the company's principal suppliers, a German manufacturer of surgical equipment, invited George and the marketing director to Cologne for a factory visit and to attend a medical and pharmaceutical trade fair. George asked Faye if she would like to accompany them.

"That's ridiculous," said Derek, when, as they packed the dishwasher that evening, she told him about the invitation. They'd been married for almost a year by then. "George just wants to get you into a hotel on your own."

Faye was shocked. "What? Why would you think that?"

"Oh, please. Don't be so naïve. Why else would your boss want you to travel with him?"

"Because he believes—he says I'm good at spotting trends. At predicting what our clients want and what will sell. I'd be—"

Derek snorted as he overfilled the soap cannister. "Right! 'Spotting trends.' That's one way of putting it." He hesitated. "I'm surprised you'd even consider it; after what you told me about him, about George."

Faye looked at him, narrowing her eyes.

"Don't say you've forgotten *that,* too?" said her husband.

She had, Derek insisted, become increasingly absentminded since joining the sales team. It was, he said, as if she was so preoccupied with work that she regularly forgot things she told him and worse, things he told her. Faye was surprised. She wasn't forgetful about other things in her life. But when she considered how much time she spent thinking about work, even when she wasn't there, she realised it was possible it dominated her thoughts. She vowed to herself to be more mindful at home with Derek. But clearly she hadn't been attentive enough, because she had no idea what she'd told Derek about George that might discourage her from travelling with him.

"I'm sorry, love, but I don't know what you're referring to. What did I say about George?"

He drummed his fingers on the kitchen counter. "Of course, that's convenient."

Faye glanced down. "Sorry."

"You told me that George was quite the ladies' man. That he couldn't keep his hands to himself."

She stared at him, horrified. "But he's not. He's nothing like that. George is—"

"Hey!" he said, holding up his hands. "I'm only repeating what you told me."

Faye began wiping the kitchen counters. She felt lightheaded. What was wrong with her? Why would she spout such nonsense about George to Derek? Surely he was mistaken. But then why say such a thing?

The next day, she told George she'd rather not go to Germany.

"Why?"

She swallowed. "It doesn't make sense. I mean, I should be here handling key accounts while you're away, shouldn't I?"

George peered at her from beneath his bushy eyebrows. "Hmm. Everything okay at home?"

"No. No, it's nothing like that. It's just—"

"It's okay. I think it's a pity, but it's okay."

When, after seven years with the company, Faye left GNS Medical Supplies to give birth to Zach, she'd been sales manager for two years, following George's promotion to director. She and Derek owned a three-bedroomed house not far from where he'd grown up and close to the schools he'd attended, which was just as he wanted it, insisting that his offspring would attend the same schools as he and his father had.

"I wish you hadn't resigned," said George, when he took her to lunch shortly before she left. "We would have given you unlimited maternity leave."

"It wouldn't be fair."

"You will come back though, won't you? There's no one who loves selling medical equipment like you do, and no one who does it better."

She blushed and smiled.

GNS Medical Supplies was sold to a multinational company two years later and its range absorbed into that of its new owner. Faye lost touch with George, Ellen and Cynthia.

There's no one who loves selling medical equipment like you do, and no one who does it better. It was silly, she knew, but George's words were imprinted on her mind. She'd never said them out loud, but sometimes replayed them in her head. Even so, the memory of her old colleague's praise and her record of success at GNS—her monthly sales figures were unprecedented—hadn't been enough to persuade Faye she was capable of returning to the workplace when Zach started school. Neither did reminiscing convince her that she'd achieved anything remarkable, particularly when held up against what Michelle had accomplished.

"Hi."

It was Clare. Faye dropped the lid back on the box as if she'd been caught shoplifting. Food! Why was she staring at the food when the girl returned?

"Hello," she said, wishing she was able to respond more coolly. "You're okay . . . um . . . feeling better?"

"Yes, thanks."

There was an awkward silence.

Clare shrugged off her jacket and put it on a bench. "I guess we're here for the night?"

"Ja." Faye looked outside. "It doesn't look like it'll let up any time soon."

"I hope the others are okay."

"They are, I'm sure of that. If the river was flooded, they would've returned by now. No doubt they'll be a little hungry if the rangers aren't able to reach them either, but otherwise, they'll be fine."

Clare nodded. "What were you doing?" she asked, tipping her head towards the food containers.

"Just having a look, seeing what I have."

"Were you going to cook?"

"Maybe." Faye shrugged. "I was bored. Thought I might as well do something."

"Can I help you?"

"Of course. I wasn't sure what I'd make. Perhaps pasta with cream and cheese."

"That sounds good. Let's have a look what we have in our box. Mom packed it, so . . ."

"Ah! In that case!"

They chuckled.

It was Clare who suggested adding more ingredients to the cheese sauce—she'd found shallots and cacciatore in one of the boxes Michelle had packed.

"But won't your father be annoyed if we eat his meat? He might have plans for it," said Faye.

"He has no idea what's in here. Anyway, we won't use it all," replied Clare, taking a cutting board from the box. Slim and grey, it looked like it was made from slate.

Faye leaned forward for a closer look. "Is that—"

"No, it's not stone. I thought so too, at first, but it's some sort of modified natural material. No common garden camping utensils for *my* mother."

"Stylish," replied Faye, taking a tin plate to slice the shallots on.

"You must've noticed the cooler box?" Clare gestured towards the black and white container, which—elegant, modern and clean among the other dusty, worn coffers—looked like it had misunderstood the dress code.

"Yes. Derek and Bruce were admiring it and playing with all its nifty digital functions last night."

"Dad's embarrassed by it."

Faye gave a small laugh. "Do you cook at home? With your mom?"

"No." Clare frowned slightly. "Dad and I cook together. Mom prefers doing it alone. Says it's more work showing us how to do things her way than doing them herself."

"Oh."

Faye wasn't sure what more to say. The sound of chopping, the *clank-clank* of the steel and the *thud-thud* produced by Michelle's high-tech board, seemed to accentuate the pause.

"Do you and . . . um . . . Derek cook together?" Clare asked eventually.

"No. God, no. I mean, he's a good cook, but we never do it together. He reserves his cheffing for special occasions. Usually when people are coming over. Gives me a shopping list. I deliver the ingredients and then make myself scarce. Until it's time to clean up."

"Sounds like he and my mother have a similar approach."

The women were quiet for a moment; as if contemplating the idea.

Clare continued, "Actually, I remember Zach's birthday one year. We must have been eleven or twelve. He, Derek, I mean, had just been to Holland and cooked us a Dutch meal."

Faye massaged the back of her neck. "Oh! What a nightmare that was. You kids turned your noses up at the herring. Then the croquettes exploded and the poffertjes were burnt. Poor Zach! What an awful birthday."

"Derek was so angry and it gave us the giggles. Alice, Linda and I set off the boys, but Derek sent Zach to his room. Poor guy. On his birthday. And it wasn't even his fault."

Faye remembered how angry and humiliated she'd been on Zach's behalf. She'd followed Derek to the kitchen after he'd yelled at their son.

"That's not fair, Derek. The girls were giggling, not Zach. And honestly, they're kids and this," she gesticulated to the mess in the kitchen, "it hasn't worked out. Let's round them up and go to the Spur for a burger. It's a pity it didn't go the way you planned, but there's no—"

Her husband spun around, the veins in his temple pulsing. "I'll take the others to the bloody Spur! You and Zach can laugh at me all you like while you clean up. 'The girls were giggling, not Zach.' Do you hear yourself? What is it about Clare that riles you? Hmm? What?"

Faye was dumbfounded. What was he talking about? Clare? She hadn't mentioned Clare. She'd said, "the girls," meaning Clare, Alice and Linda. She stared at him. Her mouth was dry, her head whirring. Derek glared at her for a moment and left the room.

Now she tipped the shallots into the pot where they sizzled in the butter. "Yes, that was a birthday best forgotten," she said, without looking at Clare.

"I'm sure every family has them," said the girl.

When the pasta was ready, Faye produced a half bottle of red wine.

"We didn't finish this last night," she said, taking a corkscrew to the stopper that had been pushed back into the neck. "I think a full-bodied cabernet will go well with our dish, though don't quote me on that. Derek's the wine fundi in the family."

She gathered two mugs.

"Will you have some?"

Clare was quick to respond. "No thanks."

Faye poured some wine into one of the mugs.

"Actually, yes, please. Just a little," said the girl.

Faye placed the pot of pasta in the middle of the table. Clare handed her a plate. They sat as close to the fire as possible. The older woman spooned pasta onto her plate and then, as if having forgotten to do so earlier, jumped up to add wood to the fire. When she sat down again, she ignored the small helping of food on Clare's plate and raised her mug.

"Cheers! Here's to the rain petering out soon and us being rescued tomorrow." The stainless steel mugs touched with a solid clunk.

"Though I hardly feel deserted here," said Faye.

Clare looked around the lapa, where the flames flickered orange and yellow against the stone walls and the paraffin lamp on the table alongside them pattered quietly, as if in tune with the rain.

"No, it's not too bad at all."

Faye, chewing, nodded.

"In fact, we're not alone. Look. We have dining companions."

Clare's head was tipped up towards the roof. Faye followed her line of sight to the rafters where she saw what looked like, at first glance, a gathering of grey-brown rats hanging by their tails, their eyes glinting in the light of the fire and lamp. Then she saw their wings.

She swallowed with a small shudder. "Eew. Bats."

"Yes." Faye heard the smile in Clare's voice.

"I hope they stay in their section of the restaurant," she said.

"They will. Or they'll fly off into the night. Perhaps they're put off by the rain. They're probably usually hunting by this time, which is why we didn't see them last night."

Faye look a long sip of wine. "Can't say I missed them."

"They won't come near you. Poor things have such a bad reputation. Except in China, where they're honoured and symbols of good luck and happiness."

"I like that. Maybe it means the rain will stop and we can join the others tomorrow."

Clare turned away from the bats and began eating slowly. Faye scooped two more spoons of pasta onto her plate. The food was delicious, but she didn't mention it.

"That reminds me; I met some bush pigs today," she said instead.

"Really? During the day? That was lucky. I recall my grandmother telling me that you generally only spot them at dawn or in the evening. Did the others see them?"

Faye described her encounter with the pigs, not bothering to conceal how afraid she was, and how silly she felt when the animals fled in the opposite direction. Clare's laughter was loud and whole-hearted.

"I'm sorry, I'm sorry," she said, trying to catch her breath. "But the image of you running out of the trees and pigs disappearing into them is hilarious. I'm sorry."

She put her hand on her forehead and began laughing again.

"Stop it," said Faye, giggling and pointing at the bats. "You're going to scare them."

Clare looked up, still chortling. "No, no. They're fine. Not batting an eyelid."

That set them both off once more.

When they stopped laughing, Faye told Clare about the birds.

"You're probably right," said Clare. "They were Knysna loeries. The red you saw when they flew away is to distract predators. Hunters think they're chasing something green, but suddenly it's red. It's confusing and gives the loeries a chance to escape."

"Really? Fascinating. You know a lot about birds." Faye glanced up the bats. "And animals."

"Just what my grandmother told me. I wish I remembered more. Paid more attention. She loved loeries. Did you know that they're monogamous? Like swans. And the turtle dove and some species of eagles."

They were cleaning up, laughing again as they tried to avoid getting wet while catching water splashing from the roof, when Faye realised how well Clare had eaten. She'd helped herself to seconds and they'd polished off the rest of the wine. She wondered how the young woman felt about herself. Would she hate herself when she thought about it later? Purge? Michelle said she wasn't bulimic, but how could one be sure? The illness was all about secrets.

"Thanks for supper," said Clare, stacking the clean pots and plates on the counter. "I really enjoyed it."

"Me, too." Faye kept her eyes down. "I haven't laughed so much in a long time."

"I haven't enjoyed my food so much in a long time."

"Really?" This time, Faye did look up.

Clare hesitated. Faye wondered if she regretted having spoken about food, but she continued. "It was just so . . . normal. I felt like myself."

"Oh. That's good . . . isn't it?"

Nine

Although Grootkloof Cabin was an easy walk from the river, it took the group almost an hour to get there. Diane bent her arm and held it against her chest, nursing the pain in her shoulder. The gashes in her forearm and chest were not as severe as they'd appeared and, after some bandaging by Bev, who was counted upon by her friends to always carry a carefully curated emergency kit, the bleeding ceased.

Derek's injury was more serious. For a while, as he lay on his back, the rain washing over his face, his friends discussed how they might build a makeshift stretcher to carry him to the cabin. Eventually, he pulled himself up, grey-faced from the effort.

"No. That's enough drama for one day," he said. "My back is not broken. I've possibly dislocated a vertebra, stretched some ligaments. Come. Help me."

Once he was on his feet, Derek accepted Diane's hiking poles but, even leaning on them and after Bev's painkillers kicked in, he shuffled slowly and rested frequently.

"Go ahead," he said, when the others waited for him beneath the jumble of trees that lined the jeep track like a dishevelled boulevard. "Don't treat me like a special needs person."

His friends exchanged glances and ambled on. They didn't stop again but moved so slowly they might as well have. Derek pretended not to notice. Although the trees provided some shelter, it wasn't enough to keep the group from being perpetually drenched. The squelching of his socks in his boots reminded Derek of a hike he, Michelle and Diane had undertaken on the mountainside near home when they were teenagers.

It had been a sunny, windless day and, after they'd walked for more than two hours, they stopped at a small dam a few kilometres from the end of the trail. Stripped to their underwear, the youngsters cavorted in the water for a while and then lay in the sun to dry. Diane sat up first.

"We should get going. My folks expect me for lunch," she said.

"Really? I'm warm enough for another dip," said Michelle. "A quick one?"

Diane shook her head. "You go. But quickly."

"And you?" Michelle looked at Derek.

His underpants were almost dry. "Nah," he said.

Michelle dived into the water, resurfaced and took a few strokes when Derek, who had just pulled on his shorts and boots, heard laughter and splashing. Two boys, slightly older than he, ran into the water behind Michelle. Derek glanced at Diane, surprised. They hadn't realised there was anyone else at the dam.

Derek and Diane watched as the boys, their heads close and their voices muted, glided towards Michelle, who was the facing the other way. Derek stood up as the strangers drew closer to her. He recognised the surprise in her voice.

"Hey!"

The boys chortled as they advanced. Michelle tried to swim around them. They blocked her, still laughing. The distance made it difficult for Derek to see what they were doing to her. He walked towards the water, fists clenched.

"Excuse me!" shouted Michelle. "Don't you dare touch me again!"

Derek didn't remember diving into the water or swimming to where the others were. But suddenly, he was there, shouting and lashing out at the boys. They were startled—then amused.

"Cool it, man," said the larger of the two, pushing Derek away. "We were just teasing."

Derek swam towards him, bent his knee and shoved his boot into the boy's groin. His yowl of pain echoed across the water as he reeled backwards, eyes wide and face pale. The other boy lunged for Derek, grabbing him around the neck and pushing him under the water. Derek kicked and punched, but his attacker was stronger and heavier. For a moment, beneath the water, Derek imagined he'd drawn his last breath. Suddenly though, the boy released him and he shot to the surface, Michelle's voice in his ears.

"Get away, you damn idiots!" she yelled.

Derek spluttered and looked around. The boys were making their way to the edge of the dam.

"Idiots!" he echoed.

Michelle glared at him and swam towards Diane.

The girls were silent as Michelle dressed. They walked on. Derek followed, his boots sploshing and his wet khaki shorts rubbing uncomfortably against his inner thighs. His heart was still racing and he wasn't quite sure if his lungs had recovered. All he could think about, though, was Michelle and how the boys might've touched her.

"Hey, Mich," he called, as they approached the gate at the end of the trail. "Are you okay? I mean . . . erm . . . did they hurt you?"

Michelle spun around. "Just don't talk to me!"

"What? Why are you mad at me? I came to—"

"God, Derek! I was okay. They were just messing around."

"But—"

"The one's hand accidentally skimmed my arm when I tried to swim past him. I was joking with him. They weren't doing anything."

"I didn't know . . . you shouted and I thought—"

She took a deep breath. "God. He could've drowned you."

He walked towards her. "But he didn't. I managed—"

"Because I fought him off you, you idiot! God! Boys!"

Michelle stormed off. Derek stared at Diane.

"I don't get it. What did I do wrong?"

Diane shrugged. "She knows those guys. They're her brother's friends."

"So? They're arseholes. I didn't know. How was I meant to know? I thought they were, they were . . ."

Diane turned and followed Michelle.

They never spoke of the morning at the dam again, but Derek didn't forget it. He longed for the day that Michelle would apologise for her behaviour and thank him for coming to her rescue. She might've known the boys, but that didn't mean they wouldn't harm her. He had saved her and he would do the same again.

Now, as he limped to the cabin, his boots similarly sodden, Derek thought about how calculated his response to Diane had been earlier, versus the way he'd instinctively plunged into the dam to rescue Michelle from the boys. He missed her. If Michelle had needed rescuing from the river, he wouldn't have hesitated. And, if she'd been watching from the riverside, he'd no doubt have been at Diane's side much faster. He wished Michelle hadn't had to cancel.

If anyone was surprised to find that neither Clare and Faye nor their supplies had made it to Grootkloof Cabin, they didn't mention it. Indeed, the group had been largely silent since leaving the river. Their examination of the Grootkloof site was perfunctory. Unlike the previous day, when they'd taken their time to admire and discuss Heuningbos Hut and its pretty location, the hikers were subdued as they walked up the stairs into the lapa, which was more or less a replica of the one at Heuningbos. Bev and Helen checked the cabin and bathroom. There were plenty of beds and the gas to heat the water was connected. They'd be okay.

Sheets of rain obscured the view like milky waves across a disconnected television screen. Sluicing every surface it met, the shower was clearly not a passing squall and looked set to continue for hours. Although the temperature hadn't yet dropped by much, Derek was pleased he'd told his friends to include space blankets in their daypacks. They'd need them overnight.

Bruce, who'd carried Diane's pack and stayed at her side since the river crossing, lit a fire. The hikers dug into their bags, using what they could to towel themselves off. They unpacked food they hadn't had time to eat yet and unwrapped it, laying sandwiches, fruit, nuts, crackers, cheese and energy bars across the table in something of a mishmash buffet to share. Derek watched as his friends ate, no one with much gusto. He had no appetite at all.

Bev handed him two packs of tablets. One contained painkillers and the other, anti-inflammatories. He hobbled across the room, sat on a bench against the wall and swallowed another one of each with a slug of whiskey—not the first since they'd arrived at camp—from his hip flask.

An antique from the nineteenth century, the flask was the only thing Derek had asked for when his siblings were sorting through their father's belongings. It had been on a bookcase in his father's study for as long as he could remember. His father had inherited the flask from an uncle, but never used it. Derek liked the image of himself as a gentleman bootlegger with expensive taste in style and alcohol. Now though, he didn't care about the flask; he was simply grateful for the tingle and burn of the whiskey on his tongue and the warmth of it in his stomach. He lay back, eased his aching vertebrae against the cool surface of the bench, and waited for the alcohol and drugs to take the sharp edges off his pain and thoughts.

The incident in the river had shaken him. He'd put his life and those of his friends at risk by not taking the ranger's advice. Thank God he'd been the one to go to Di's rescue, even if he had hesitated. That made up for his bad decision, didn't it? And if that wasn't enough, he was also paying the price in pain.

Derek was grateful that Clare wasn't there. And Faye. His wife was the only one who knew about the warning he'd received. He wondered whether the rangers had managed to reach them and what Faye might've told them. Would she say anything about him having been warned about the weather? Surely not. She'd feel complicit for not having spoken up when they left. Knowing Faye as he did, he knew she'd blame herself for not having insisted they all stay at Heuningbos. He took another swig from the flask, listening to the drumming of the rain as it poured off the roof and onto the stone stairs.

"Anyone for a game?" asked Geoffrey, wielding a pack of playing cards.

Derek gave a dismissive wave. Helen placed her arm over Bev's shoulders and guided her towards Geoffrey. Bruce offered to refill their water bottles and, when they declined, sat at the table to play. Diane made her way to where Derek lay, his head propped on his backpack.

"Are you okay?" she asked.

"Getting there." He held up the flask. "Want some?"

Diane manoeuvred one of the tree-stump stools closer and sat down. "Actually, I can't think of anything better," she said, taking the flask from him.

"How are your injuries?" asked Derek.

She took a small sip and handed it back to him. "Fine. Lots of blood for a couple of minor gashes, really. My shoulder's starting to feel better. You took the brunt of it. God, I was scared. I thought that was it."

She shook her head and closed her eyes. Derek saw the tears before they rolled down her cheeks. He lifted the flask to his lips.

"If you hadn't come—"

"It's okay, Di. We're okay. Hey, we survived. We have a great tale to tell."

"But it could so easily have ended badly. I mean, *really* badly." She wiped her eyes and stared at him. "I don't think I've ever been so afraid."

"I know."

He held the flask to her. She shook her head.

The warmth of the liquor and fire had reached Derek's bones. They seemed to melt into the stone, taking most of the pain with them. He smiled.

"We're okay."

Diane tried to return his smile. It was more of a grimace.

"Where do you think Faye and Clare are? Still at Heuningbos? Or would the rangers have taken them somewhere else?" she asked.

"I don't know. It's hard to say whether they would've had rain on that side of the valley and how it might've affected the rivers. I mean, this is totally unseasonal."

"So everyone says."

"Either way," he continued, "they'll be fine. Better off than we are, given that they'll have our supplies from last night if the rangers didn't get to them in time."

"Yes. There's that. Though, strangely enough for me, I'm not hungry."

"Me neither. I wonder if Clare will eat?" His tone was suddenly dreamy.

Diane raised her chin.

"What do you think about it?" he asked.

"About what?"

"Clare. And her, whatever's wrong with her."

"The migraine?"

"No. The other thing."

"Anorexia nervosa. That's what's it's called." She folded her arms. "Why does it seem so difficult for people to say? It's an illness. A mental illness."

"Yeah, that's what Mich says." He swallowed another mouthful of whiskey. "I mean, how does a perfectly wonderful, intelligent, beautiful girl go from being all of that to starving herself? How?" Derek's voice was low, peeved.

"As I understand it, it's often the wonderful, beautiful, clever girls who become anorexic," said Diane. "They're high achievers and when they decide, for whatever reason, that they need to control their diets or their bodies, they do it. The self-control thrills them. They become addicted to how good it feels."

He shook his head and looked into the distance. "Nah. She's smarter than that. That stuff happens to silly girls who worry about how they look and what boys will think."

"No, Derek. That's not how—"

"My girl would never fall for that." His words were no longer distinct. They seemed to slide into one another. "Something must've happened to her. I think she was attacked. Something major happened and she has suffered some trauma. That's what happened."

"Who are you talking about? 'My girl?' What girl?"

"Ah, Di. You must've known? Had some idea?"

"Known what? What are you saying?"

"Clare. She's my . . ." He turned his head and put a finger to his lips.

"What are you saying, Derek? Are you drunk? Stoned?"

He gave a small smile. "Maybe. A little. Come on, Di. Don't tell me you can't see it?"

"What? No. I mean—"

"Yeah. You and Mich both."

Diane leaned forward and whispered. "That's ridiculous. You and Michelle were over years ago. Are you saying that you still—"

"No. Not now. Not for a long time. But when Clare was conceived—well, ja, then."

"Jesus, Derek! You're talking such rubbish! How many pills have you swallowed with that?" She dipped her head towards the flask, which he held against his chest. "I'm going to forget you ever implied anything so crazy. I'm going to—"

"Di, you of all people, understand how it was for Mich and me. We should be—we could've—but somehow we just. . . What's that line? Can't live with her, can't live without her?"

Diane glanced over her shoulder towards the others across the room. They were quiet, heads bent over the cards in their hands. She turned back to Derek.

"You're behaving like a teenager."

"Ja. I know. I'm sorry. It's just that since Clare's been ill, it's been driving me nuts. Mich's in denial about what must've happened to her. Geoff is clueless. My God, I even drove to the university to see her. I was . . . I was planning to find out for myself . . . find out whoever hurt her and beat the living daylights out of him."

"What? You didn't! That's insane!"

"I know, I know. I got there, but I didn't say anything. I saw how it would freak her out if she found out that I, and not old Basson's Garden Services, am her—I mean, have you seen her with Geoff?"

"Stop it." Diane's fists, resting on her knees, were clenched.

"Today, in the river, when we, well, it made me think. I want her to know, Di. If something had happened . . . Just because Mich doesn't want me, doesn't mean—"

She leaned closer and hissed in his ear. "Geoffrey is Clare's father. I don't know why you're spouting this nonsense and why you think anyone would believe you. You're nuts, drunk, high, whatever, and this is dangerous. And what about Faye? Have you forgotten you have a wife? And a son? What would this farce do to them?"

Derek blinked and lifted the flask to his lips.

"Thank you for saving me," she said, standing up. "But my God, you're an idiot and you don't deserve the love you get, not from any of us. Pull yourself together. Let this be the first and last time you ever mention or even think such nonsense."

As she walked away, Diane heard Derek say, "You're a good friend, Di. Mich is lucky to have you."

Ten

The sound of the rain on the roof was more muted when Clare awoke, as if the droplets were smaller and the wind chasing them, calmer. It was the kind of *pitter-patter*, white noise that, in other circumstances, might've enticed her to burrow back under the covers and snooze a while longer. Instead, she glanced at the bed on the far side of the cabin. Faye lay motionless, facing the wall.

A pair of Cape robin-chats with their distinctive orange breasts and grey bellies hopped about on the lawn. The larger of the two stopped when he spotted Clare open the door. He sized her up with eyes shining brightly in the black band that ran, Zorro-like, from his beak to the side of his head. As she stepped onto the grass, the bird emitted a shrill call and the pair flew away.

The water was boiling when Clare saw Faye walking towards the lapa. Although she wore her jacket, her head was bare. Clare realised that, while the clouds remained dark and low, the rain had stopped.

"Morning," said Faye. She held up her palms. "Yay. But I'm not sure it's going to stay away for long. Shall we nip down to the stream to see how full it is?"

They carried their coffee with them, treading carefully over the rivulets that ran down the slope in braids and spinning eddies. The earth was dense and sticky beneath their boots and, as they reached the edge of the yard, Clare saw the orange-grey robin-chats flit from the trees. They alighted on the lawn where a pair of hadedas, dull grey but for the occasional glossy bronze glint of their wings where the light touched them, were already determinedly pecking for worms in the sodden soil in their percussion-like way.

The water swirled fast and turbid a few centimetres below the bridge, burying all but the largest boulders and giving off a muddy, mineral scent. Faye looked upriver and then down.

"No longer a stream, that's for sure," she said.

"Is it much higher than yesterday?"

"Absolutely. And to think there was barely enough water here for me and Bev to dab ourselves with when we arrived."

They watched quietly for a moment. Clare swept a bushel of reeds that had been washed onto the bridge into the water with her boot.

"What do you think it means for the other rivers?" she asked.

Faye shrugged. "Probably that they're impassable. It's possible that bridges have been flooded, damaged."

"So, impossible for the rangers to reach us?"

"Perhaps. It's hard to be sure without knowing the route they'd take by car. And how the rivers lead into one another."

"Bloukrans being the largest, right?"

"I think so."

Clare glanced at Faye, thinking she might have more to say but she remained still as she looked beyond the bridge to where the path led up and around the hill.

"I wonder if my father and the others will be able to go on?"

"I'm guessing but, if this," Faye tilted her empty mug towards the water, "which was a trickle two days ago, is anything to go by, they'll be stranded for a while, too."

"Stranded?"

"It'll be okay. The water will subside in a day. Maybe two. We'll be collected and reunited soon enough."

"So we wait?"

"I don't think there's an alternative. Do you?"

Clare shook her head and turned towards the path. "I'm going to walk for a bit."

"Where?"

"That's the route you took yesterday, right?"

"It is."

"Perhaps I'll see the pigs," she said.

Faye chuckled. "Okay. I'll wait in the lapa in the unlikely event the rangers do make it. Will you . . . erm . . . go far?"

"Do you think it's possible to see the Bloukrans from the top of the ravine? To gauge how full it is?"

"Maybe, but that's quite a hike," said Faye looking pointedly at the sky.

Clare handed her the empty mug. "I'll turn around if it starts raining again."

❧

She did want to see the wild pigs. She was also curious about how full the river was. But that wasn't really why Clare wanted to walk; she was anxious to exercise.

For a while, she'd tried to convince herself it was okay because she'd done nothing the previous day, but the truth gnawed at her. She had to work off supper. The pasta swimming in cream, cheese and cacciatore! My God! What was she thinking? And the wine? Almost a mugful! That was around three hundred calories.

Clare glanced over her shoulder. Faye was out of sight. She began running.

The hill was steep and her hiking boots heavy. Despite the clouds, she was soon hot. Clare couldn't remember the last time she sweated while exercising; that bodily function, she'd discovered, was reserved for the night-time horrors of an anorexic. She wasn't perspiring as she jogged up the path. Even so, she was warm enough to stop and, while running on the spot, she removed her rain jacket and tied it around her waist.

By the time she reached the top, Clare had run for more than half an hour. Her feet ached from the unfamiliar motion of the boots and, worried she might develop blisters, she slowed to a fast walk. The expanse of veld, flat and open, made breathing seem easier. It was windless and, with the clouds so low, the vegetation seemed to be waiting for something to happen. Stepping around the bigger puddles that dotted the trail, she decided to continue for another half hour before turning back. That would give her an hour's proper workout, plus however long it would take to return to Heuningbos.

Although she doubted others would believe her—if she dared tell them—Clare felt sure that she had turned a corner in her illness. While she had moments of weakness, like when she snapped at Faye yesterday and only just managed to restrain herself from doing sit-ups on the first night of the hike, they were fewer and far between. She believed that she was resuming control. That was the plan. The only way she'd fully recover would be to prove to herself she was stronger than the illness.

The solution had come to her when she returned home from varsity for the first time and saw the effect of her illness on her father and mother. It wasn't that her parents hadn't known she had lost weight since leaving home. The news had reached them months previously when one of Michelle's colleagues, whose daughter was a student at the university too, mentioned it.

"Sweetheart, I believe you're terribly thin," said Michelle, when she called Clare that evening. "So thin, people are talking about it. What's that about?"

It hadn't been difficult to reassure Michelle over the phone. Her mother, a runner, was delighted Clare had become serious about the sport and, yes, of course runners were on the thin side. Michelle dismissed the information as ill-informed gossip, probably instigated by someone who wished that they themselves had the kind of drive required to get leaner so they could run faster and farther. She said as much to Geoffrey. It was he who discovered they'd been wrong not to ask more questions.

When a bony girl with long hair listlessly dragged two bags towards him at the airport, Geoffrey stared beyond her, looking for his daughter among the other passengers appearing between the automatic sliding doors. Even when the girl planted herself in front of him and said, "Dad! Hello!" it took several seconds before Geoffrey recognised Clare.

That night, as she was about to tap on her parents' bedroom door to say good night, she heard weeping. It was her father.

"I don't understand," he said between sniffs. "What happened to her? What happened to our girl?"

Clare didn't hear her mother's muted response. She turned and ran down the passage. She'd never seen or heard her father cry. He was her rock. The man with a solution for every problem and a disposition strong enough to shoulder any troubles. She had broken her father. She'd shattered the strongest person she knew. She felt faint with shame and self-loathing.

"You need to see someone, sweetheart," said her mother the next day. Geoffrey had left home early. "A doctor. A specialist."

"No," replied Clare.

Michelle blinked, frustrated. "You know you're unwell, ill, don't you?"

She nodded.

"So you need someone to treat you, to help you get well. It's *that* simple."

"No. I have to do this myself, Mom."

Michelle stood up and walked to the window. They were in Clare's bedroom, the room she'd occupied since she was six. The room where she'd become Katy Perry as she sang into her hairbrush. The room she'd asked her father to paint dusky pink when she turned thirteen.

"Purple? You want a purple room?" he had teased.

"It's dusky pink, Dad!" she'd objected. "Dusky pink!"

It was still dusky pink, but she'd call it purple if it made him happy.

"Clare, please," said her mother, running her hands through her glossy blonde hair. "I can't help you. I don't know what to do. You have to see a doctor. Do it for me. Do it for Dad."

But she stood firm. "I have to do this myself, Mom. I got myself into this, I can get myself out of it."

"Sweetheart, you're being unreasonable. I don't know much about this, your illness, but I don't think that's how it works. If you get any thinner, you'll have to be hospitalised and then, well, then you won't have any choice."

"I do have a choice now and you have to let me do it my way. Please, Mom."

Clare knew that everyone in her family was relieved when she returned to university after the holidays. They couldn't bear to see her eat so little, exercise so much and recede further and further into herself. Sometimes, when she tried to join in a conversation, she repeated herself. It was hard to stay focused. They stared at her with pity and annoyance. She was an embarrassment. Angus, seventeen at the time, said as much.

She was slicing a boiled egg for breakfast when he walked into the kitchen and tossed his tog bag on the table. He glanced at her plate.

"Jeez, Clare! An egg? Are you sure you should?"

She ignored him.

"You're a freak, did you know that? Wherever I go people ask, 'Hey Angus, what happened to your sister? Where's she going? She's kind of disappearing.' It's embarrassing. I mean, who are you? Get a grip, Clare. Please."

She didn't respond. What could she say? He was right; she was an embarrassment, but he didn't realise the full extent of it.

Now, more than two years later, Clare was certain she was getting a grip. Wasn't she? She'd not only got her degree, but she'd also spent those two years retracing the steps that had made her ill and trying to reverse what she had done to herself. It took longer to rewind than she'd hoped. Sometimes the tape got tangled and she had to go back a little and start over. But she was getting a grip, wasn't she?

Last night, she'd cooked with Faye. She watched Faye pour cream into a pot and stir melting cheese into it. She herself had suggested they add fatty pieces of Italian sausage. She'd eaten pasta and drunk wine, laughing as she'd done it and helping herself to more. With Faye, she hadn't loathed herself or the food. In fact, she hadn't thought much about it. She'd eaten because she wanted to. She was hungry, even though she hadn't exercised all day. Her body needed nourishing. She felt it and responded. She ate because it was the thing normal, healthy people did. The kind of thing old Clare would've done.

Afterwards, she'd gone to bed and fallen asleep almost immediately. Sure, she'd run several kilometres this morning and was marching through the veld to burn calories, but that was okay, wasn't it? She'd gained weight over the years, not a lot, but enough not to have to put a long shirt over her leggings to hide the hollows in her buttocks and the wide gaps between her thighs. The fine, fur-like hairs that had sprung up along her jawline when she was at her thinnest had disappeared. Her menstrual cycle had resumed, even if it wasn't regular yet. She was almost normal. She knew it even if others didn't.

It had happened so slowly that no one noticed. They still thought of her as the anorexic girl. She'd given up trying to explain what she was trying to do and her reasons for doing it. To others, her rationale was as delusional as her body dysmorphia. They thought that, just as she imagined the pinch of skin she held between her fingers was a roll of fat, Clare was mistaken to believe that continuing to assert her rigorous regime of self-control could reverse her condition. They thought she was deluded. Clare knew that her mother and whoever Michelle had told (definitely her father) thought that her strategy was ridiculous. They were disbelieving but, because she was no longer losing weight and her mind wasn't as scattered as it had been, they didn't fight her about it. She was ill, but she'd survive. They continued to watch her. They worried. But soon, Clare hoped, they'd realise she was the still the girl they knew because she wouldn't be ashamed of herself anymore. Her father would look at her and be proud. He'd no longer be broken. She would've fixed him. It was her responsibility since she'd wrecked him. When that was done, she could stop hating herself and become part of her family's world again.

☙

Clare checked her watch. It was almost an hour since she'd left Faye at the bridge. She should turn back. The sky was gravel-grey. Possibly darker than when she'd set off. She stopped and looked around. The woodland was visible ahead, rising dense and dark at the edge of the fynbos. She smiled as she thought about Faye and the wild pigs. To her left, the veld, stippled with a miscellany of mountain fynbos, grasses and bushes, stretched into the distance to where the mountains merged with the clouds. Not far from the path on the other side, Clare saw the edge of the ravine.

Imagining it might be possible to see down to the river from there, she made her way through the veld to the lip of the gorge. As she approached, Clare saw how dramatically the earth fell away. She leaned forward, peering over, but couldn't see the bottom of the valley. She needed to get closer to the edge. To her left, she spotted a large boulder with several substantial protea plants growing near it. She climbed onto the rock and examined the proteas. With their roots lodged in the earth alongside the boulder, the plants were sturdy and secure. Clare inched towards the rim of the boulder and grabbed the largest branch that she could get her hand around.

Leaning forward, she saw the river snaking through the canyon. Even from a distance, it was obvious the water, white and turbulent, was flowing fiercely. She and Faye might've thought the stream near Heuningbos Hut was full, but the Bloukrans River had risen above its banks. Cutting new channels through the earth here and there, it was severely flooded. It didn't seem possible that anyone could traverse it today, not by foot or in a car.

Clare gazed up the valley and onto the mountains on the other side of the river. Where was her father? She knew that Grootkloof Cabin wasn't far from the river, but was it visible from here? Seeing the faint line of the path that led from the river into the trees, she traced it into the valley. It ended at a small opening and there Clare could make out three roofs; two covered with iron and one larger one, with thatch. That's where the others would have spent the night. Were they still there? Might she spot them? Or at least see smoke rising?

She took a small step forward, her boot moving from the solid surface of the boulder into a pocket of gravel in a puddle of water. The gravel, lying in a thin layer of mud under the water, gave way beneath her foot.

The lurch was powerful enough to rip her fingers from the plant. She fell forward, tumbling off the boulder for a metre or so before her lower chest rammed into the jagged edge of a rock. The impact seemed to knock every wisp of air from her lungs but wasn't enough to stop her entirely. She rolled over and toppled again, legs and arms flailing until she landed on a ledge, her left knee taking the full force of the second phase of the fall.

She lay, stunned, trying to contain her fright and struggling to inhale, to exhale, to fill her lungs. Slowly, she told herself, slowly and deeply. That was when the pain pulsed through her. It seemed to come from muscles that held her ribs together, ribs which seemed to click as if disconnected. She breathed shallowly and fast, holding the oxygen in her upper airways. Her heart pounded, her head spun and her knee throbbed as though someone had pounded it with a mallet.

Clare closed her eyes and tried to calm her thoughts. She'd be okay. She hadn't hit her head. She wasn't at risk of falling further. The ledge wasn't far from the top and, if she was careful, she could crawl back to safety. As she pushed herself up, a dagger of pain stabbed through her and she passed out.

Eleven

She sat on the stairs leading into the lapa, shovelling muesli and long-life milk into her mouth. It was tasteless and required more chewing than it deserved. Faye remembered why, at home, once Derek left for work, she ate toast heaped with butter and marmalade rather than her husband's preferred breakfast cereal.

"Breakfast is not about savouring textures and flavours," he'd insisted when, early in their marriage, she'd tried to introduce other things to the table in the morning. "It's about fuelling your body as quickly and effectively as possible. There's no time for cooking and relishing food at breakfast."

Faye didn't agree. She was happy to get up in time to make omelettes with cheese and mushrooms and pancakes with apple and cinnamon. But she didn't argue. Neither did she comment on how accurate Derek's assessment of muesli was. Introduced as a morning meal for patients by a Swiss doctor in the early 1900s, muesli wasn't, she thought, food at all; it was medicine.

Before Zach was old enough to go to school, Faye would wait until Derek had bolted down his muesli and left before she and her son went into the kitchen to create their own more interesting breakfasts. It was her son's introduction to cooking.

Later, when he'd begun school, Zach ate breakfast with Derek.

"Eat your muesli, Zach. It contains everything you need to get going. There's no time for toast or eggs. We'll be late," his father would grumble.

Knowing that his mother typically filled his lunch box with interesting snacks, Zach didn't complain. So, muesli it was for Zach, too, until he left his parents' home and became master of his own meals. Faye, however, turned to toast. Now, as her jaw ground its way through another spoon of rolled oats and rubbery almonds, she thought about how many years that had gone on for; a life measured in solitary mornings of toast and marmalade. It was, she thought, only marginally better than a life measured in endless mouthfuls of muesli.

A bird, dark grey with orange on its breast and outer tail feathers, hopped on the grass on the edge of the yard, stopping occasionally to duck his beak into the ground. A robin, thought Faye, picturing illustrations she'd seen on Christmas cards from her mother's friend in Britain. Clare would probably know. She watched the bird, noting the white above his eyes, and willed him to call so that she'd have more information to share, but he was quiet.

The clouds had gathered again, dulling the light with their crowding and affirming her earlier hunch that more rain was imminent. With her jaws exercised and bowl empty, Faye left the lapa and followed the track behind the cabin. She wanted to be outdoors for as long as possible and was curious about the state of the road.

With parallel ditches of varying widths and depths, the tracks resembled seasonal riverways rather than a roadway. Boulders had been excavated by the rushing water, creating glistening, smooth-edged obstacles in the earth, which made Faye think of the plump seals she'd seen sunning themselves on the harbour walls in Cape Town. Sections of the road had been washed into deep dongas on the side, leaving wide gashes in the earth. Where the tracks levelled out, the water had deposited patches of silky, squishy mud. It was difficult enough to navigate by foot, let alone in a car.

Faye stopped on the crest of the hill and looked down to where the track swept to the east, disappearing around the corner and reappearing in the valley below. There she saw how the stream, now a river, had flooded the road and the surrounding basin, depositing large piles of debris left and right. It was difficult to gauge the depth of the water, but it didn't look passable. She would, she thought, probably be obliged to chew her way through another bowl of muesli the next day. Or perhaps Clare would have something more interesting to offer from her and Geoffrey's boxes of supplies.

She'd hoped to find the girl back at Heuningbos when she returned and, as Faye approached the lapa and heard the clank of a plate and the thud of something falling on the stone floor, she was pleased.

"Hey! You're back," she called as she climbed the stairs.

The eyes, light brown and close-set, that met hers were not Clare's. A large baboon sat in the middle of the table, knees splayed and genitals exhibited. He'd ripped a corner off the muesli box and was pouring the contents down his throat. Behind him, a marginally smaller baboon had the plastic top of the milk carton in his mouth and was peering into the box. Several other members of the troop were sniffing and tugging at the containers on the floor. The smallest among them sat alongside Michelle's fancy cooler box. Turning her head to the side, the monkey ran her tongue across the lid.

Faye froze. She might've been unsure about the intentions of the wild pigs the previous day, but the baboons' ambitions were clear; they wanted food. She also knew how vicious these animals could become if they felt cornered. She felt a spatter of frustration. What had she been thinking by leaving the food out? The information in the trail guide was unambiguous:

"Do not feed animals or leave food accessible to them. Animals that are fed can become reliant on humans, lose their natural instinct to find food and even become aggressive. Food left for collection at cabins and any waste should be secured so that animals cannot get to it by any means."

The bins at the cabin had animal-proof lids and the containers the hikers had brought were secure, but Faye had left the cardboard cartons containing the muesli and milk on the table. She'd lured the animals into the lapa.

As if sensing her reproach, the large male stopped guzzling the cereal and, box clutched to his chest, stared at her, his furry brow low across his eyes. Faye swallowed. What was he thinking? What was his plan? Should she turn and run? Drop her eyes and slowly walk backwards down the stairs?

Before she settled on a decision, the baboon opened his cavernous mouth to display two pairs, bottom and top, of terrifyingly long, yellow fangs and emitted a deafening bark-roar, which seemed to come from the pit of his belly and, with the lapa as echo chamber behind, reverberated across the valley.

Faye thought her knees would buckle as the baboon, with Derek's box of muesli still firmly in his hand, leapt neatly off the table. Followed closely by the others, he loped to the far corner of the shelter, hopped down the stairs and cantered across the lawn. As the troop, the little cooler box-licker trailing at the back, vanished into the trees, Faye sat down, breathing heavily.

⊰⊱

Hours later, Clare still hadn't returned. Faye, who'd cleaned up the mess made by the baboons and lugged all the boxes to the cabin where she could lock the door and windows, had given herself a deadline: if the girl wasn't back by three o'clock, she'd head out on the trail to look for her. It was one thing to give Clare her space, but another to be left to worry for so long.

She wondered if she'd find the young woman close by. Perhaps she was at the stream, behaving like a sulky teenager who couldn't get her way. Faye thought about Clare's obvious annoyance when she had appeared at the cabin the previous day. She'd wanted to be left alone. But then, after they'd had such an enjoyable evening, Faye had imagined Clare had reconsidered her attitude. Obviously not.

It worried her that Clare hadn't eaten all day. She would, she decided, put some food in her backpack just in case, when she found her, Clare agreed to eat. But what? What would the young woman be most likely to accept? Faye had noticed Clare's daypack under her bed in the cabin. Would it be rude to open it and look at what hiking snacks she'd packed for herself? If there was anything there, she'd know what the girl would be most inclined to eat. It wasn't really snooping if the intentions were honourable, was it?

She peered out the window to check that Clare wasn't approaching and picked up the bag. It contained a water bottle; space blanket; beanie; small canvas bag holding tweezers, matches, plasters, headache tablets and lip-ice; thick notebook with pencil attached to it with string; small packet of peanuts and raisins; an apple; and two energy bars. The bars were similar to those Faye had packed for herself and Derek. Faye also had nuts and oranges, the latter of which would hopefully be an acceptable exchange for Clare's apple.

Pleased with her ingenuity, she was about to close Clare's bag when curiosity got the better of her conscience. She glanced out the window again and, again seeing no one, took the notebook out of the bag and opened it.

It was a day-by-day account of the food Clare had eaten, calories in brackets alongside each item and the total consumption each day. Daily exercise undertaken was also recorded. Faye grimaced. Poor kid. Was this what it was like to be anorexic? Obsessive control and monitoring? Clare had included additional notes here and there.

"Butter on Provita today. First time in two years!"

"Upped weekly intake by an average of 165 calories per day. Getting there."

"Felt lightheaded on run. Need to add protein to morning meal. Look into shake."

"Department tea party. Managed okay."

Faye tried to imagine what it was like; being so fixated on every morsel that passed your lips. The notes were cryptic. "Upped weekly intake . . . Getting there"? It seemed that Clare was trying to get herself to eat *more*, rather than less. Was that why she was recording everything? She flipped back to the beginning of the book. Clare had begun it more than two years ago. Initially, it was all about recording food items, calories and exercise. There were only a few notes. She turned the pages slowly, scanning Clare's tiny scribblings.

"Went to cheese and wine do with Mark. He pressed me to eat pickled gherkins. Insisted vinegar has fewer calories than wine. Joker! I managed one."

"Feeling up to half marathon but only if I can pick up half a kilogram before month end."

Then it jumped out at Faye.

"Lunch with Derek Mackenzie. Chicken salad with creamy dressing."

She stared at it. "Lunch with Derek Mackenzie." She read it again, as if she might be imagining the words. Clare's cursive was small, but she'd kept the pencil sharp and her writing was neat. "Lunch with Derek Mackenzie." Could Clare know another Derek Mackenzie? Perhaps. But, aside from "Mark," Clare hadn't noted any other names in the journal.

Faye looked at the date. Mid-March less than two years ago. Clare would've been away at university. Derek was at work. What was he busy with at the time? Was that when his company was sorting out the project in Port Elizabeth? When he flew to the city several times over about three months and spent a few nights there each time? The city that was about an hour's drive away from Clare's university? It made sense. Derek would have been able to visit Clare at the time. But why? Why would he visit their friends' teenage daughter? Faye pictured her husband and the young woman at a restaurant. Clare, with her chicken salad and Derek, across the table, leaning forward, his large, knobbly hand covering the girl's tiny one with its skinny fingers. She felt ill. It was an image she recognised.

Zach was to spend the weekend with a friend at the boy's family's holiday house at Hermanus. They'd be leaving directly from school and, as Faye ate her toast and drank her coffee that morning, the weekend stretched before her like a dark tunnel with no light in any direction. Derek usually went into the office on Saturdays to catch up on paperwork. When he returned, he'd watch sport on television. Sunday mornings were for golf with two of his colleagues.

Faye phoned her mother to invite her for Sunday lunch, but even Veronica had plans for the weekend.

"What about today, then?" said Faye, hating the desperate intonation of her voice. "Zach's away for the weekend and I'm free."

"That'll work, dear" said her mother. "But let's go to a restaurant for a change. My treat."

It was always Veronica's treat on the rare occasions mother and daughter dined out together. Faye hadn't said anything, but she sensed her mother knew how reluctant she was to spend Derek's money. She might even have guessed her son-in-law liked it that way.

Veronica suggested the Woodcutter's Garden Bistro.

"If we get there early, we can decide whether to sit inside, on the porch or in the garden depending on the weather," she said.

It was a mild autumn day and the women were happy to follow the waitress to a shaded table tucked away near a tangled mass of climbing roses with a few late blooms holding out until winter. The flowers reminded Faye that her roses needed pruning and she was pleased to have at least one task to get to over the weekend.

They'd eaten and ordered cappuccinos when Faye excused herself and walked through the garden towards the restaurant building to use the bathroom.

"Through the door and to your left," said the waitress, as she walked down the stairs with their coffee.

She saw Derek from the doorway, his lean head with its thick, wire-straight hair unmistakable. He was at a table against the wall on the far side of the room with a woman whose shoulder-length auburn hair fell forward, hiding half her face as she laughed at something Derek said. He leaned forward, lips still moving and placed his hand on hers.

Faye stared, holding her breath. Her mouth was dry and she felt cold. Why was she standing in the doorway? She shouldn't be there. She shouldn't have seen him. She should go. A waiter with a tray of desserts stepped in front of her and then stepped back.

"After you," he said, indicating she should enter. "It's that way," he added, nodding his head to the left.

Knees shaking, she made her way to the bathroom. She stumbled into a stall, closed the door and leaned against it, breathing heavily. She tried to gather her thoughts. Perhaps she was mistaken. Maybe it wasn't Derek but someone who resembled him? She heard the door swing open and someone go into the stall alongside her.

Faye stood up. She should get back to her mother before Veronica came looking for her and, God forbid, also saw Derek. Or the man who looked like Derek. She opened the door and, washing her hands, looked at herself in the mirror. Her face was pale. Her lipstick needed reapplying.

A toilet flushed and the stall door opened. The woman with the man who looked like Derek stepped out, petite and confident, and wearing a pair of bright yellow stilettoes that picked up the colour of the sunflowers on her dress. She smiled at Faye as she opened a tap. Faye blushed and looked away. The girl was younger than Faye had imagined her to be from a distance. Was she even in her twenties? She left while Faye fumbled in her handbag, looking for her lipstick. Shortly afterwards, Faye followed, ducking her head in the other direction as she left the restaurant.

When she and her mother made their way to Faye's car minutes later, she spotted Derek's navy-blue BMW.

"You were at the Woodcutter's Garden Bistro today," she'd said that evening, as she added a second potato to Derek's dinner plate and handed it to him.

He took it, eyes fixed on her face. "I was," he said, his voice even. "How did—"

"My mother and I were there for lunch."

"Why didn't you say hello?" Still staring at her, Derek picked up his knife and fork. "Well?"

She looked down.

"Faye . . . Faye . . . Please Faye. I was there with the intern. It was her final day. I took to her lunch as a formality."

"A formality?" she mumbled. "You take all your interns to lunch at the end of their stint? I didn't know."

"Yes, I do. As you well know."

Did she know? Was it something *else* she'd forgotten? She bit her lip.

"We invest a lot in these kids, work closely with them—"

"Closely?"

"God, Faye! I'm not going to entertain your insecurities and suspicions. The scenarios you make up."

"Make up? I saw you with your hand on her—"

"Your imagination is sick, Faye. You're not well. I've told you before; go and see someone about it. I'll pay."

"I am not ill, Derek. I know what I saw."

He pursed his lips. "There's nothing I can say that'll convince you when you're like this. If you—"

"What do you mean, 'like this'? When do I—"

"That's *exactly* what I mean. You won't listen so there's no point having this discussion."

Derek scooped food onto his fork and put it in his mouth. Faye stared at him. She had no appetite. He chewed and swallowed.

"Please, Faye. Don't be one of *those* women. The kind who make up problems so that their lives seem more interesting than they are. You have nothing to worry about. Whatever you think you saw today and whatever conclusions you leapt to, you're mistaken."

She pretended she believed him. After a while, it seemed to her she did. It was okay unless she allowed herself to interrogate her thoughts, which she tried not to do. But now, staring at the note, "Lunch with Derek Mackenzie," it was difficult.

Faye shoved the notebook back into the bag, closed it and pushed the backpack beneath the bed.

Twelve

B y the time Derek woke up, the others had long since left the cabin. He hobbled onto the stone deck and looked around. With the clouds having lifted, the view over the trees and onto the peaks across the valley was vast. The vegetation nearby was leafy and vibrant while, in the distance, the mountains looked like the faces of weather-beaten old men, lined with cracks, crevices and caves.

He leaned against the railing and rubbed his back. It was stiff and sore, as if someone had folded him in half, lain him on the floor and bounced on his shoulders. The shrill call of a sunbird pierced his already throbbing brain. His mouth felt furry and his neck ached.

Although he couldn't see them, Derek could hear the others talking in the lapa. Bev and Helen had walked to the river to see whether it had subsided.

"If anything, it's risen," said Bev. "There's no way we would've dared try cross it in its current state."

"Never," said her wife. "And we're not just saying that because we're still traumatised by what happened yesterday."

There was mumbled accord before Diane announced that she'd found four sachets of instant coffee in her daypack. The news elicited a cheer and Bruce offered to boil water so they could share the find. Coffee might help, thought Derek, walking slowly down the stairs.

"Hey," said Bruce, as Derek shuffled into the lapa, pain shooting through his lower back with every step. "Just in time for your half cup of coffee. How are you feeling?"

"I'm afraid my hiking ends here."

Bruce collected the mugs. "Really? Damn, that's unfortunate."

"I could probably make a few kilometres of easy terrain, but today's route is hairy. There's no way I'm up to it."

"We've decided none of us are up to the original route," said Geoffrey, pointing to the map spread on the table. "We're not going to chance another river crossing, particularly since it looks like we might be in for more rain."

Derek felt a modicum of relief. At least he wouldn't miss out the main trail.

"What's the plan then?"

They gathered around the map.

"We thought we'd take one of the escape routes," continued Geoffrey. "This one is the shortest and will take us to the road that leads back to the rangers' office. It's still quite a distance and we might encounter problems at the bridges, but it's the most practical. Ideally, we'll meet the rangers with Clare and Faye once we get to the road. Of course, since we don't know how badly damaged the road might be, it's just wishful thinking."

"But what about this ascent?" said Diane, her finger on the map. "If Derek isn't up to the original route, he won't be up to this section either."

The group was quiet. It was true. The escape route avoided the river, but there was no way of avoiding the precipitous, rocky climb up to the road. Derek bent towards the table to take a closer look. He'd barely bowed as the tension hit, causing him to groan loudly. He placed his hand on his lower back and straightened slowly. His face was grey.

"You guys go. I'll wait here until it's possible for a vehicle to get to me. Just leave me all the painkillers you have," he said, with a weak smile.

"We don't all have to go," said Geoffrey. "Whatever we decide, the original route is out. We'll lose at least a day today and we need to find out where Clare and Faye are. If any of us are going to continue—if the weather settles and it's possible—we need to give them the option of continuing, too."

"Faye won't go on," said Derek matter-of-factly. "She'll stay with me. Get me home."

Diane looked at him, eyes narrowing. For a moment, no one said anything.

"Okay. Who wants to go? Who wants to stay? What makes the most sense?" said Geoffrey eventually.

"I'd like to go," said Diane, still looking at Derek.

The others turned to her, expecting an explanation. She said no more.

"We'll go with you. Won't we, Hel?" said Bev.

Helen nodded. "The sooner we can get to the road and talk to the rangers, the sooner we'll get help to Derek and find out if it's feasible to continue on an alternative route."

"And get to the food," added Bev.

"And find out where Faye and Clare are. Shall I stay?" asked Bruce, glancing at Geoffrey and Derek.

"No one has to stay with me," said Derek.

Geoffrey looked at him. "I'll stay," he said. "Bruce, you go. I'll wait with Derek."

Diane shuffled her feet. "But don't you want to get to Clare?"

"Of course, but since we don't know where she and Faye are, there's no guaranteeing going will mean I will see her sooner."

"Whatever you decide is okay with me," said Derek, hand on his head now. "I need to take some more pills and lie down. Safe travels. See you when I see you. Goodbye."

The others murmured their good wishes and goodbyes, except Diane, who looked at her boots. Derek glanced at her briefly, sighed and shuffled towards the cabin.

"I'll sort out the painkillers for you," said Bev, following him.

As he lay waiting for the tablets to take effect, Derek thought about Diane. She'd made it clear that morning she was still angry with him. He shouldn't have told her that he believed Clare to be his daughter. But the combination of the trauma of the crossing, pills and whiskey had muddied his thoughts. Also, if he was perfectly honest, he'd longed to have someone to talk to about it ever since he'd worked it out.

He'd always imagined, given that his, Diane and Michelle's friendship was significantly older than their connections with the others, that Diane would be the most sympathetic. She knew that Derek had loved Michelle ever since the three of them met at primary school. He didn't like to dwell on the fact that Diane also warned him against his feelings for Michelle for almost as long.

"Get over her," said Diane: Derek had put his fist through a cupboard door when he discovered that Michelle had agreed to go to the matric dance with someone else. "You two are too alike to ever be a couple."

"What do you mean? She's nothing like me. I'd never do something like this to her!"

"Bullshit, Derek. What about sticking your tongue down Shona Morris's throat at that braai last term?"

"That's because Michelle chose to go away for the weekend at the last minute."

Diane shook her head. "You'll never get it right. It'll never work. You think you love her, but you want to possess her. She might love you, but no one will possess her."

But Derek and Michelle did get it right. Or rather, Derek thought they did, for a few weeks when they began university. With Diane around less—she and Bruce had recently begun dating—and in their new environment, Derek and Michelle relied on one another for company between classes and during social events. So much so, in fact, that those they met on campus believed them to be a couple. They were invited to parties together, where they arrived and left together. One night, after copious plastic cups of cheap wine, they kissed.

When Derek told Diane about the kiss, she warned him against it happening again. "It'll end badly, Derek. Especially for you, I suspect."

He didn't listen. He and Michelle took it further and were happy, drifting together on a raft of passion and naïveté, until Derek, hormones and ego optimised, had said to Michelle, "I knew you'd come to your senses one day."

The next day, when they met on the library stairs as usual, she told him she no longer wanted to be romantically involved with him.

"I know it might be weird for a while, but we've been friends for so long and this was just a little detour, so I'm sure our friendship will survive," she said, patting his arm and looking into the distance.

"What did I do?" wailed Derek into the phone to Diane that night.

"I knew it was a mistake," she replied.

"It wasn't. It's not. She'll come to her senses."

"Whoa! Derek! I hope you never say that to Michelle."

"What? What do you mean?"

"That she'll 'come to her senses . . . and be with you.'"

He was quiet.

"No? Seriously? You already said it?"

"It's just a phrase. I was joking."

"That's not how it comes across. It makes you seem controlling."

"Controlling?"

"Yes. And it's not the first time you've revealed this side of yourself to Michelle."

"What do you mean?"

Diane said nothing.

"Tell me, Di. What are you talking about?"

She sighed. "Remember when we were in grade eleven and you told Michelle that you were worried about her because you'd overheard someone say her outfits were slutty? And then we called you on it later, after we'd confronted the guys you had accused and they denied it. You backtracked and claimed you never said it. Tried to tell us that we were imagining things."

"I was an idiot," mumbled Derek.

"Yes, but the thing is, you were trying to control Michelle. At least that's how she saw it and I wouldn't be surprised if that isn't what she feels now."

"That's ridiculous, Di. I'll explain it to her. I was joking."

Derek tried to speak to Michelle but she fobbed him off. It wasn't long before she and Geoffrey began dating and shortly after that, Derek introduced them to Faye.

Of course, that wasn't the end of it for Derek and Michelle. Although he never mentioned it to anyone, not even Diane, Derek believed that he and Michelle would end up together. She would, he told himself, "come to her senses again."

When he and Faye, who'd been dating for several months by then, were invited to a braai at Michelle's parents' home along with their other friends, Derek suspected nothing. He'd thought of their house, not far from his parents' place, as a second home. So, when Michelle's father produced a bottle of sparkling wine and Geoffrey stood up after they'd eaten and told the gathering that he had proposed to Michelle and she had accepted, Derek was dumbfounded.

"Are you okay to drive?" Faye had asked as they walked to their car later.

"Of course. Why wouldn't I be?"

"You haven't said a word since the, erm, news."

"Don't be ridiculous. You're imagining things."

He drove her home without saying another word.

A few weeks later, Derek proposed to Faye.

Michelle and Derek didn't discuss the weeks of passion they'd shared when they were students. But he never gave up trying to catch her eye, hoping to recognise a glimmer of longing. She and Geoffrey had been married for three years, and he and Faye for six months less, when they eventually spoke of it. They were at an alumni dinner and found themselves alone at the table for a moment.

"You're looking as gorgeous as ever," said Derek, tipping back a third glass of wine.

"Why, thank you, kind sir," said Michelle, leaning forward to clink her glass against his. "You're not looking too bad yourself."

"Ah! Is that regret I hear?"

She giggled. "Well, we did pretty well together for that short time, as I remember it."

Derek raised his brows.

Michelle blinked. "Well? Didn't we?"

"Do you think about it a lot?" he asked, his heart thumping in his ears.

"Don't you?"

He nodded.

Derek phoned her at the work the following day. He expected her to laugh or worse, apologise for her behaviour and blame it on the wine, but he couldn't help himself. To his surprise, she didn't brush him off. To the contrary, she agreed to meet him for lunch later in the week. Then, the following week, they met at a hotel where they made love. Afterwards, as they lay in post-coital silence on the hotel bed with the curtains drawn on a sunny day, Michelle burst into tears and, to Derek's horror, apologised.

"This is madness," she sobbed. "I'm so sorry I dragged you into it."

"What do you mean?"

"Geoffrey and I have been arguing."

"About?" asked Derek, daring to hope that she'd told her husband about him.

"He wants to give up his job to start a garden services business. It's driving me crazy."

"Oh? But what does that have to do with me?"

"Nothing. It's just that I've been so damn miserable thinking about him giving up a great job—he's in line for a promotion, for God's sake, and could be a director within ten years—to drive a bakkie around the suburbs."

Derek didn't care if Geoffrey cleaned sewers for a living. He shook his head, confused.

"He's so stubborn," she said, pulling her panties over her feet. "Says he wants to be his own boss and provide employment and training to unskilled people."

Derek grabbed her arm. He didn't want her to leave. "I don't care about Geoffrey."

She brushed his hair back and kissed his forehead.

"Don't make a scene, please Derek. This is hard enough. I'm sorry I'm such an idiot, but let's pretend I'm not. For everyone's sake. Let's forget this ever happened. I'm truly sorry. You're such a good friend."

Two months later, Geoffrey and Michelle told their friends she was expecting their first child; Clare.

⚶

Wishing they'd get a move on and leave him in peace, Derek closed his eyes and tried to block out the chatter of his friends outside the cabin as they prepared to leave. Did they really have to agree on every aspect of their endeavour? Why didn't Bruce take the lead and get the women moving? Democracy seldom worked in groups. Someone had to take control.

Then at last, he heard Helen's voice above the others: "Right. Let's go. See you soon, I hope, Geoffrey."

"I'll be a second." It was Diane.

Derek heard footsteps in the cabin. He didn't open his eyes. He'd said his goodbyes. They came closer. He sensed a body near his. It crouched and for a moment he thought whoever it was, was going to touch him. He almost flinched. Then he heard the sound of his bag being pulled from beneath his bed. He opened his eyes.

"Damn. You're awake," said Diane, squatting alongside him.

"What do you want?"

"Your flask."

"What?"

She unzipped the bag and looked inside it. "Well, I'm damned if I'm going to leave you here with Geoffrey, Bev's ample supply of drugs and your whiskey after last night's performance."

"Don't be ridiculous," he said, non-plussed.

Diane stood up, slipping her hand into the pack and rifling around. "Where is it?" she asked.

"I have no idea. I finished it last night."

"I don't believe it. It's a big flask and there was plenty left when we stopped talking."

He shrugged. "I continued drinking. It was the only way to dull the pain. Or perhaps I spilled some. I don't know. It's gone. Look in the lapa."

She dropped the bag on the floor. "Sure. I'll look. My God, Derek, if you say anything along the lines of what you told me last night to anyone ever again, I can assure you that you will lose every friend you have in this world."

"If it's not true, why does it upset you so much?"

Diane glared at him. "You really are the most selfish arsehole I've ever met," she said, turning and leaving the cabin.

Derek closed his eyes and stroked the flask, which he'd tucked beneath his space blanket.

Thirteen

For a moment, as she recovered consciousness and her vision cleared, Clare thought she'd fallen again. When the view of the boulder and the proteas fell into place, she realised she hadn't moved. The clouds seemed closer, as if they'd drawn together to peer down at her. She recognised a tiny pink erica struggling to survive in a narrow cleft in the rock. A succession of raucous cries made her look up. A small bird swept by, closely pursued by a pair of crows.

She knew she'd have to sit up. This time she'd do it slowly. She lifted her torso using her right arm, keeping her left elbow tucked into her side to protect her ribs. There was no rush, she told herself. Slow and steady. Move and rest. Breathe. Pay attention. Do no harm. Remain conscious.

Finally upright, she placed a hand on her head, tapping her skull lightly and running her fingers through her hair to confirm she hadn't hit her head. There was neither bruising nor blood. The fainting must have been caused by shock, pain or a combination of both. Leaning slightly forward, she straightened her right leg. It, too, seemed unscathed. The problems were on her left side, primarily her knee and lower ribs.

Clare was crying with exhaustion and pain by the time she had pulled herself the short distance along the ledge to where she was able to drag herself up and over the boulders, and across the rough ground to the summit. Her skin bled where it had been shredded by the jagged earth and stubbly vegetation. She lay on a patch of bare ground until her breathing and tears stilled. She pictured the route to the cabin. Would Faye come and look for her? If she did, they would miss one another if Clare wasn't on the path. She had to get there as soon as she could.

Uncertain her injured knee would support any weight at all, she thought of standing and it made her stomach churn. Clare sat up and looked around for a stick she could use as a crutch. The mountain fynbos was short and bushy, and the trees too far away to have deposited any suitable branches. She'd have to make do without support. How could she test her knee? She thought about what her dad had taught her years previously.

⨞⨞

Nine-year-old Clare had accompanied her father to meet a new client. They stood and surveyed the man's yard, which, following renovations to the house, resembled a building site rather than a garden. The client pointed to a messy ditch running from an overflow pipe off the roof.

"That's going to be an issue every time we have rain," he said. "You'll probably have to put a pipe underground."

"Hmm. Not necessarily," replied her dad. "There's more than one way to skin a cat."

Her father went on to propose lining the drain with river stones and planting the edges as if it were a natural waterway. It would be beautiful. The client was delighted.

As they drove home, Geoffrey glanced at Clare. "Is something wrong? You're very quiet."

She shook her head but contemplated the question for a moment. "I can't stop thinking about you skinning a cat," she said, eyes straight ahead.

"What? Oh, Clare! I'm sorry. It means there are more ways than one of solving a problem or reaching a goal. I wanted to—"

"I know what it means, Dad. I just don't like it. I mean, poor cat. Who would do that anyway?"

"Okay. I won't say it again. Let's think of another way of saying the same thing."

They tossed ideas back and forth, many of which were ridiculous. By the time they arrived home, father and daughter were worn from laughing. They settled on an alternative; "There's more than one way to pick your nose."

Clare thought about her father and his unflagging resourcefulness now, as she sat, unsure of how to safely rise so she could test her knee. She needed a helping hand or a crutch. Neither were available.

"Come on, Clare. There's more than one way to pick your nose," she said.

What would she do if she was at home facing the same challenge? She thought about it for a while, deciding she'd manoeuvre herself to a chair or couch and pull herself onto it. From there, it would be possible to rise on one leg, get her balance and then carefully put the other leg down to test it.

The boulder she'd fallen from would do, only this time she'd stay on the safe side of it. She was about to drag herself to the rock when she noticed a large paw print in the sand. It was a typical cat print with four clear, clawless toe pads. Clare placed her hand above it; it was larger than her palm. Leopard, she thought, wishing her father was there to discuss the thrill of the find with her.

She pulled herself along the earth, heaved herself into a sitting position on a part of the rock that was the approximate height of a chair, and slowly rose on her right leg, bending from her hip to support herself with her right arm. Once she felt steady, she tried to straighten her left leg. The pain in her knee was jarring, but settled when the leg was straight. She lifted her torso, leaning very slightly on her left leg. It didn't give way. She was able to move upright, albeit slowly and with more of a hop than a step. A walking stick, however rudimentary, would help a great deal, but at least, until she found one, she'd be able to get back on the path and head towards Heuningbos.

It wasn't easy to make her way through the fynbos. With no clear path, Clare had to zig-zag her way around the plants, trying to avoid catching her injured leg on any of the bushes. The short distance to the path took almost an hour to cover. She tried to reassure herself with the knowledge that, now upright, she'd almost certainly see Faye or whoever else might walk along the path and be able to call out to them. Even so, she was relieved to arrive at the path where walking would be easier.

With the edge of the forest less than a hundred metres in the other direction, Clare felt a tug of regret she wouldn't hike there on this trip. She briefly imagined hobbling to the trees and lying in the undergrowth. Navigating the veld had exhausted her. A nap would be pleasant. But she had to get back to the cabin. She needed help and shelter.

The path, with its sandy surface and silver puddles, lay ahead. It was hard to imagine that, just hours ago, she had walked so freely upon it after running up the hill. Clare felt cold at the thought of not being able to run. How long would it be before she recovered? How would she manage without it? There was only one person who would understand how difficult it would be for her not to run. Mark.

❧

"It's weird how I find the thought of going for a run terrible," said Mark, when she met him in their usual spot under the sprawling wild fig tree near her res. "If it wasn't that I knew you'd be mad with me if I didn't pitch, I'm not sure I'd have the willpower to do it."

"Really?" she said, as they took off. "After all this time, you're telling me you don't actually like running? Why do you—"

"No, no. You misunderstand me. I like running and I *love* having run. That feeling of having done it is incredible, afterwards. But I hate the thought of having to run before I get here."

"So, don't think about it; just do it."

"How do you not think about it?"

"You're asking me?" said Clare. They laughed and ran on.

Mark was the only person Clare joked with about her condition. She had met him in a lecture early in second year when he sat next to her and, dropping his books with a thud, said, "Ah, the thin girl who runs a lot."

She looked at him, trying to gauge his intentions. He smiled, pale blue eyes twinkling, "I don't mean anything by that. I have sisters who I miss teasing when I'm away. I'm Mark."

When the lesson was over, he followed her out of the room. "Can I come running with you sometime?" he asked.

"Um . . . why?"

"I think I'd like it. I want to try."

"You're not a runner?"

"Not yet."

"Well, I—"

"I tell you what; I'll meet you for a run this afternoon and if I can't keep up with you or you hate having me for company, I'll never ask to join you again."

She agreed and told him where and what time he should meet her. She was surprised when he arrived beneath the tree promptly. He was wearing boardshorts and tennis shoes. They ran for an hour, Mark talking practically non-stop the entire time. When they arrived back at the tree, Clare felt she knew him.

"I'm sorry for you," he said, only mildly breathless, "but I really enjoyed that. Can we do it again sometime?"

Clare nodded.

"Excellent. Thank you. See you tomorrow."

She waved and he turned to go, but changed his mind, stopped and looked back at her. "You know, my older sister was anorexic years ago. There's no way she could have run like you do."

"Is that why you want to run with me? Because you find it fascinating that I'm up to it?"

"No. I mean, yes, I do find it interesting. Hey, you're interesting.

But that's not why I want to run with you."

She tipped her head.

"I want to run and I don't want to do it on my own," he said.

"So, join a club."

"I just did. The Clare Club. See you tomorrow!"

Although she didn't describe her shame in detail to Mark, she didn't hide everything from him either; not the way she did with others. Perhaps because of his sister, he was perceptive and understanding without her having to explain. In fact, he was the only other person— besides her mother—who Clare told about her reverse-anorexia approach. Initially, although his arguments differed, Mark was as dubious about it as Michelle had been.

"Hmm, ja," he said. "I can see why your mother is not convinced. The thing with anorexia, unlike illnesses like, say, depression and obsessive compulsive disorder, is that sufferers typically spend a lot of their time not actually wanting to get better. Even when they recognise they're ill, they cling to the illness."

"But—"

"I'm not saying that's what you're doing. But it could be what your mother believes when you try to explain you're going to continue using what drives your anorexia to get better. She might find it hard to believe."

"She does."

They were quiet as they ran up a short, steep hill. Mark continued on the descent.

"Also, what worries me about your approach is you're not addressing the actual problem," he said. "In a way, you're reinforcing it. I mean, your problem is you're addicted to control, isn't it? By controlling yourself even more, if that's possible, you're affirming your behaviour is okay."

"Wow. You're quite the expert on the subject."

"My family likes to dig deep when one of us has a problem."

"Clearly. The thing is, I don't know if it's an addiction, but even if it is, controlling whatever it was that made me anorexic is the only way I am ever going to believe in myself again," she said.

"Therapy, with a psychologist and a dietician, worked for my sister. You still have to do the work yourself in therapy," said Mark. "It's not like one of those vibrating weight-loss machines that promises to shift kilograms while you passively lie there."

"I know, but it depends on someone else, others, helping you, showing you how. I need to do this on my own."

"Okay. But don't you think it might be easier if you accept help? Also, you might recover faster," he said.

"It's not important how long it takes; what matters is I do what it takes so I like myself again."

"You're hardcore."

A week after they met, he bought himself a pair of running shoes and shorts. She was surprised by how much she looked forward to running with him, and the relief she felt from being able to talk so openly about her anorexia. If Mark ever worried about her eating too little and running too much, he never mentioned it. That's not to say he didn't quiz and tease her about her habits. He was the only person who noticed when she gained a few grams and congratulated her when he saw her eating more than usual or daring to eat food she wouldn't have previously. Many of her eating milestones happened when she was with Mark. She smeared butter on a Provita for the first time in eighteen months as they snacked together before a long run, and ate a spoonful of peanut-butter when he dared her. It was also Mark who convinced her to eat a tiny block of chocolate on her birthday.

They sat together during the one lecture they shared and they ran most days. Aside from that, Clare and Mark didn't see one another. He told her about girls he was keen on and asked her advice about approaching them.

For Clare, it was the ideal relationship. She'd cut herself off from the friends she'd made during her early days at university and didn't make any new ones aside from Mark. She couldn't bear the idea of being watched and worried over. She didn't want to explain herself to anyone else and she didn't believe she would make a good friend until she had overcome her anorexia. Mark didn't give her a choice and Mark was a running friend, which was a different kind of friend. But even that changed.

They had known each other for almost two years and, with their final exams a few months ahead, Clare knew her running days with Mark were nearing the end. He was leaving to do a post-graduate degree at another university and Clare would return home and look for work. She knew she'd miss him and wondered if they'd stay in touch. He, it emerged, was thinking the same.

"I met your old boyfriend over the weekend," he said, as they ran on the path near the river. "William?"

"Oh. Will. How is he?"

"Still hung up on you, I think."

"That's ridiculous. How did you discover you both know me?"

"He's seen us running."

Clare shuddered. She hated the idea of Will watching her run and making whatever assumptions he was bound to make. She was curious though, why Mark would think he was "still hung up" on her. She hadn't seen Will since he'd cast the pitying look in her direction at the end of first year. She knew Mark wouldn't make her suffer the indignity of asking him to explain himself and kept quiet until he inevitably went on.

"He was at a birthday party of a mutual friend on Saturday, saw me and asked if you were there. I had no idea who he was. Turned out he has seen us running together and thought we were a couple. I said no, which was obviously a relief to him."

"Why do you say that?"

"Because he then proceeded to tell me how you and he had been an item."

"That doesn't mean he's still hung up on me, Mark."

He didn't say anything for several paces. Then, "Would it be so weird?"

"What? Will being hung up on me? Of course. We've been—"

"No. Us? A couple?"

Clare nearly laughed but caught herself in time. Mark was a joker and a tease, but this wasn't his kind of humour. Was it?

"Are you joking?" she asked, looking straight ahead.

"Do you want me to be?"

They finished the run in silence. Clare's head whirled. She wasn't sure what to think. Mostly, she was sad. She realised her running days with Mark were over even though the term hadn't come to an end yet. She also wondered what had happened to suddenly make him decide he was interested in more than running with her.

"Listen, Mark," she said, as they pulled up at their tree. "It's never been like that for us. Just because you meet a guy who I was with for a short while years ago, shouldn't change the way you see me."

He stepped in front of her. His face was red from running and his eyes shone. "Is that really what you believe? That meeting William made me think of you as girlfriend material? I truly hope I'm not that shallow."

"No! You're not. It's just I . . . I didn't know you felt like that."

"Nor did I, until recently. But let's forget I said anything."

"Well—"

"Unless you'd rather we didn't? Forget, I mean."

"No. I mean, yes. I don't know what to say, Mark. I've never thought of you that way."

He ran his hands through his hair. "That says enough. Says it all, really."

"Mark—"

"No. Jeez, Clare. Don't say anything more. It's . . . it's enough. I'm a klutz. I've got to go. See you around."

He walked away, head bowed.

They didn't run together again. Nor did she see him in lectures. She missed their runs. Their easy banter. About a month later, shortly before she packed up her room to go home, Clare saw him standing beneath the tree when she returned from her evening run. He was wearing boardshorts and flip-flops.

"Hey," she said, smiling as she glanced at his feet. "You've given up running?"

He nodded. "Ja. It's not for me."

There was an awkward silence.

"I'm leaving tomorrow so I thought I'd come and see how you are. Say goodbye."

"Oh. Wow. Thanks. I mean, I'm fine." She rubbed her shoulder, suddenly aware it was stiff. "How are you? How were the exams?"

"All good. Thanks." He lowered his head, raising his eyes to look at her. "You look—really well. Are you—"

"Yes. I'm getting there. I have my moments, but I think it'll be okay."

"Great. Look, I have to get going, but if you ever come to Durban . . ." Mark shrugged.

"I'll look you up. We can go for a run."

He looked away. "Sure. Bye, Clare."

She drew in a long breath, checking it as the pain nudged her ribs. It took another moment before she was able to step-hop forward. Perhaps she'd contact Mark when she got home. But what would they have to say to one another if they couldn't run? That was their thing. They ran. They talked. It stopped when he wanted more. No. *She* stopped it when he wanted more. Perhaps, if she wasn't so afraid, they'd still be running and talking.

Afternoon slid towards evening. She limped on. Surely Faye would be looking for her by now? At her current pace, it would be dark well before she got to the Heuningbos. How she would manage the rocky path down to the stream in the fading light, Clare didn't know. A spritz of liquid on her forehead made her look up. The mountains were shrouded in cloud. She untied her jacket from around her waist and put it on, groaning as she moved. The drops fell soft and steady.

fourteen

Faye saw the woods and felt the rain at the same time. Given how cloudy it was, she wasn't surprised by the latter. The trees, however, startled her. She had followed the same path the previous day but now, distracted by what she'd read in the notebook, hadn't realised now how far she'd walked.

She had expected to find Clare much closer to the cabin. Would the girl really have gone as far as the forest? What was she thinking? Had she walked all the way to the Bloukrans River to see how flooded it was?

It was when she took her eyes off the trees and focused on the path again that Faye saw the figure. Hood up and head down, the person approaching leaned heavily on a stick that was too short and crooked to offer any real support. The walker's progress was slow and jerky, like that of a geriatric for whom motion was arduous. Faye recognised the red jacket, thin legs and bony hands. It was Clare. She ran to her.

"My God! Clare!"

The girl raised her hooded head. "I was hoping you'd come. I'm not sure . . . I'm—"

Tears shimmered in Clare's eyes and she swayed against the silly stick. Faye tucked herself beneath the girl's right arm, taking the branch from her. Clare leaned onto Faye's shoulder, wheezing and crying. The older woman patted her lightly, noticing how bloody and dirty her bare legs were. They stood for a moment, rain dripping from their jackets. Clare shivered and sniffed, raising her left arm slowly to wipe her nose.

"I'm sorry," she said.

Faye shifted so she could look at the girl. "It's okay. What happened? Your leg?"

"And my ribs. At first I thought my knee was gone. But here." She gestured towards the left side of her chest. "It's more painful here."

"But what—"

"I fell." The tears ran. "I was stupid. I'm sorry. I went to the edge," she tilted her head towards the ravine, "to look down at the river and fell off a boulder."

"Into the ravine?"

"I landed on a rock, on my chest, and then fell a bit further onto my knee. I was lucky. Really."

"Hmm, perhaps. But you can barely move."

"I know. I'm sorry . . . the pain. And I'm so cold."

Faye took a deep breath. It was late. It was raining. Clare was shivering, bowed by pain and probably in shock. Heuningbos was about two hours away at a normal pace.

"Let's see how fast we can move if you lean on me."

Clare straightened and staggered forward. One step, two, three. The path was narrow and it was difficult for Faye to walk alongside and support her. Clare grimaced with every movement. They persevered for less than a metre before stopping. Faye was breathing heavily and Clare's face was grey and wet, whether from sweat or rain, the older woman wasn't sure.

"Perhaps you can find me a better stick? Among the trees maybe?"

Faye shook her head. "I don't think you're up to getting back to the hut tonight. Not in this weather and not in your state."

"But—"

"Clare, think about it: this is the easy part. I can't see how you are going to manage going downhill. You must've noticed on your way here how steep and rocky the path is."

"Yes."

"If we go into the trees, I'll build us some kind of shelter. We can stay there tonight. I have my space blanket."

"Surely I can make it. To Heuningbos. I just need a better stick." Clare was crying again.

"We'll be okay for the night. Hey, weren't you the girl who *chose* to sleep out in the open a night ago?"

Faye didn't say how worried she was about Clare's injuries, particularly the pain she described around her ribs. She'd learned how dangerous rib fractures could be after Veronica had suffered two broken ribs in a car accident years ago. Although the doctor who had attended her mother in the emergency rooms told Faye most patients with fractured ribs didn't suffer complications and said the breaks, though painful, healed well over about six weeks, that wasn't the case for Veronica. A few days after being discharged to recuperate at home, she was rushed to the operating theatre. It emerged her ribs and everything around them were so badly damaged she'd bled into her lungs. The injury could've been fatal. The memory worried Faye. It was important to get Clare checked out as soon as possible, but she didn't want to make things worse by letting the girl exert herself.

"Do you think my ligaments are gone?" asked Clare after, having turned towards the trees, they managed only a few metres before she needed to rest again. "In my knee, I mean."

Faye looked at her boots, which, she realised, were not as waterproof as the salesperson had promised. "I don't know."

"It folded under me as I landed."

"The good thing is there's not a lot of you to land on it."

As soon as she'd said the words, Faye wanted to take them back. But Clare gave a small smile.

"Ha," she said quietly. "Something positive about being anorexic at last."

Faye gave a snuff of a laugh. "Come. Let's get out of this rain. How's your jacket holding out?"

"I'm not sure. I'm so cold, I don't know whether it's because I am wet or just cold."

"Your ribs, do they hurt when you breathe?"

Clare nodded.

"Worse now than earlier?"

"I don't know. Perhaps. It's just that it's so tiring to walk when I can't breathe easily or put any weight on my knee. It's hard to pinpoint which is worse."

"I understand. But the pain—around your ribs—is it concentrated in one place or spread wider over your chest?"

"Mostly on the side." Clare looked at her. "Why? What does it mean?"

"I don't know. I just wondered."

They moved slowly towards the trees, quiet for a moment.

"You brought your daypack," said Clare. "I wish I'd been as smart."

"You didn't think you'd need it."

"Did you?"

Faye remembered about how angry she'd been as she'd thrown handfuls of energy bars and crackers, packets of nuts and two oranges into her bag. Since finding Clare, she'd not thought about the notebook. Of course, she'd thought of little else up until that point, reciting countless variations of what she'd say to Clare when they met. Things like, "So, you and Derek, huh? How long has *that* been going on? I hope he at least waited until you were of legal age?" and "Are you crazy, Clare? You deserve much better."

Now, with the girl's bony arm across her shoulders, Faye felt nothing but numbness about Derek. She'd known, even as she marched away from the cabin fantasising about the ruthlessness she'd mete out once she found Clare, that if she and Derek were secretly involved, it was not because the girl had initiated it. She wondered how Derek had played her and why he'd done it. Was it because he couldn't have Michelle?

Derek had told Faye about Michelle on their first date. He'd invited her to a movie and they'd gone for milkshakes afterwards.

"So, you're doing a business degree? Accountancy?" he asked. She nodded.

"And you're taking economics, right?"

"Yes."

"You must know my ex-girlfriend? Michelle Lowe?"

"No, I don't think I do. Is she also doing business?"

"No. Law. But she has to do economics this semester."

"It's a large class. Her name doesn't ring a bell."

Derek wouldn't leave it. "Long blonde hair? Wears it with a fringe?"

"No. Sorry."

"Often wears denim shorts and probably sits in the back of the room. You can't miss her laugh. She doesn't seem to pay attention to what's being taught but afterwards you discover she didn't miss a word."

Faye swirled the milkshake with her straw. "I'm really sorry, Derek, but I don't know your girlfriend. I mean, ex-girlfriend."

He cackled. "Ex-girlfriend, please!"

She bent her head and took a long drink, wondering how long she'd have to sit there before it would be polite to leave.

"Ex-girlfriend," Derek repeated. "Thank goodness. She's high maintenance. Very insecure. I couldn't handle it."

"Of course not," she said quietly.

He jerked his head up. "What do you mean?"

"I was just agreeing with you."

"Do you want to meet her? You should meet her. Then you'll know what I mean."

"Why would I want to meet your ex-girlfriend? This is a very strange conversation. I'm not sure—"

It was as if Derek had got the exact response he wanted. He reached across the table and placed his hand over hers. He was smiling.

"It's okay. There's nothing to be insecure about. I'm over her. You'll see."

By the time Faye said goodbye to him that evening, she had decided not to see him again. Two days later, she arrived home from lectures to find Derek drinking tea with Veronica, a large bunch of red roses on the coffee table between them.

※※

"No sign of the rangers, I guess?" asked Clare as they shuffled towards the forest, their heads close together with the rain dripping off their hoods and onto the path ahead.

"No. I walked down the road for a bit to where I could see the bridge; it was completely submerged. The river was still raging. There's no way they would have been able to get to us today and now, with this . . ."

"I'm sorry." Clare's voice was quiet.

"Don't apologise. It was an accident. Sure, it would be more comfortable to wait out the weather in the hut, but we'll make a plan."

"And head back in the morning. When it's light and hopefully dry. Right?"

Faye lifted her free hand and gave a thumbs up. She didn't say what she was thinking; that she'd rather Clare waited until a medic had checked her before she undertook the rocky descent to Heuningbos.

The light was fading when they reached the forest. A few metres in, the shower stilled and was replaced by sporadic spatterings of water, which fell onto the forest floor, gathering in pools between the leaves. Faye recognised the fallen tree she'd leaned against to drink when the pigs had appeared and helped Clare to where it was low enough to sit.

"Thank you," said the girl, her face softening with relief as she eased herself onto the soggy log.

Faye took her water bottle and some tissues from her bag, and wiped the blood and dirt from Clare's wounds.

"Let's take your jacket off and check your arms too," she said.

"They're just grazes from the fall and from dragging myself up the ravine."

"I know, but I want to make sure before it gets dark."

Clare nodded.

When she'd daubed and inspected Clare's abrasions and was satisfied they were superficial and not too filthy, Faye handed Clare the water and took an energy bar from her bag.

"Eat this. I'm going to make a shelter for us."

Clare drank and, as Faye turned to survey their surroundings for a suitable spot, she heard the wrapper crinkle and snap open.

Why she had any idea about how to build a shelter in the wilderness wasn't clear to Faye. Perhaps she'd seen something on television or read a book about it to Zach. It didn't matter; she was grateful for the knowledge, whatever its source. Faye knew she should cover an area just large enough to accommodate her and Clare. If she made too large a shelter, it would be difficult to keep warm. She also knew the weather generally moved from west to east, which meant the opening should face east. That way, they'd not only be shielded from the wind and rain, but they'd also benefit from the warmth of the sunrise.

She didn't have to look far for a fallen tree with bare branches that provided a good frame for the place she pictured. She snapped off several smaller branches and twigs, using her boot to hold down the larger pieces as she twisted and broke them. Scooping out the undergrowth and debris to level the floor reminded Faye of raking leaves with Veronica in the garden when she was a girl.

"Rustle around on the top first to give the snakes and other goggas a chance to escape," her mother had said.

After she'd "rustled around on the top" with a stick, Faye created a space suitable for the two women to lie in. She used the same stick to warn other goggas of her intentions before gathering armfuls of the driest leaves she could find to build an organic mattress. Picturing her mother in hospital after the accident, Faye also made something of a backrest to prop up Clare.

It was like making a nest, she thought, picturing the flock of weavers that she watched building their nests in the willow tree in their garden every season. She wondered if Derek, like many of the birds' dissatisfied partners in the willow tree, would have found her structure lacking and pull it apart if he were there? She was pleased he wasn't.

After stacking pieces of wood and leaves against the outer frame of the shelter to cover it, she stood back to inspect her work. There was a *drip-drip-dripping* sound, and she noticed the leaves above were funnelling the rain directly into the shelter. The offending branch was too high to move or break. Looking around, Faye noticed a tangle of creepers hanging from the next tree. She realised she might be able to loop a creeper around the offending branch and tie it back.

It took Faye three attempts to hook the creeper vine around the branch. She finally managed it by holding onto the creeper while climbing into the neighbouring tree. With the branch hooked by the creeper, she climbed down and tied the leaves out of the way. The dripping stopped.

"At last," she said. It was almost dark and, although she was warm from her efforts, Faye knew that it wouldn't be long before she felt the cold of her wet clothes.

"I'm done," she called, turning towards where she'd left Clare, but the young woman wasn't there.

"Clare?" she called again, walking towards the fallen tree and looking around.

Clare was lying parallel to the log, her breathing fast and shallow, tears coursing down her cheeks.

"What happened?" said Faye, crouching alongside her.

"I saw you struggling and wanted to help."

"You fell trying to stand up? Trying to walk to me?"

"I don't know," she sniffed. "I tried to move but everything went black. My God, it's sore."

Clare's arm shook as she held it above her chest. Faye swallowed. She was afraid of what might be happening to the girl, how her broken ribs might've punctured her lungs, or worse, damaged her heart. She had to get her out of the rain and into the shelter.

"Will you try and stand with me here to help you?" she asked.

Clare nodded.

"We're going to take it really slowly. Rest whenever you need to. It's not far to go and we'll get there if we're careful."

"Why would I have passed out again?"

Faye exhaled. "I don't know. Shock. Exhaustion. You're sure you didn't hit your head?"

"I'm sure."

Holding onto Faye on one side and the log on the other, Clare was able to stand. They made their way to the shelter. Once there, Faye helped Clare to the ground where, in a sitting position, she inched backwards under the branches.

"You mustn't lie flat," said Faye.

"Really? I'd like to."

"No. You'll breathe better if you stay propped up. Rest your back against those leaves."

After fetching her backpack, Faye crawled in alongside Clare.

They sat side-by-side, listening to the lilting sound of the rain high above on the canopy and the plunking of the larger drops as they landed on the muddy earth closer by. The air was still and the light fading. Clare shivered. Faye dug into her bag and unwrapped her space blanket.

"Are you okay," she asked.

"Yes. It's, erm, cosy."

"Well," said Faye, "at least there are no bats in the belfry."

fifteen

The forest was noisier by night than Clare imagined it might be. The shushing of the rain and shuffling of the leaves made her think of childhood holidays on the coast. She recalled the thrill of waking to the crashing of the waves and the way they hissed as they swept the sand. Back then, the sound carried the promise of hot, grimy hours of play with Angus and Linda, of learning to body surf with her father and the unusually carefree tinkle of her mother's laughter as she lined up her brood to apply sunscreen. Now, with the foliage sticky and warm beneath her bare legs and her parents' friend lying beside her, Clare felt damp and queasy with dread. She hoped the two painkillers Faye had given her would expedite sleep but pain and discomfort prevailed. She shifted her hips.

"Warm enough?" asked Faye, who'd insisted on covering Clare with her space blanket, maintaining that she, in a jacket and trousers, would not need it.

"Yes. Thanks," said Clare, wondering what other ingenuity Faye might conjure if she'd said otherwise. The older woman's resourcefulness had surprised her. Clare hadn't pictured Faye as someone who would know how to erect a shelter in a forest with nothing but what nature offered. Yet, within half an hour, she'd created a refuge that not only held off the rain and wind, but was also relatively comfortable. Clare couldn't imagine her mother being as inventive and capable under similar circumstances.

They spoke simultaneously.

"How did you—"

"I didn't tell you—"

"Go on," said Clare.

Faye went on. "About the visitors to the lapa this morning."

Her descriptions of the baboons at Heuningbos, particularly the large male with the muesli and the little one licking the lid of Michelle's showy cooler box, were amusing. Clare wished it wasn't excruciating to laugh.

"It ended well but honestly, the alpha male terrified me," said Faye. "Those fangs. That roar. Even though I told myself he wouldn't attack me if I didn't approach him, I was petrified. I hadn't realised how large they can be. He was magnificent. Terrifyingly magnificent. But afterwards, when they left and my knees stopped trembling, I felt I should thank him for taking that awful cereal with him."

Clare smiled, thinking about how she'd almost pointed out the distinctive leopard claw-marks on a nearby tree as Faye helped her to the shelter earlier. The bark was slashed in several places, leaving deep wounds and scars. The older lacerations had oxidised and turned brown. Other more recent gashes were white. A few were so freshly inflicted that the resin glistened in the evening light. Clare recalled the leopard pawprint she'd seen near the ravine. They were in leopard territory. She was about to mention as much when she remembered how Faye had responded to the pigs and bats the day before. The older woman would, thought Clare, be unnerved by the evidence of the big cat. She'd insist on going elsewhere. They'd have to walk on and Faye would have to build a new shelter. Clare neither wanted to move any more nor did she want to create any more work for Faye. So she said nothing and, as Faye recounted her fear of the baboons, she was pleased she hadn't.

"I meant to ask," said Faye. "Did you see the Bloukrans River before you fell? Do you remember?"

"I did. Got a good view of it. It was overflowing. Made the stream near the cabin look like a trickle. I think I also saw Grootkloof Cabin."

"Really? You saw it clearly?"

"I saw the path leading to it and its roofs. I was trying to get a better view when I fell."

"Ah. So, is it close the Bloukrans River then? Grootkloof, I mean?"

"Pretty close. Not on the river bank, though. I guess half an hour away or so."

The rain continued pattering the canopy.

"I wonder where they are now?" said Clare, almost as to herself. "My poor dad. I've given him enough to worry about and now this."

"Geoffrey will understand."

"I know, but he, well, he takes on so much. It's hard to watch."

"What do you mean?"

Clare pictured the look on her father's face when, at the airport, he hadn't recognised her until she stood in front of him and spoke. She recalled the sound of his sobbing later and thought about how seldom he looked directly at her, as if seeing his daughter was too painful to bear.

"He makes me feel ashamed of what I've become," she said. "Ashamed of how weak he thinks I am."

"Your dad? Surely not. He's—"

"He doesn't mean to, but . . ." Clare regretted having initiated the conversation.

"How then?"

The shelter was quiet but for the rain.

The girl emitted a tiny, shaky sigh. "I've let this illness consume three years of my life. I should've sorted myself out by now."

"Is that how it works though? Is it possible to simply sort yourself out? Aren't you being hard on yourself?"

"I don't think so. It's just that I'm so ashamed of how ashamed my father is of me. And how hard it is for him to hide that shame. Does that make sense?"

Faye was quiet and lay so still that Clare wondered if she'd fallen asleep. Perhaps it was for the best; too much had already been said. Then she felt a hand on hers, giving it a gentle squeeze.

"I'm not inside your dad's head, but I do know him. And I'm a parent. I don't believe your father is ashamed of you. He's far too understanding for that. Too compassionate. I don't doubt that it hurts him to see you ill and that he'd love to wave a wand and make all well. That's what parents want, to make their children happy, even if it costs them. But Geoffrey is not ashamed of you."

"How could he not be?" The words were carried by another sigh. "I'm ashamed of me."

"What would it take to change that? To get rid of the shame?"

Clare moved her hand and swallowed. Even that hurt.

"I have an idea, something I've been trying for a while, actually. The two people I've told think it's silly, just an extension of the anorexia, but I think it'll work for me. It *is* working, mostly."

"What is it?"

"You'll probably think as my mother does; that I'm ridiculous."

"Try me."

Clare explained how she believed she could use her relentless need to be in control to reverse her illness. She told Faye how she set goals and added calories and different foods to her diet every week. She explained how she monitored her achievements and rewarded herself with exercise.

"I thought, if I can't beat my compulsion, why not make it work for me, help me recover?" she said. "If I'm disciplined enough to get it right, I might even recognise myself again and like what I see. The person I used to be."

Faye didn't interrupt and, when Clare stopped talking, she remained silent. Clare wondered once more if the older woman had fallen asleep. But that wasn't the case.

"I get it," said Faye. "I can't say whether it will work because I'm not an expert, but it makes sense. The thing is, you say you're trying to find the person you were; the one you recognise and like, right?"

"Yes."

"Well, I'm not sure that's possible. You aren't the same girl. None of us stay the same as we experience life. We change. We evolve."

"I know. I'm not asking to be naïve and seventeen again; I just want to be able to look at myself and feel proud, happy, so others can feel the same. I can't think of any other way of getting rid of the shame."

She heard the leaves crinkle as Faye shuddered.

"Are you cold?" asked Clare.

"No. No. Not at all. I just, well, have you ever asked your dad if he's ashamed of you? In so many words, I mean."

"I don't have to. It's obvious. Also, Derek told me."

There was louder scrunching sound as Faye shifted her weight. "Derek? What would Derek know about how your father feels about you?"

"He said my mother told him."

"Your mother told Derek your father was ashamed of you?" Faye spoke slowly.

"Apparently."

"That doesn't sound right. I mean, why?"

"Why? Because it's how people feel about anorexia—when someone they know is anorexic."

"No, I mean why would Michelle, your mom, tell Derek?"

"I don't know. Because they've been friends forever and talk every day about everything? That's what he said, anyway."

Faye was quiet. Clare wondered again why she'd opened up to Faye. Mark was the only other person she'd ever spoken so freely to about her condition. Even then she'd been more guarded. It had been a weird day. Perhaps the shock and the painkillers were to blame.

"I think I'm going to sleep now."

"Oh. Okay. Good. Yes. I hope you sleep well. Wake me, Clare, if you need me. Please," said Faye.

Clare eventually drifted off and slept deeply for several hours. When she woke up, her body stiff from guarding against the tiniest movement, it was still dark. The pain though, was worse than the stiffness. Every joint, muscle and nerve seemed connected to her rib cage, where the agony was channelled and then radiated back out like the talons of a bolt of lightning, clenching and burning. Even turning her head hurt.

Hoping to distract herself from the discomfort, she tried to identify the sounds of the forest. She heard the thunking of raindrops falling from the leaves onto the wood and soil. The *splats* were overlaid by the chirruping of crickets and croaking of frogs. An owl called from way off. Clare wondered if it was the same owl she'd heard while sitting on the stairs at Heuningbos on the first night. She also made out the plaintive *whue-whe-whe-whe-whe-whue* of what she took to be a fiery-necked nightjar. She listened for other sounds, imagining footsteps when a branch cracked or leaves crunched. She pictured genets, caracal, wild pigs and honey badgers slinking hesitantly through the undergrowth as they detected the unfamiliar smell of humans in their territory. When the snapping and scrunching sounds were louder, she imagined the almond-shaped, yellow eyes and twitching, rounded ears of a leopard. Her heart sped up at the thought of the cat's large, furry paws stealing closer to the shelter.

"Leopards might be the smallest of the big cat family, but they are the stealthiest and the most elusive," said her grandmother, when she'd accompanied the family on a trip to the Kruger National Park.

Faye's breathing was deep and rhythmic. Clare wondered if the older woman would have slept at all if she'd mentioned the leopard. She thought about their conversation and about how the darkness and their proximity had made talking easier. How ironic it was she'd insisted on being as far away as possible from her parents' friends on the first night and yet now, compelled to lie within millimetres of Faye, she found solace. How kind the older woman had been. How eager to understand. She wondered what Faye might say if she knew the full extent of her shame and how she'd let it ruin the most important friendships she'd known.

≈≈

Clare, Buhle and Maryanne met at playschool and were best friends throughout their school years. Buhle and Clare made formidable doubles partners on the tennis court. Buhle and Maryanne danced in the same hip-hop troupe. Maryanne and Clare were members of the school orchestra and all three sang in the choir. They spent weekends together, formed a study group, cried on one another's shoulders and celebrated each other's successes. Although their interests took them on different paths when they completed high school, the trio never imagined being anything other than best friends. Then Clare came back to town after her first year at university almost twenty-five kilograms lighter.

The friends had agreed to meet at Gino's, the pizza restaurant where they'd spent most Friday nights throughout their teenage years. Although Clare hadn't seen the others since she left, they'd all been in touch regularly during the months Clare and Buhle had been studying in different towns and Maryanne had taken on an internship with an interior decorating company. Her friends were already seated when Clare arrived. Maryanne saw her first. She covered her mouth with her hand and nudged Buhle, who gaped as she recognised her friend. The two girls exchanged a glance as they stood to embrace her. Buhle spoke first.

"My God! Clare! What have you done?"

She hugged her friends briefly and sat down.

"I'm sorry. I should've warned you. I . . . I lost weight," she said, suddenly wishing she hadn't agreed to meet them. She knew her weight loss would surprise them, but she hadn't anticipated their shock.

Maryanne gawped, speechless.

Buhle leaned forward and took Clare's hand. "What happened? Why?"

"I've been running . . . a lot."

"Running?"

Maryanne still hadn't said a word. Clare nodded. Buhle shook her head, her eyes shining.

"No," she said. "You don't get *that* thin from running. No matter how far you go. Have you stopped eating? Altogether?"

Clare looked at her hands. "No, not altogether. It's just—"

Maryanne leaped up, sending her chair crashing to the floor and ran out of the restaurant. Buhle stood.

"I'll be back," she said, following their friend.

She wasn't. Clare waited but neither Buhle nor Maryanne returned. About twenty minutes after they'd left, her phone pinged with a message from Buhle. "MA's not well. Have taken her home. Will call tomorrow to reschedule. Sorry. B."

Buhle phoned the following evening. Clare almost declined the call. Shortly into the conversation, she wished she had. Buhle tried to explain.

"She's freaked out, Clare."

"Freaked out?"

She sighed. "My friend, have you seen yourself?"

Clare was silent.

"You were always the one who was so together, who kept me and Maryanne cool, kept us keeping on. It never occurred to us that you were so concerned about your appearance."

"That's not—"

"I mean, you always looked great and we imagined that, well, it's like we didn't know you and now . . ."

"Now what?"

"Geez, Clare, I don't know want to say. It's a shock, what's happened to you."

"I'm sorry."

"Hey. No. I mean, you don't have to apologise. It's not like you did this to us on purpose."

Clare felt cold, despite the fact that it was a warm, windless day. "No."

"It's just that it's a lot to deal with."

That stung. Clare hadn't realised how upset her friends would be by what had happened to her, what she'd done to herself. She should have anticipated it—particularly given the way her father had responded—but she hadn't. Unlike the friends she'd made when she arrived at university, Maryanne and Buhle had known her for decades. She'd assumed they'd try to understand. At least ask the kind questions caring friends ask one another. Try to help. Be there.

"Yes," she said, collecting herself, "it's a lot to deal with."

"Ja. I just . . . I just don't know what to do. Maryanne is—"

"No, listen," said Clare, but she wasn't sure how to say what she wanted to say. How humiliated she felt about letting her friends down. How embarrassing it was to go from being the one who supposedly had everything under control to the one who was completely out of control—and whose appearance was a billboard to the fact. Buhle and Maryanne didn't know what to do. Neither did she. The only thing she could do was to protect them from further embarrassment. She'd done this to herself. She was the one who should pay the price.

"It's okay. We'll get together when, erm, you guys feel better," she said.

"What? No, Clare. That's not—"

"It's okay, Buhle. I've got lots to sort out over the holidays. Tell Maryanne I hope she feels better."

She'd ignored her friends' repeated attempts to contact her after that, telling herself she was doing so for their benefit. They were ashamed of her. She was ashamed of herself. Even if they had been interested in finding out, how could she explain what had happened to her? She didn't know. It was just easier for everyone if she didn't inflict her misery on her friends.

Faye had emptied her daypack, rolled it up and placed it under Clare's knee to support the injured joint. Initially, it had felt comfortable. Now the canvas dug into her flesh. And, while the pile of leaves Faye had arranged for them to rest on were more comfortable than she'd expected, Clare was now stiff and longed to move, but she daren't. Everything ached. The most intense pain, though, came from inhaling and exhaling. Who knew that breathing could cause such agony? She wondered how she would make it back to Heuningbos.

Although the rain continued whirring in the upper boughs of the trees, the light was changing. She looked over her feet, through the opening of the shelter and beyond the trees to where the sun lit the clouds from behind. The darkness in the shelter separated her and Faye from the rest of the world and yet, because it comprised pieces of the forest, it seemed that they were also part of the place. Connected. A nest in the trees. A spot in the forest. A place in the world.

She heard Faye sit up and moan quietly. "You're awake," Faye said, rubbing her neck. "Are you okay?"

"Yes," said Clare, going for the default before she realised how pointless it was to pretend. "No, I don't think I am."

"Even more painful than yesterday?"

She gave a tiny nod. "It's so uncomfortable to breathe."

"Did you sleep at all?"

"Yes, a bit."

Faye peeled an orange and gave it to her. "You need this before you take more painkillers."

She didn't ask Clare if she wanted to eat or what she'd prefer. The orange was followed by an energy bar, water and painkillers. Clare didn't resist. It was as if, without asking or even anticipating that she might not be welcome, Faye had simply stepped into the bubble Clare had created to hold the world at bay. It was meant to be a place where she could remain numb, put life on pause. Others had seen it, but now Faye ignored it and Clare was grateful.

"Look," said Faye, as she took the bottle from her. "The rain has stopped."

Sixteen

There was something about the combination of the morning light slanting through the cabin window and the stiffness of his joints that reminded Derek of the phase of his life his mother referred to as "Derek's Meningitis Days."

He was six when he fell ill. It was only when he was rushed to hospital for the second time that doctors diagnosed the illness and began treatment. After several complications and weeks of handwringing and prayer from his mother, little Derek was laid up for more than two months. Eventually, fully conscious and with less fever, vomiting and headaches, the boy's recovery became a time of love and loss, which, though no one suspected it then, shaped the man he became.

Discharged from the hospital, home in his own bed and alert to daily life once more, Derek was delighted to have his mother to himself. By the time he awoke to the sun's rays sloping through his bedroom window and the ache in his joints duller than it had been the night before, his father and siblings had left for the day. As the third born of four, he wasn't accustomed to a tranquil house or the full attention of a parent. His mother, tearfully grateful to see her son regaining his health, clucked about and cosseted him. She trotted to his bedside, delivering whatever he desired whenever he called. She fed him, held cups of juice to his lips and read to him. When he needed (or demanded) to be bathed, she squandered her favourite bubble soap, turned the tub into a mountainous pool of perfumed foam, and stood by as he soaked, adding hot water at his command.

Mother Mackenzie charmed him with her own stories about a superhero called "Derek the Strongest." She also snuck a television set into his bedroom during the day, a treat made more exhilarating because his father believed that watching television from bed was almost as abhorrent a deed as discussing money in company. Derek basked in the adoration and servitude of his mother. He never felt fonder of her than he did when she, her face puce from the effort, heaved the television set back to the study before the others returned each afternoon. But, as much as he enjoyed his mother's undivided attention, Derek soon took it for granted. It was, however, the double loss that he suffered at the time that he would feel more keenly in years to come.

His father was a stern, quiet man who, raised by elderly parents, believed children should be infrequently seen and even more rarely heard. As such, Jock Mackenzie wasn't reared to converse or reveal much about himself to others. In fact, he seldom made known his emotions. However, when he witnessed his third born (and second son) mewing in agony and repeatedly losing consciousness while a group of doctors huddled around his bed muttering their bafflement, Jock was moved. So much so that it had required several gulps to dislodge the lump in his throat.

Derek's mother spent more time at the hospital than at home during the weeks that followed. When he was with her during that time, Jock watched wordlessly as his wife paced the room, squeezing the blood from her fingers and fretting about the boy as if no one else existed. Her other children took care of one another and Jock took care of himself.

For a while, when Derek was home convalescing, Jock continued his silent surveillance. He knew how close they'd come to losing their son and was pleased the boy was on the mend. He needed his mother.

One evening, however, as Jock arrived home from work, he heard Derek call for her. She scurried from the kitchen, waving briefly at her husband as she noticed him in the hallway. He followed and stood near the doorway as his wife went to the boy's side.

"Can you tell me another story, Mother?" asked Derek. "I'm bored."

"I will, dearest. After supper. I'm half done cooking dinner."

"But that'll take ages and I'll be tired by then. Can't you—"

Jock stepped into the room. "Your mother is busy, Derek. Why don't you read a book if you're bored?"

Derek and his mother glanced at one another before she turned to her husband.

"He doesn't read yet, dear," she said.

Jock raised his brows. "Really? Well, that's another good reason for him to get out of bed and go back to school as soon as possible."

"The doctor said he needs a few more weeks."

"If he's strong enough to demand entertainment at home, I venture that he's well enough to sit in a classroom."

"Soon enough, dear," said Derek's mother, giving her son a nervous smile as she led his father away.

He wasn't sure what passed between his parents after that but the following week, the boy returned to school. Two weeks later, his teacher intercepted Mrs Mackenzie when she arrived to fetch her children and told her the school was concerned about Derek: he was so far behind he might be unable to catch up or keep up with his classmates. It would be better, said the teacher, if he stayed home for the rest of the year and returned the following one to start grade one afresh.

Derek was delighted by the news. It meant being home alone with his mother again and watching daytime television. Jock was incensed.

"He and his teacher will simply have to work harder so he can get back on track," he said. "His brother and sister can help him in the afternoon, too. How hard can it be to catch up on two months of grade one work?"

"It's just that it's important he gets a good foundation, they said. He's missed some crucial steps," explained his mother, wringing her hands once more.

His father would have none of it, and the boy was bundled off to school again the next day. The months that followed were alienating and confusing for Derek. Resentful of the fact his parents had dismissed her recommendation, his teacher largely ignored him. In addition, with his classmates having established friendships while he was ill, Derek sat alone on the wall at break times so he could see the road, lest his mother should come by. Surely she'd rescue Derek the Strongest?

When the year ended, Mr and Mrs Mackenzie received a letter from the school principal. He wrote, "We regret to inform you that Derek has not met the minimum standard required to progress to grade two and will have to repeat grade one next year."

It was the first time he heard his father say, "That boy will amount to nothing."

When he returned to the same classroom with the same teacher scowling at the board the next year, Derek was a year older and, he believed, a year wiser. He looked around and saw versions of his younger sister. He resented being among them, and was annoyed that no one seemed to care he was the boy, Derek the Strongest, who had triumphed over "a very bad disease" the previous year. When Tom de Klerk dared to climb on "his wall," Derek shoved him off. Tom fell on the tarmac and broke his arm. Mr and Mrs Mackenzie were summoned to the principal's office to discuss their son's anti-social behaviour.

"You've mollycoddled him," Jock told his wife as they drove home, Derek sniffling on the back seat. "It's your fault the boy will amount to nothing."

Just as Derek had had no friends the previous year, he was friendless once more; this time because he was feared. That changed when tiny blonde Michelle Lowe arrived at the school halfway through the year. Although the others warned her about Derek, she ignored them.

"Why do you always sit on the wall?" she asked him, as they lined up to return to class after morning break one day.

"Because I can't smell you from up there," he sneered.

"I think it's because you think no one wants to play with you."

"It's because *I* don't want to play with *them*, stupid!"

"If you change your mind, you can play with me and Diane. Just as long you don't—"

"I don't want to!" he snapped.

Michelle sighed and looked at him, her large, round eyes blinking fast. When she spoke again, she did it slowly, enunciating each word. "You can play with me and Diane, as long as you don't think we will put up with any of your nonsense. Think about it."

Derek didn't respond. He was overwhelmed by Michelle's pluck, her confidence and her gold curls and smooth skin, which he hadn't noticed until that moment. Mostly though, he was struck by the intensity of her eyes, which seemed to look straight though him and knew everything.

The next day Derek joined Michelle and Diane on the playground and the threesome was established. When he asked his parents if he and the two girls could watch a movie instead of having a party for his birthday that year (and for many years that followed), Jock scowled.

"Don't you have any male friends?" he asked. "Get one or two of them to come along, too."

"No," replied Derek as he ran from the room.

Derek's mother took the three to movies on his birthday. The following Saturday morning, Jock woke Derek early and told him get dressed.

"We are going fishing," said his father, as if it was something they'd done before.

The boy dressed and went to the kitchen where he stared at his mother, hoping at least for an explanation from her. She didn't look at him, but handed his father a basket.

"Your lunch," she said. "Good luck!"

Jock drove Derek to a farm that offered trout fishing, including the hiring of equipment. They were receiving instructions on how to fly fish, which even Jock was finding hard to follow, when a man arrived with a boy Derek's age.

"Ah, David. Good," said Jock.

The man, it was revealed during the morning, was a clerk at Jock's factory. The fishing, Derek realised, was a ruse to introduce him to a boy his age. He and Philip were meant to become friends. Philip was as indifferent to fishing and making new friends as Derek was. The day, which ended early when Philip got a hook stuck in his foot and his father rushed him to a doctor, was a disaster. The only thing, bar Philip's foot, that anyone hooked was the branch of a tree alongside the lake. The only time the boys spoke to one another had been to say hello when they were first introduced.

"There was no effort. No effort at all," said Jock, as he dumped the basket on the kitchen table in front of his wife that afternoon. "I'll not waste any more time on the boy. He'll amount to nothing."

But still, even though Jock liked Derek's friend Michelle, he never stopped hoping his son would pal up with members of his own gender. Surrounding oneself with ambitious males was, he believed, important to "getting ahead in life."

"I don't know why you let it get to you, Father," said Derek, by then a teenager. "You always say I won't amount to anything, so why would a few male friends make any difference?"

Now, at Grootkloof, with the birds (Derek didn't try to distinguish them) increasingly clamorous outside, the cool quiet of the cabin and the fuzzy-headed after-effects of the whiskey and pills, he was reminded of another incident with his father. It happened during Derek's first year at university when he was suffering the painful jolt of waking each morning and remembering that he and Michelle were no longer together. For a while, he imagined if he went to as many parties and wooed as many girls as possible, Michelle might become jealous and regret having broken up with him. It was at one such party when, already far gone on alcohol, he took a freshly-lit joint from someone and made a show of sucking on it until it burnt his fingers. When he was still out cold on the couch in the party house at eleven the next morning, someone called his parents' home.

The first thing Derek remembered hearing that morning was Jock's voice in the room.

"What happened here?"

"Erm, well sir, I think he overdid it last night," said a young man, presumably one of the residents of the house.

"Give me specifics, lad."

The room was quiet for a moment until a girl spoke up.

"He'd been drinking, a lot, for several hours and then smoked an entire joint. That's, erm, dagga. You know, cannabis."

"I know what it is," said Jock, his voice low.

The man resumed. "He went a bit odd, sir. Angry and very loud. Shouting at everyone and saying things that made no sense to any of us. Then he stood on the table and started demanding that someone go and fetch his girlfriend—"

"Michelle Lowe," interjected the girl quietly. "Hard to forget the name."

"Ja, that was the name he shouted again and again. Anyway, no one here knew her but that didn't stop him going on and on about her. I guess after a while we ignored him and he, well, fell asleep. We didn't expect to find him still here today, though."

The pair helped Derek to his feet and to the bathroom where he threw up several times, before they loaded him into Jock's car. Not a word was said on the drive home. Mrs Mackenzie came out to meet them when they drew up in front of the house, her eyes darting nervously between father and son. Jock got out of the car and walked inside.

"This is it," he said, not bothering to look at his wife. "This is what your son has amounted to: nothing."

When Jock died less than a year later, father and son were barely talking to one another and there was certainly no evidence that the older man had changed his opinion of Derek.

Now, as he sat up in the cabin and dragged his legs over the side of the bed, Derek pictured his father's face and imagined his voice: "Just as I predicted, you've amounted to nothing."

Derek glanced at the floor where his hip flask and the last pack of the painkillers lay. The pain in his back had eased but still, he hoped the rangers would make it that day so he'd have access to more analgesics by nightfall.

Seventeen

Faye was surprised when Clare spoke so openly about her anorexia. She wondered if it was the darkness, their isolation, the after-effects of the girl's accident or because she and Faye were on the periphery of friendship that prompted her to talk. She settled on it being a combination of all of these things. Aside from loosening up for a bit while they'd eaten supper with the bats overhead the previous night, Clare had been subdued, aloof even. Her reticence ebbed as they lay side-by-side on the damp forest floor. Faye was pleased the girl felt she could confide in her, but that didn't stop her heart pumping faster. She knew little about eating disorders aside from what Michelle had told her. What if she said the wrong thing? Upset the girl? Made things worse for her?

Then Clare spoke of how ashamed her father was of her; confirmed, she said, by things Derek said. Faye was stunned. The notion of her husband understanding Geoffrey's emotions was ridiculous. The only thing more implausible was that Geoffrey was ashamed of his daughter. Nor did it make any sense that, even if it were true, Michelle would disclose something so private about her family to Derek. And, in the unlikely event she had confided in him, why would Derek repeat such hurtful information to Clare? Even if her husband and the girl were involved in a relationship that might afford him some kind of prerogative, it was cruel. As belittling as he might be about his wife, Derek wasn't heartless.

Faye's mind whirred with questions, to none of which she gave voice. Where were they when Derek told Clare about her father's shame? Lunching near the university? How had the conversation come about? What did Derek mean when he said he and Michelle, "Talk every day about everything"? Was that even possible? Faye wasn't aware Derek and Michelle spoke to one another outside the times the Mackenzies and Bassons met as couples or families.

But it was Clare's description of her own shame that shook Faye most. In fact, her muscles contracted and released in such rapid succession, she shuddered. She literally shook. Indeed, Clare's words struck a chord. No, it was more than that. The entire orchestra played and the refrain was loud and clear.

"I just want to be able to look at myself and feel proud, happy. So others can feel the same."

Careful not to move when Clare finally stopped talking and her breathing slowed to indicate sleep, Faye repeated the girl's words to herself.

"I just want to be able to look at myself and feel proud, happy. So others can feel the same."

❧

Faye tried to picture herself in front of a mirror. The full-length one Derek had installed inside his cupboard door would do. The thought of standing there made Faye flinch, pinch her eyes shut and turn her head. She didn't want to have to look at the depleted version of herself she was sure she'd see. Like an old cloth, wrung dry and, twisted and knotted, abandoned in the sun, what she saw was brittle, faded, worthless. There was nothing about the idea that made her proud or happy. Faye felt only shame.

During her early days at GNS, she'd dreamed of training others as George had trained her, passing on what she knew and loved. She wanted to see others uncover unexpected things about themselves and discover skills they didn't know they possessed. She remembered the thrill of it. But Faye never returned to work. Instead, she'd stayed home, become dependent on Derek and, as he told her, "Morphed into an overly sensitive soul, prone to paranoia, and also forgetful and easily confused."

What had happened to make her that way? Had she really changed that much? Did Derek exaggerate? Or was he entirely mistaken, as her mother had argued during one of Faye's last conversations with her in the hospice.

"Hello, Mom," said Faye when Veronica had opened her eyes to find her daughter sitting at her bedside.

Veronica blinked. "At last. I was wondering when you'd come. It's been so long."

"I was here yesterday. We shared one of those cupcakes from Zurelli's that you enjoy. Remember?"

Her mother tapped the side of her head with a finger. "Tsk. Of course. It's the worst thing about getting old; you can't get anything to stick."

"Don't worry about it." Faye took one of her mother's hands in hers, glancing at its translucent skin. "You've done well. Even at my age, I can't get things to stick."

"Says who?" Veronica squinted at her. "Derek?"

Faye smiled, but her mother drew her balding eyebrows together.

"You mustn't let him bully you. It's unpleasant and it worries me. Greatly."

"Oh, he doesn't, Mom," said Faye, patting her mother's hand.

"But he does, Faye. He does. And is he ever wrong? I mean, he says you're forgetful and, what's the word? Erm, delusional? Yes, delusional." She shook her head. "And when he's wrong, obviously wrong, does he apologise? Ever?"

"We don't argue. I don't want to argue."

Veronica turned her hand and gripped Faye's fingers with surprising strength. "I'm not going to be around for long so I'm going to tell you this now. And yes, I know; it's as hard for you to hear, but you—"

Faye swallowed. "No, Mom. Please don't. It's not—"

Her mother ignored her, speaking louder. "You have *never* been forgetful. You are not delusional. Or confused, suspicious or obsessive. Or whatever else Derek accuses you of being. You are my strong daughter, the one who was my rock when Dad died and who has always been caring and reliable. Always reliable. Always capable."

Faye leaned forward and laid her head on her mother's hand to hide her tears. "I know, Mom, I know."

But she didn't know. She wished she believed in herself the way her mother did.

A little later, Faye left her mother and walked down through the hospice passages, feeling frustrated. Veronica was dying and deserved peace. She shouldn't be worrying about her daughter. Faye never discussed her marriage with her mother or anyone else. Had Veronica drawn her own conclusions or had Derek discussed Faye's shortcomings with his mother-in-law? Why? Because he was worried about her and hoped that her mother might join him in trying to convince her to seek help?

She'd sat in her car in the parking lot, trying to calm her thoughts. Of course Veronica would defend her daughter. She was biased, old and couldn't see Faye's faults the way Derek could. But what of their son? Was Zach more objective? Was that why, as the years passed, Derek had toned down his criticism of Faye when the three of them were together? Still, that didn't mean Zach was unaware of how things were between his parents.

"Mom," he'd said one evening as she prepared supper and he did his homework. "Why doesn't Dad give you pocket money every month like he gives me?"

She looked at him over the tomatoes she was chopping. "Why would he do that?"

"Then you could buy yourself things you like, like books and lipstick."

"I don't need lipstick and I get books from the library."

"You used to sometimes wear lipstick, and if you could buy books, you could join the book club with Alice and Clare's moms."

"I could, I mean, I can buy books. Dad wouldn't mind if I bought books."

Zach looked at her. "So why don't you?"

"The book club meets on Tuesdays, which is when Dad has his Toastmasters meetings."

The boy tilted his head.

"Besides," she continued, tipping the tomatoes into a pot, "the library has plenty of books."

"I think Dad should give you pocket money," mumbled Zach, head down again. "I'm going to ask him to."

"Please don't, Zach. I don't want you to. Please don't." She hoped he didn't recognise the panic in her voice.

"Okay. But, Mom, when I get a job, when I'm working, I'll give you pocket money."

Faye went to her son, wrapped her arms around his shoulders and hugged him. They never spoke of it again, but from then on, on every birthday, Christmas and Mother's Day, Zach presented his mother with a voucher from a bookshop.

⋙⋘

Now, as she lay on a bed of leaves in a forest in the mountains, it was clear to Faye. Her mother had died nursing worries about her. Her son pitied her so deeply he'd used his pocket money to buy her vouchers, hoping she'd join her friends' book club. (She bought the books but didn't join the club.) No wonder Faye was ashamed. She'd let her mother and her son down. She was weak and had failed them. She'd allowed her life to be derailed and landed up in scrapyard of worthlessness. How had it happened?

When she fell in love with Derek, Faye imagined that being with him and his equally self-confident and ambitious friends would somehow elevate her, make her stronger, more assertive. As Derek's wife and adopting his friends as hers, she would, she'd thought, live a fuller, more rewarding life. One in which she'd be a woman with opportunity and influence. In that regard, she might certainly have been delusional. Instead of building her up, the marriage had depleted her.

Even if Veronica was right about Derek having coerced his wife into believing that she was weak and needy, Faye had bought into the notion. She'd existed so long within his assessment of her that she no longer saw beyond it. Could she rebuild what had been chipped away over two decades? Was there a way to be happy and proud again? To be willing to face the mirror? *Oh, to have the same grit as the tiny girl alongside to me. To have a plan and the resolve to make it work.*

The shelter was dark, the gloom helped not only by the cloudy night and dense forest, but also by the layer of leaves and branches Faye had assembled to keep the rain and wind out. As she'd settled in alongside Clare before nightfall, she'd wondered briefly if the darkness and sounds would play tricks on her imagination and make her too nervous to sleep. It was only two nights ago that she'd sat outside at Heuningbos and seen Derek switch off the light in the cabin, believing she would never be brave enough to sleep outdoors. Yet here she was. Not just outdoors in a makeshift shelter, but in a forest—with an injured girl.

Faye looked around for the shadows she'd imagined might transform into unwieldy shapes with fangs and claws. They were nowhere to be seen and she was not afraid. Moments ago, she'd chastised herself for being helpless and insubstantial. But Faye had built a shelter in the forest. Clare was injured, dangerously so, but Faye had worked out how to protect her, acted on it and, for the moment, they were both alive and dry. She wanted to sit up, punch the air and call out in victory. Instead, Faye smiled and closed her eyes. She should sleep. Faye wasn't afraid and if she wasn't afraid here and now, in the middle of the night in a forest in the wilderness with a gravely injured girl depending on her, why should she be afraid of anything that might lie ahead?

The sun etched the edges of the clouds on the horizon. Faye looked over her boots through the trees towards the glow. Night had passed and she had slept. She sat up and glanced at Clare.

"You're awake. Are you okay?"

The girl's face was pale with a bluish tinge and her breathing laboured, but she gave Faye a small smile. "Yes. No, I don't think I am."

"Even more painful than yesterday?"

She barely nodded. "So uncomfortable to breathe. A bit woozy."

"Did you sleep at all?"

"Yes. Several hours, I think."

Faye pressed her lips together. The girl shouldn't move. A punctured lung could explain her colouring and the light-headedness: she wasn't getting enough oxygen. There was no option. Faye would have to leave her to find help, and she'd need to get going soon.

She peeled an orange, handed it over, and was pleased when Clare ate it and an energy bar, followed by painkillers and water. The bottle needed refilling. Faye looked outside.

"Look, it's stopped raining. I'm going–"

"Shh," said Clare, staring out of the shelter into the trees.

Faye stared at her. Was the girl hallucinating? She turned and followed her gaze.

The sunlight glistened on the manes of the wild pigs who, twenty metres or so away, were snuffling and rootling in the undergrowth. They gave no indication of sensing the women's presence.

"My friends," whispered Faye. "You see, they exist."

Clare's mouth curved into a tiny smile and she nodded.

They counted seven large animals and four piglets who tip-toed in a line through the brushwood. They were quiet but for the muted sounds of their trotters and rummaging in vegetation and earth. Clare and Faye watched until the animals disappeared from sight.

Clare closed her eyes. "We haven't missed out on everything on this trip then."

"I know what you mean." Faye turned to face her. "I'm going to go now. First to get more water and then to find help."

"Shouldn't I try—"

"No. I don't think you should move."

"Will you go back to the cabin? Wait for the rangers?"

"No. Yesterday I saw how badly the road was damaged. It'll take them ages to reach us that way. I'm going to follow the trail into the ravine and see if I can't raise help quicker the other way."

"To Grootkloof Cabin? Where the others are? Or were?"

"Yes. It's possible, with the weather as it was, that they're still there, which would be helpful. That's why I want to get going now."

"But the Bloukrans is also flooded. I saw it. It's huge."

"Yes, but if I remember correctly, there's a rope crossing at the bottom of the ravine. I've got to try. If it doesn't work, I'll turn back."

"Are you sure it's—"

"Yes."

Clare's lower lip quivered. Faye rested her hand on the girl's shoulder.

"It's the best we can hope for. You can't move. You must stay as still as possible. Don't move. At all. Understand?"

Clare closed her eyes and gave a small nod.

Faye took the bottle to a puddle on the path and filled it with rainwater. She placed it alongside Clare with the bag containing the nuts, crackers, energy bar and remaining orange. She didn't remind Clare to eat; she knew the girl would, if she could.

She adjusted the empty backpack beneath Clare's knee and straightened the space blanket over her.

"Thank you, Faye," said the girl. "You're amazing."

"I know," she replied. "I'll see you soon. Then you can tell me again."

Eighteen

"What's your verdict, Geoff?" asked Derek, as he stepped out of the cabin and spotted his friend sitting on the stairs. "Is today the day we'll be rescued?"

Geoffrey glanced at him, wondering why, after all these years, it still annoyed him that Derek was the only person who addressed him as Geoff. "My friends, Geoff and Mich," he'd say. No one else called Michelle "Mich" either.

"Depends on whether the others met up with the rangers yesterday. But if they had to hike all the way to the offices, it's unlikely they would have made it in a day."

"The rain last night wouldn't have helped."

"No, but it's stopped now so—"

Derek snorted. "The eternal optimist. God, I hope they come. I've had enough of this place."

Geoffrey had had enough, too. Not of the place. In other circumstances, a cabin built on the edge of the mountain with a forest stretching into forever out back, and the mountains standing watch in front would have been idyllic. Sharing the spot with an injured, curmudgeonly and half-sauced Derek, and the uncertainty of knowing where the others were however, soured the experience. Geoffrey had tried not let Derek's complaining—primarily about his back pain, the weather, his wasted vacation time and how hungry he was—aggravate him the previous day. He had been grateful the injured man had spent most of it on his bed. Geoffrey had used the time to explore.

At some point over the past century or so, parts of the area had been planted with exotic trees, including pines and gums. More recently though, the indigenous vegetation had reclaimed its place in the earth, mingling with the alien plants to create a kind of hybrid jungle where the spikey European conifers were entangled with purple-flowered creepers and yellowwood saplings that struggled alongside the blue gums.

In other places, where they had been undisturbed for hundreds of years, giant trees grew gnarled and twisty amid groves of leafy ferns, lichen-covered rocks and mossy logs. There was something magical about the groves, something whimsical that reminded Geoffrey of the illustrations in one of his children's favourite picture books about fairies and forest animals. He had sat on a rock in a particularly peaceful spot and looked intently at the scene, trying to imprint the arrangement of plants, textures and colours on his brain so he could recreate it back in the city. He wouldn't have minded disappearing into the forest again, but it seemed Derek was stronger today.

"You're feeling better then?" he asked.

Derek scowled and placed his hands on the small of his back. "Ja. Ja. I think so. I hope so. Thank God for Bev's mobile pharmacy. Wouldn't cope otherwise. Definitely couldn't sleep without the drugs."

Geoffrey glanced at him. It was almost midday. Derek had certainly managed to sleep. "Are you feeling up to walking to the river with me? I want to see whether it has subsided?"

"I'm probably up to it, but why bother? It's not like it's going to make any difference to us."

Geoffrey gave a half shrug. "It'll give us some idea whether we'll see anyone today or if we'll have to wait another day."

"And then what? I mean, if we have to stay? Are you going to try and convince me to eat dodgy-looking mushrooms again?"

"Something like that."

Geoffrey had mentioned that he'd seen several different types of mushrooms on his walks, some of which he believed were edible. Derek said he doubted a guy who operated a garden services company was qualified to distinguish edible fungi from inedible. Geoffrey didn't respond, having long ago learned to ignore Derek's assumed authority on all things.

"See you later then," he said, getting to his feet and heading towards the river.

As he walked down the track, Geoffrey thought about his friends and the entangled lives they led. People from outside the group often commented on how wonderful it was they had been friends for so long. Michelle, Diane and Derek had known one another almost all their lives and, while the others had been drawn in by one of the three at different times, they'd all been connected for nearly twenty-five years. It was, he thought, mostly good, but sometimes it seemed not entirely healthy.

There was something about having the same friends for so long that blurred the boundaries. It was akin to being part of a family, which sometimes meant having to tolerate people even if you didn't really like them. Just like you didn't call out an uncle for an inappropriate remark because you didn't want to upset his sister— that is, your mother—being part of a tight group of friends made it difficult to call someone out without treading on collective toes.

In theory, being alone with Derek, as they had been since the previous morning, was the ideal time for Geoffrey to challenge the man. He could've told him how annoying his jibes about his business were, asked him to use his proper name and told him to stay away from Clare. Faye wasn't around to be embarrassed and Michelle wasn't there to feel protective towards the man she'd known since she was six or seven years old.

Derek and Michelle had a complicated relationship that seemed to be something apart from the rest of the group, and sometimes defied reason. Geoffrey asked her about it once as they were driving home after meeting their friends at restaurant to celebrate Bruce's fortieth birthday.

"I know you and Derek were an item for a while at varsity and it doesn't bother me, but I am curious about why you broke up?"

She looked at him, surprised by the question. "Pfft. I don't remember the specifics but we decided we made better friends than, erm, romantic partners."

"Fair enough."

"What makes you ask after all these years?"

"It occurred to me tonight that you're the only one among us who is immune to his digs. Actually, it's not even that you're immune; more that he doesn't try and taunt you at all."

"Really? I hadn't thought about it."

Geoffrey gave a disbelieving snort. "What's your secret?"

"Probably because I called him on it when we were kids."

"Called him on what?"

"His low self-esteem. And the way he tries to disguise it by being a bully."

Geoffrey huffed. "Derek has low self-esteem? Are we talking about the same person? Derek Mackenzie?"

"Why do you think he always has to have the last word? Be the centre of attention?"

"Seriously? Why would he have low self-esteem?"

"Hmm. I'm not sure. It's not something we've ever really discussed. I don't think he'd acknowledge it. Perhaps it's because he felt he never measured up to his father's expectations. His mother doted on him but his father dismissed him as a failure. I think it affected him greatly—even if he doesn't realise it. But I'm guessing, really."

"His father? I didn't know. But you said you 'called him on it.' What did you say?"

"Geoffrey! Why the interrogation? I don't remember. It was ages ago. We were kids."

They'd arrived home and he hadn't pursued the subject. Michelle's answers made sense; Derek didn't bait Michelle because she never rose to it and perhaps because he felt she knew him best and saw parts of him others didn't. Her theory that he had low self-esteem was consistent with what Geoffrey knew about bullying behaviour: those who don't value themselves put others down in order to feel better about themselves.

For a while, after his conversation with Michelle, Geoffrey pitied Derek. He felt, although they had moved in the same circles since university, he should make an effort to get to know him better. He invited Derek to meet him for drinks after work twice, and once to join him for a round of golf. Derek declined all invitations and Geoffrey realised getting to know each other better wasn't something the other man wanted. He was Michelle's friend and Geoffrey was an extension of her. So be it, thought Geoffrey, and so their association continued as before. It was no surprise, then, that the men hadn't connected during their day together, away from the others, in the Tsitsikamma. Geoffrey had however, imagined Derek might somehow express appreciation at his willingness to stay with him. He hadn't.

Although the clouds hadn't cleared completely, they no longer looked threatening. Perhaps the hike could still be rescued, even if it meant being transported further along the original route and only walking the last two days. While he was initially disappointed Michelle couldn't make it, Geoffrey was pleased his daughter had agreed to join him. He'd enjoyed the first day's hike with her. It was a chance for them to get to know one another again after she'd been away at university for the past three years. They'd always been so close, but with her illness and the miles between them, things had changed. He realised she was no longer the same young girl who, during the school holidays, would jump into his bakkie and travel to his clients with him, watching him work alongside his team, and asking him to explain what he was doing as they worked.

"You're not thinking about becoming a gardener, are you?"

Michelle asked pre-teen Clare when the girl had told her mother about the tree that Geoffrey had transplanted that day.

Geoffrey had looked up from the sink where he was washing his hands, interested in his daughter's response.

"I don't think so," said Clare. "But I wouldn't mind becoming a botanist."

Michelle raised her brows. "Hmm. Not sure what botanists do outside of academia. Is there any money in it?"

Clare hadn't studied botany. Instead, she'd graduated with a degree in environmental science and was hoping to find work that focused on sustainable energy. Geoffrey was proud of her, her interest in the environment and the fact that she wasn't driven primarily by money. Of course he worried about her health and wished that she hadn't got so thin. He tried not to watch what she ate and reassured himself he was no longer worried she would starve herself to death like he had been when she first came home. She wasn't out of the grips of the illness, but neither was she entirely in its clutches. Geoffrey hoped that, as soon as Clare found a job that tested and engaged her, she would find she didn't have the time or inclination to obsess about her diet and exercise.

He wondered, thinking about his own high school obsession with rugby, whether Clare was genetically predisposed to compulsive behaviour. Success in the sport was a badge of honour among Geoffrey's friends and peers and their families. Before he reached his teens, his agility and enthusiasm meant he was always chosen for his age group's first team. At high school though, his slight physique and medium height put him at a disadvantage. He wasn't brawny enough for the squads of rangy, rough-edged youths who fought their way over, under and through one another in the feature games on Saturdays.

When Geoffrey mentioned his dissatisfaction about his body at the dinner table, his father responded, "Not everything comes equally as easily to everyone."

Geoffrey thought it was a fair observation and set his mind and body to adapting. He downed a mixture of three raw eggs, two mugs of milk, rolled oats and spoonfuls of peanut butter every morning and trained on the sports field alone before daylight. He worked out at the gym for two hours almost every day and joined the wrestling club to hone his scrumming skills. He declined his friends' offers of cigarettes and beers when their parents weren't around, and was in bed by nine-thirty every night to ensure he was up to training the next day. It was a routine he followed diligently for three years. At last, in his final year at school, Geoffrey was seconded from the B-team to the A-team for a major game.

"Geoffrey," said the coach, as the boys lined up to run onto the field, "this is your reward for never giving up. Enjoy it!"

Less than ten minutes into the first half, the boy (or was he already a man?) playing lock for the opposition, tackled Geoffrey with such force that both the radius and ulna bones of his right arm broke. He never played rugby again.

There were other examples of his single-mindedness, including his determination to leave banking and start a gardening business. The decision almost cost him Michelle. She was appalled by the idea of him giving up a well-paid, prestigious job with a leading banking group for something as menial, poorly-paid and risky as starting yet another garden services company in the suburbs.

"I don't know you anymore," she'd wailed dramatically. "Three months ago you told me Xolani said you could be part of the executive committee within three years. Now you're saying you want to drive bakkie loads of compost around for the rest of your life."

"I don't want to live my life indoors, staring at a computer and attending an endless series of meetings about money and people I will never meet."

"It's like you're having a midlife crisis and you're not even thirty. Why are you doing this to me?"

Michelle had tried to talk him out of the idea for more than week and when she realised he wasn't backing down, she stopped speaking to him and moved into the spare room. Then she disappeared for a few days and, when she returned to discover Geoffrey hadn't changed his mind, she sobbed and threatened to leave him for good.

"God, Michelle! I hope you don't. It would break my heart and it's not what I want. But I won't keep doing something I loathe to keep you happy because I'd end up hating us both."

She left the house again, but returned that evening. They didn't talk about it again until Geoffrey told her he'd submitted his resignation letter a few weeks later.

"Well, I hope you know what you're doing," she said, "because it's not just about you and me anymore."

He stared at her, mouth agape.

"Yes, I'm pregnant."

It was one of the best days of his life.

⊰⊱

The track through the trees to the river was dotted with puddles. Watching the sun fighting its way through the clouds, Geoffrey felt hopeful a vehicle would arrive within the day to fetch them. He was anxious to see Clare. It wasn't only that he felt responsible for her, but they'd undertaken the trip together. He hoped they would be able to salvage the next two days and continue the hike, even if the others couldn't join them. Of course, Derek wouldn't be up to it, which inevitably counted out Faye, too. Faye. Thank God she'd disregarded his instructions and gone back to the cabin to be with Clare. Geoffrey was not sure how he would have coped knowing his daughter was either alone and stranded at the cabin, or elsewhere with strangers. The fact that Faye was with her was comforting. It was one of the reasons he'd offered to stay with Derek. If Faye could selflessly return to be with Clare when she was ill, how could he, with a clear conscience, leave Faye's ailing husband alone?

As he drew nearer, Geoffrey heard the rushing of the river, punctuated by the solid knocks and cracks of deadwood against the rocks and the lapping of agitated water against freshly excavated dongas. He realised then it was likely he and Derek would have to wait it out at Grootkloof Cabin for at least one more day. The Bloukrans was angrier even than he recalled it being when the surge had suddenly appeared and almost taken Diane with it.

He took his cap off and scratched the side of his head as if trying to dislodge the image of Diane being flung against the ropes and then with Derek and Bruce, the three edging their way towards him in the swirling mass of water and debris. What idiots they'd been to cross and yet, as they'd sat around the fire in the lapa hours later, not one of them had conceded their foolishness. Did they think saying it aloud would be to admit culpability? Or were they just in shock? Would they ever speak freely about it?

The trees opened onto a flat, wide stretch that ran parallel to the river. Geoffrey walked downstream to where the rope hung. Remarkably, both sections of the cable had survived the flood. The lower line had ensnared a messy orb of logs, reeds and branches, which, pulling the rope taut across the water, seemed to taunt the river as it was tossed back and forth.

Geoffrey sat down, his feet dangling over the bank directly opposite the ropes. It was where the group had briefly assembled after the crossing, thanking their lucky stars, God and whoever else they might've believed was involved in saving their lives.

There was something hypnotic about the way the water hit the entangled mass and tugged at the rope. Staring at the bobbing debris, he almost missed the pair of blue duikers who gave him a quick look before scampering into the dark shadows of the undergrowth on the other side of the river.

Nineteen

"Faye is afraid of her own shadow," was Derek's refrain. Yet, here she was, walking through the wilderness alone. And not for the first time, either. Two days ago, she'd made her way back to Heuningbos to Clare, and the next day she'd headed out to find her when she didn't return from her walk.

That's not to say that Faye didn't move cautiously as she headed through the forest for the Bloukrans River. Her eyes scanned left and right, taking in the red and white alders, Cape Chestnuts and yellowwoods, and noting the shadows and how they moved. Where the trail traversed open patches of veld, she took in the bunches of fluffy white flowers that lined the way and the musty scent of buchu. Faye watched for the solid forms of buck, pigs and baboons in the bush and, where the rays shone weakly on the ground, for sunbathing snakes. Vigilance was good in the bush, she told herself. It didn't mean she was afraid, did it?

Faye only discovered she was inclined to be fearful when she met Derek. She remembered the first conversation they'd had about it a year into their marriage when he told her he was going on a white river rafting weekend with his work colleagues.

"Nice," she'd said. "A team-building thing?"

"Not really. More of a company outing. Partners were invited but I knew it wouldn't be your thing."

"Oh?" She looked at him, confused. "Why not?"

"Two days of white river rafting? You'd hate it. It would terrify you."

"What? Why?"

"You told me how easily afraid you are and how much you dislike the feeling," he said.

"I did? I don't remember—"

He'd wrapped his arms around her and drawn her to his chest. "It's okay. You don't have to be superwoman. I'll take care of you."

A few months later, the subject came up again. They were saying their goodbyes in the street outside the pub after meeting Diane and Bruce after work.

"Ah, Faye, I nearly forgot," said Diane. "Bev asked me to mention she's getting a women's book club together. Are you interested?"

"Yes. Absolutely. I'll give her a call."

"Good. She was thinking every second Tuesday night of the month."

Derek stepped forward and put a hand on Faye's elbow. "Hmm. Nights. That's going to be a problem."

The women turned to him.

"Faye's afraid of driving alone at night," he said. "But perhaps one of you other girls could give her a lift?"

"What? I'm not—"

"No, no, you're right, love," said Derek, steering Faye in the other direction and calling over his shoulder to Diane. "We'll work something out, Di! Bye!"

"I'm afraid of driving alone at night? Since when?" asked Faye, as she pulled the seatbelt across her chest.

"Didn't we agree that it was safer that you didn't do it? I mean, you can't drive properly—I mean, confidently—if you're afraid."

"We discussed I should lock the car doors when I drive alone at night."

"I said it would be safer. You seemed uncertain. Nervous. I'm just thinking about you. It worries me to think of you driving around at night on the verge of a panic attack."

Faye had no sense of ever having panicked, but said nothing. When Bev called her the following week to discuss the details of the book club, she told her friend that she'd had second thoughts and wouldn't participate after all.

As the trail looped back into the trees, passing through a lush fern gully where water droplets hung onto the tips of the luminous green fronds like tears, Faye quickened her pace. She was anxious to get back to Clare, whether she'd found help near the Bloukrans or not. It was a slim one, but the chance that the others had had to spend two nights at the Grootkloof Cabin wasn't one she could let pass.

The ravine announced itself abruptly as the path wound downwards. Cleared of leafy padding by the rain, the earth was saturated and slippery. Faye broke a branch from a fallen tree and fashioned it into a walking stick. Even so, she was obliged to slow her pace and ignore the fairytale impression created by the gnarled roots, frilly ferns and light shining through the trees, and keep her eyes trained on the path instead. In some places, rocks and roots, freshly exposed by the eroding waters, and deep dongas created obstacles, forcing Faye to either slow down even more or beat her way through the undergrowth to get around them.

As she navigated one such detour, she stepped onto a large boulder. She didn't notice that most of the soil beneath it had been washed away. The rock came loose under her weight and Faye was catapulted forward into a bush.

With thorns embedded in her hands, arms, neck and chest, she remained propped half upright in the plant for a moment, unsure of how to move without being further impaled. She was bleeding from several perforations and her heart was pounding from the fall. As she slowly unpicked her flesh from the barbs, more blood flowed.

Her walking stick had also become entangled in the thorn bush and, after extracting it, Faye shuffled down the path until she came across a puddle. She sat, picked the remaining thorns from her flesh and, dipping her buff in the puddle, daubed her wounds. Several continued bleeding. Faye stood and walked on, unable to ignore Derek's voice in her head.

"Were you ever tested for dyspraxia as a child? I've never known anyone as clumsy."

"What do you mean?" she'd asked.

"Surely you've noticed the scratch on your car door?"

"No."

Derek waggled his eyebrows. "It's there. You can't deny that."

"I haven't noticed it," she said, making her way into the yard where her car was parked.

He followed. "It looks like you caught it on a pillar."

With the blue paint scraped away over about the length of a pen to reveal silver metal and an indent deep enough to create a shadow, the scratch wasn't easy to miss. Faye crouched and ran the tip of her finger along it.

"I'm flummoxed. I, well, surely I would have heard it happen?"

Derek pursed his lips and nodded.

"It doesn't make sense. I can't think where I would have connected with anything lately. I've only—"

"That's the point though, isn't it? You don't notice things. You're clumsy."

Faye felt her eyes well up. She bowed her head and examined the damage again. She felt silly getting tearful about the car, but she'd been so careful with it since he'd bought it for her four years earlier. It even worried her when Derek used it for golf every week. Particularly since he always had a few drinks in the club house afterwards. She blinked the tears away and stood up.

"Perhaps when—"

"Don't apologise. It's okay. I'll call the insurance on Monday and get it seen to. Hopefully they won't raise our premium too high."

She was clumsy again when she broke the coffee machine.

"I did explain how one inserts coffee pods into the machine, didn't I?" asked Derek, as he burst into the bathroom one morning.

"Yes. It's simple."

"Exactly. Then how did you manage to stuff it up again?"

"I don't think I—"

"You forced the capsule tray closed. It's cracked."

"It was fine last night. At least, I didn't notice anything."

"That's the problem; you don't notice anything. Which explains why it's broken. Why so many things in this house get broken."

"Wait a minute," she said, putting her toothbrush down and turning to face him. "That's not—"

"I know, I know. It's not fair. Don't worry about it. Derek will buy another one. Derek will sort it," he snarled before walking away.

What would he say if he saw her now, with her wounds and bloodied blouse?

"What have you done *now*, you clumsy woman? You've ruined your shirt!"

It was in that instant, as she continued down the ravine, that Faye realised that she would leave Derek. At first the thought, contained and clear, surprised her. Then it soothed her. It's possible she'd toyed with it before, particularly since Zach had left home, but she'd never allowed herself to settle on the idea. *Why now?* The answer came quickly. She was not afraid. Or was it that she was no longer afraid? Never afraid? It didn't matter. What did matter was that at last she knew for sure she was not afraid.

She thought about how much had changed since she'd returned to Heuningbos to wait with Clare. Was it really only two days ago? How remarkable that a guileless decision could have such consequences. If she'd continued the hike with the others, Faye wouldn't have had to test her courage. She would've followed Derek. She would still believe herself to be his version of her. "Nobody knows you like I do," he'd continue to say. She'd believe it. Feed someone the same narrative for long enough and they forget the truth exists. It had taken just two days in the wilderness without him for Faye to realise her husband didn't know her at all.

Derek would laugh when she told him about her decision. He wouldn't believe her. Then he would protest. Loudly and indignantly. There was no doubt about that. He would tell her how she'd suffer without him and how ashamed their son would be of her. She would, she resolved, tell Zach as soon as possible about her decision to leave. She wasn't sure exactly how her son would react, but she suspected Zach would be okay, perhaps even a little proud of his mother.

Her husband would also threaten her with poverty if she left, which would be another ruse. Although she hadn't worked for two decades, their house had been paid for by her earnings at GNS. She'd consult a lawyer quickly, too. She'd be prepared so that Derek could not intimidate her. She'd have the answers. She'd give them voice. She'd leave.

But first things first. Clare was her priority now. Once the girl was safe and the drama over, they'd go home and Faye would tell Derek that she was leaving. Then she'd leave—and start living again.

The terrain had levelled out when Faye heard the river. It was hidden behind a dense bank of tall reeds, but the proximity of the water made her want to call out. What if the others were on the other side and could hear her? She jogged along the path between the cliff and the reeds and, as she paused at the sign indicating the river crossing, two duikers appeared from the other direction, stared at her for a moment and sped out of sight. She made a mental note to tell Clare about them.

Her spirits sank at the sight of the water. There was no way, rope or no rope, anyone would be able to cross it. Tempestuous and muddied, the river rushed, carrying with it clumps of vegetation and deadwood. Where it wasn't swirling around boulders, tapping the lower branches of trees or streaming smoothly with lava-like power, the water created deep eddies that looked large enough to swallow a duiker—or a person. Faye stared, disappointment tugging at her gut. She'd wasted hours hiking in the wrong direction. There was no way she could traverse the river to get to the Grootkloof Cabin to check if the others were still there. She'd return, immediately.

The thought of climbing back up the ravine made her weary. Steep and slippery, it wasn't going to be easy. A drink of water would help. She walked to the edge of river, knelt and, scooping water in her hand, drank. As she leaned back, preparing to stand, Faye looked upstream. A flash of red caught her eye. A cap. A red one like Geoffrey's. There was someone sitting on the bank.

She jumped to her feet, keeping her eyes on the figure as if it might disappear if she looked away. The boulders on the edge of the river were slippery and, where the water was close to the bank, Faye held onto the plants and eased her way upstream. Finally she saw the ropes ahead of her and, as she gripped one with both hands to support herself, she called out.

"Geoffrey! Geoffrey! Over here!"

He raised his head, eyes widening as he saw her. "Faye! Hey!"

"My God! I am so relieved to see you," she shouted, trying not to cry. "We have to get help to Clare."

Geoffrey jumped to his feet, whipped his cap off his head and held a hand behind his ear. "What? I can't hear you."

"Clare needs help."

He shook his head. The sound of the river was drowning her words. He looked left and right and pointed slightly downstream from where Faye had approached through reeds. The river narrowed there and the water was deeper, less turbulent and quieter. Geoffrey kept pace with her from the other side as Faye inched her way back along the narrow bank and over the wet rocks. She sighed with relief as they both arrived at their designated spot on opposite sides of the river.

"What happened?" shouted Geoffrey.

It took Faye a moment to realise he was referring to the bloody punctures on her body.

"It's nothing—an encounter with some thorns. But—"

"Are you sure? It looks pretty brutal."

She was touched by his concern and self-consciously tugged at the lapels of her shirt.

"I'm fine. But Clare—"

"Where is she?"

Faye stepped as far into the water as was safe. Her boots and socks were already drenched from manoeuvring through the shallows. "She's had an accident. Injured her knee. But it's her ribs that I'm worried about. I think they're broken. And—"

"What happened?"

"She fell."

Geoffrey, almost knee deep in the water, leaned forward. "Where is she?"

"In the trees. The first part of the forest after Heuningbos Hut."

"The trees? You can't get her back to the cabin? To Heuningbos? Surely—"

Faye shook her head. "I don't want to risk moving her. Her chest, her lungs—"

Geoffrey wrung his cap in his hands. "You think they're punctured?"

"I'm not sure, but . . . yes, it's possible. I—'

"My God, what are we going to do?"

Even over the distance, Faye recognised the panic in his eyes. "You have a copy of the maps, right?"

"Yes, but we can't risk crossing any of the rivers. We tried—"

"No. We can't. Find the shortest escape route. Get to the rangers. She needs a doctor, a paramedic. A helicopter. Whatever is required."

"A helicopter?"

Faye nodded.

"I'll go. Derek will have to wait."

"Derek?"

The sound of his name seemed out of place. Faye hadn't thought about her husband since she'd spotted Geoffrey.

"He hurt his back during the crossing. It's okay but he can't go on. The others left yesterday. To get help. To find you and Clare."

"Oh God! So they might be at the other cabin? On their way at least?"

"I don't know where they are. It's unlikely they would have reached Heuningbos by now. It's a distance to the road. But, Faye, I'm going to go now. I can't wait around wondering. If we're really lucky, I'll make it to the top of the ravine before nightfall and intercept them on the road. If I don't make it before dark, I'll sleep on the way and get going early tomorrow."

"It's that far? The escape route? And a difficult climb?"

"Yes, but there's no other option."

Faye nodded.

"We should both get going, now," he said. "Will you go back and wait with Clare? Until they get to her?"

"Of course."

"Please don't leave her. I'll make sure someone gets to you. Dear God! Why did I leave her? Thank you, Faye. I don't know what to say . . . "

He was pacing, his cap wound into a ball in his hands.

"I'll get back to her. You go and tell Derek what's going on. Who knows, perhaps the rangers have arrived on your side?"

"They haven't." It was Derek. He hobbled towards Geoffrey. "What's going on?"

Faye stared at her husband. It had been just two days, but it felt like a lifetime.

"Clare's injured," she said. "She needs medical attention urgently."

"What? What happened? What did you do?"

Geoffrey turned to look at him. "She fell," he said. "We have to—"

"Fell? Is that her blood?" Derek pointed at Faye's chest.

"No."

"Thank God!"

"Yes, thank God," said Faye, a cold wave of weariness washing over her. She didn't want to have this conversation or experience the hopelessness she felt when Derek was around. She wanted to get back to Clare. She wanted Geoffrey to go and find help.

Derek put a hand on Geoffrey's shoulder, leaning on him. "How badly injured is she?"

"Her ribs. Faye's worried about her breathing . . . thinks she might've perforated a lung." Geoffrey turned back to her. "Listen, Faye, just to confirm that—"

Derek transferred his attention across the river. "Her lungs? Like your mother? But that . . . that's life-threatening."

"I'm not sure, Derek. I'm not a doctor. It doesn't look good. But wait, please." Faye looked at Geoffrey. "What were you asking, Geoffrey? You must get going. So must I."

"She's on the Heuningbos side of the first forest of the trail, right? There's an open piece of fynbos just before you get there. Is that it? I want to be sure that I pass on the right—"

Derek shook Geoffrey's shoulder as if to quieten him.

"Tell her . . . " He leaned forward, placing his hands on his knees now. "Tell her that I—"

Faye ignored Derek and addressed Geoffrey. "Yes. That's right. The first section of the forest. We're close to the edge, near the opening. I think a helicopter could land there."

Derek raised his voice. "Tell her I—"

She looked at her husband. "Sure. I can guess what you'd like to say, Derek. It's one of several things I've learned over the past two days. But not now. I have to get back to her. Good luck, Geoffrey!"

"God, woman! What are you on about?" Derek was shouting now, louder than was necessary across the water. "Just bloody well listen to me!"

Faye turned and made her way through the reeds back towards the trail.

Twenty

After hours of insomnia the night before, Clare had fallen asleep to the sound of Faye departing. She'd closed her eyes and listened to the leaves crunching and twigs breaking underfoot, and, when Faye reached the path, she had recognised the sound of boots on saturated earth. The fading thuds soothed her. She closed her eyes. Faye would find help while she slept.

The forest was alive when she awoke hours later. It was as if the birds were celebrating the warmth of the sun as it fought its way through the clouds. Clare looked out of the shelter, imagining the rays on her body. She was cold and her skin felt clammy. Faye had insisted she shouldn't move, but she longed to get warm and wondered if she would be up to dragging herself out of the shade. As she leaned forward, pain shot through her lower chest, erupting into a cough, which exacerbated the agony. She sat back, breathing hard, and wiped her mouth. Her fingers came away coated with frothy white spit, which was tinged with red. Her heart was racing, her breathing wheezy, and her head spun.

Was this it? Was she dying? Would she be alone when it happened? Was this what Gran meant when she said, "We come into the world alone and we leave alone"? If it was, Clare wasn't ready. It wasn't that she couldn't be alone—she'd grown accustomed to that—but she wasn't ready to die.

After breaking up with Will, Clare had quickly learned how to self-isolate. It was essential. She couldn't bear the solicitous questions and pitying glances. She'd rather be labelled the "unfriendly, selfish girl" than the "pathetic one with the problem." If she timed her comings and goings right, she was able to avoid most of the pitying looks. She ignored the knocks at her door until they stopped completely. Clare ran before anyone else was awake in morning and again at twilight. She was the first or last to enter the lecture hall, kept her head down when she made her way across campus and spent all other hours in her room or in the remotest nook of the library. She kept her visits to the dining room to a minimum by sneaking out handfuls of fruit, which she stored in her room and nibbled on for days, cutting it into tiny pieces and chewing every morsel a hundred times. She bought her own scale so that she no longer needed to go to the gym to weigh herself every Monday.

After a while, she felt invisible. One morning, as the light brightened the horizon and Clare reached the seven kilometre point of her run, she passed two women walking from the taxi rank towards the centre of town.

"What was that?" she heard one of them ask as she ran by. "A girl or a boy?"

Even when she existed and people noticed her, she was indiscernible. Those who spotted her were unsure who she was and, indeed, *what* she was. And, if the indifferent tone of the woman who asked, "What was that?" was anything to go by, people weren't that interested anyway.

For a while, Clare was lonely. It hit her when she heard other students laughing as they passed beneath her window. Sometimes she added slices of bread to her stash of fruit from the dining room. She found a remote spot in the garden beyond the library where the sparrows gathered. Clare broke up the bread, scattered it on the lawn and watched as the little birds converged to eat. It felt good to feed them and she chuckled at how freely they stuffed themselves. Oh, to be a sparrow.

As a student, on the rare occasions when she was at home with her family, Clare often felt as if she was the girl waiting in the wings for the opportunity to join the performance. Or perhaps she was an understudy who had no idea when she might be called upon to step onto the stage and take up a starring role in her life again.

She watched Linda and Angus come and go from the house as they did things together and with friends, living their lives the way she had once lived hers, with joy and spontaneity. It was not that her siblings and parents ignored her. It seemed, though, that her place in their lives had become something they allowed for, moved around and revered. They tiptoed by, trying not to disturb the space Clare occupied in the world for fear of what might happen if they did. She was, it seemed, something of a museum piece.

At mealtimes, there'd be a knock at her door. Someone, usually Linda, would peep in. "Um . . . Supper's on the table, if you want, Clare?"

The banter and laughter would die down when she entered the room and they'd avert their eyes from her plate, desperate not to appear to be watching what she placed there and what she did with it. Someone, usually her father, would make an early effort to engage with her.

"I thought of you today when we took delivery of six quiver trees for the Walters' garden, Clare. Remember how you loved the quiver tree forest in Namibia?" he said.

"Yes, it was beautiful," she replied, loving him for making an effort.

"What's the Afrikaans name again, Dad?" asked Angus.

"Kokerboom."

"Ja. That's it. Remember Linda thought it meant, 'cocoa tree' and cried when there was no chocolate when we got there," said Clare's brother.

Clare recalled the incident and how she'd used her pocket money to buy her little sister some chocolate in the next village. She said nothing. The family laughed and the conversation went on without her.

They weren't always equally long-suffering. Angus, in particular, continued to find Clare's behaviour difficult to stomach, perhaps because, up until she became anorexic, he was her greatest admirer. She was his big sister. The fair one. The fun one. The one who always knew what Mom and Dad would want for Christmas. The one who helped him with school projects and taught him how alike girls and boys actually were.

One evening, on her way to her room after a run, Clare bumped into Angus as he came out of the bathroom. He stepped back and looked her up and down.

"Please tell me you didn't run near the sports grounds again today," he said, his top lip twisted upwards.

"Huh? Why?" she asked.

"Geez, Clare, the guys are training there. I can't deal with their comments."

She looked down and walked on. Angus followed her.

"You know, you think this is all about you, but it's not," he said, blocking her from entering her room. "Your craziness affects this whole family. We have to tiptoe around and pretend it's all okay and not say anything that might upset you. We can't live normally. My friends treat me like you've died or have leprosy. Did you know that? It's not all about you, Clare. It's about us, too. But I guess you are too selfish to notice that."

She pushed past him and closed the door. From then on, she took her meals to her room.

Angus's outburst made her think about what an unpleasant person she had become. She was obsessive, grumpy, mean, worn out and critical. Above all, as he'd said, she was selfish and self-obsessed. Everything she did and thought about concerned her, what she ate and when she ran and studied. There was no place in her thoughts for anyone else. The reality, though, was that even knowing that and acknowledging it, wasn't enough to make her accept that she might need help. She hated hurting Angus almost as much as she hated hurting her dad, but she couldn't change it. The only way she imagined inflicting less pain on them was by withdrawing even more.

Eventually, Clare grew accustomed to the solitude. Sometimes she even congratulated herself for having achieved another goal: self-rule. On the odd occasion, usually when she was trying to fall asleep, that Clare felt the emptiness of her existence and doubted she could continue fighting alone, she resolved to run further and faster the next day. Physical exhaustion, she'd learned, was a great deterrent of doubt and an excellent proponent of sleep.

There were two exceptions to her solitude: Mark, and Derek Mackenzie. The latter arrived on campus unexpectedly at the beginning of her second year. Unlike Mark, whose resolve to run with her was unshakeable (until it wasn't) and endured for almost two years, Derek visited only once, for which she was grateful. The single occasion was embarrassing enough.

How Derek knew where to find Clare on campus, she didn't know. The sight of his tall, bowed body near the steps of her residence had come as a shock. She stared at him, wondering if she was hallucinating from the pills she'd taken for the migraine she'd suffered two days earlier. She shook her head and blinked. He was still there. She hurried over.

"What's happened? My father? Mother?"

He squinted, baffled for a moment.

"No. No," he said, placing a hand on her forearm. "They're fine. I thought I'd take you to lunch."

"Lunch?" She looked around as if one of the students walking by would offer clarification.

"Is that a foreign concept to you?"

"But . . . why?"

"I'm here for work. Thought I'd come and see you."

It was odd. Clare couldn't imagine why her parents' friend, her friend Zach's father, would visit her, let alone propose lunch. She had no intention of going anywhere with him.

"I have lectures—"

"Not now."

She stared at him. Did he know her timetable or was he assuming the university broke for lunch? She wished she'd said she had a lunchtime seminar.

"Come. We'll be quick. I reserved a table at the bistro in High Street."

She'd gone, unable to find a way out without being rude. It was even more awkward than she had imagined it might be.

"So, I wanted to talk to you about something," said Derek as they waited for their order. (Chicken salad! Her heart pounded at the thought of it.)

"Oh. Okay."

Clare knew Zach and his father had argued about the anthropology degree he had decided to enrol for at a university in Johannesburg. She wondered if Derek might want to discuss his son's choice with her.

He leaned forward, trying to catch her eye. "The thing is . . . Mich, I mean, your mother, is worried about you."

What? Had her mother sent Derek Mackenzie to talk to her? Why would she do that? She and Michelle had discussed her illness at length before she returned to university. What more could there be to say? Clare nodded slowly, looked at him and held his eye. She wished her father was there instead.

"She says, your mother says, that you've got thin because . . . um . . . you're ill. But I—"

"My mother spoke to you about my—about me?"

Derek took a long sip of water. "We're friends. We talk every day."

"Did my mother ask you to visit me?"

"No! Goodness, no. She doesn't know I'm here."

"My father?"

He looked down and shook his head.

"I know." She felt her throat thicken. "I've hurt him terribly. I hate myself for that. I'm sorry. He's the last person I'd want to hurt. But I'm getting better. I'm going to make it up to my father."

"Well—"

"He's ashamed of me, isn't he? Did he say that? Or was it my mother?"

"Mich—"

"I knew it. My poor dad. I'll make it up to him."

Derek was staring at her. "No, that's not . . . he's not—"

He was interrupted by the waitress who placed their food on the table. When she left, Derek leaned back in his chair and placed a serviette on his lap.

"I just wanted to check that you're okay," he said. "That—um— that whatever happened to you hasn't happened again."

"What do you mean?"

"Whatever happened to make you stop eating. If someone hurt you—or something."

"No one hurt me. That's not how it works. Not for me anyway."

He stared at her, eyes darting. For a moment, Clare thought he was going to challenge her. Did he *want* her to have been hurt by someone? Would it make it easier for him to understand why she was anorexic? But why did he need an explanation? He and her mother had known one another their entire lives. He, Faye and her parents moved in the same circles, but that didn't explain his visit, the uneasy lunch and his . . . his prying.

"If you don't mind, I don't want to talk about this," she said, picking up her knife and fork.

"Do you talk to Geoff, I mean, your father about it?"

She shook her head. He gave the faintest trace of a smile and began eating.

They didn't discuss her parents or her problem again, self-consciously navigating their way through the lunch by chatting about her studies and how Zach was doing. Derek seemed to have accepted his son's decision or, if he didn't, made no comment on his disapproval. The conversation was stilted, and when Clare said she had to rush, Derek didn't try to delay her. She was relieved when they said their goodbyes, additionally so when he didn't suggest they do it again.

She'd never mentioned Derek's visit to her parents. Neither did she and Derek ever speak of it. However, she never forgot how she managed to almost finish her chicken salad with its unidentifiable and therefore unknown caloric-value dressing. It was a victory and, she knew, a tiny turning point in her recovery. She thought of how the information would baffle Derek if she ever told him about the significance of their lunch.

⋐⋑

Now, as Clare's heart slowed and the discomfort in her chest eased, she felt for the space blanket and pulled it over her once more. As she glanced up, she saw something move on one of the thicker branches Faye had used for the frame of the shelter. The light glistened on shiny scales. Her heart quickened again. Was it a snake? A venomous boomslang perhaps? Then she noticed the reptile's long, clawed toes. It was a skink.

Partially concealed by the dying leaves, the creature was on the hunt. Clare watched as it lifted its snakelike head and stared into the twigs with intense concentration. She scanned the branch for its prey, but saw nothing. Suddenly, the skink darted its head forward and, with whatever it had caught firmly in its jaws, chewed and swallowed. She might have involuntarily moved or murmured her applause. The reptile looked at her for a moment and scuttled away.

Clare ached all over. She longed to adjust her position on the cold, damp ground, but the pain, breathlessness and bloody coughing she'd experienced when she moved earlier warned her against it. It wouldn't be much longer, she told herself. Faye would come with help, hopefully her father. She wasn't going to die on the forest floor after falling from a rock. She'd be okay. She had to be; she hadn't done anything with her life yet.

Twenty-One

I t was as if the river carried Derek's words away with it when Faye turned her back on him and hurried away through the avenue of reeds. She couldn't make out what he was saying. Neither did she try. She wanted to get back to Clare. Geoffrey would send help and she needed to be there to make sure the rescuers found the girl. There was no time for anything else. Faye didn't want to think about her husband and his irrelevant ramblings but, once on the path that ran parallel to the river, she couldn't help picturing him as he'd surprised them by appearing alongside Geoffrey.

He was pale and stooped and, given the way he rested his hands on the small of his back as he walked and then, when he stopped, on his knees, clearly in pain. It was as if he was holding himself together. Faye's instinctive response was concern. She wished she could help ease his pain. But then, when Derek began shouting across the river, she turned numb. His voice was loud and demanding, as if what she and Geoffrey were discussing no longer mattered. Derek's needs and directives had to be heard. It didn't occur to him he might not be a priority at that point, have all the facts or be in control of things.

As he'd grown more agitated, the words had run together. Faye wasn't sure whether it was because he was becoming increasingly incoherent or because she had stopped listening properly and allowed the noise of the water to flood her ears instead. She wished he'd shut up so that she could clarify things for Geoffrey. But Derek had bulldozed on, drowning their voices with his. Even by his standards, his behaviour was bizarre. What was going on? Her skin prickled as she recalled how Derek had dismissed the blood smeared across her neck, chest and arms when she'd confirmed it was hers. Not even her blood mattered to him.

Once she was sure Geoffrey knew where to find Clare, Faye had turned away and left. She didn't want to hear Derek's voice anymore; not across the river and not in her head. She'd steeled herself against it and walked away. But now, as she made her way along the river towards the path that would take her back up the ravine, she felt an emotion she didn't immediately recognise.

At first, she imagined the churning in her stomach was due to hunger. Her knuckles were stiff. Her fists were clenched. Then she realised she was also grinding her teeth. Her jaw was tight. Something was rising in her gut. Clamping and gnashing her molars was her way of controlling the feeling, destroying it before it revealed itself. What was it? What had she suppressed for so long that she longer recognised it?

Faye was angry. No. The feeling was stronger. It was fury. She couldn't remember when last she had allowed herself to be angry, let alone furious. And, as the emotion pushed its way into her chest and her heart pounded, she realised she could no longer ignore it. She didn't want to. She spun around and retraced her steps, a hot energy surging through her.

She was walking back between the reeds towards the river when she heard Derek's voice. He was shouting, even louder than before. This time, she listened.

"Yes, that's what I said, Geoff! Clare is my daughter. Ask Mich who consoled her when you were driving her nuts with your plans to leave the bank and become a gardener! That'll explain it. And God knows I would have done a better job raising her than you. She wouldn't be . . . be whatever she is now if I'd been around for her!"

Faye's heart seemed to thunder in time with the river. She stopped and, concerned her legs would give way, leaned on her walking stick. Clare was Derek's daughter? No. It didn't make sense. How could it be possible? Derek and Michelle's romance pre-dated the girl's birth by years. Or was Faye mistaken? Surely she would have known? Suspected something? There was nothing about Clare that suggested she had any of Derek's genes. Physically, she was a fragile, feminine replica of Geoffrey with Michelle's hair. Neither was there anything in her personality Faye recognised in her husband. Derek was irrational. He must be ill. Perhaps he'd hit his head during the river crossing? She should have asked Geoffrey exactly what had happened. There must be some mistake. But why would Derek claim such a thing? How could he be so cruel?

She thought how specific he was about the timing. He'd referred to more than twenty years previously. That was when Geoffrey had left the bank to start his business. Faye tried to remember the time, where they were and what was happening in their lives. Had she and Derek ever discussed it? Talked about Geoffrey's decision? How did Faye find out about it? Then it came back to her.

GNS Medical Supplies had been awarded the distribution rights for a range of cancer screening equipment made in Canada. It was a big deal and the launch demanded a great deal from George, Faye and their sales team. Although she and Derek had had supper together at home every night, she'd been rushed and tired and hadn't given him much attention during the fortnight of the launch. The afternoon when it was finally over, Faye left work early so she could prepare Derek's favourite meal. It would be good to relax and catch up, she thought. By the time he got home though, she'd packed it away in the fridge and was getting ready for bed.

"I told you I'd be out this evening," he said.

It was possible, she thought; she'd had a lot on her mind.

"It's okay," she smiled. "We'll make up for it over the weekend."

Derek sat on the side of the bed and took her hand. His eyes darted left and right as they were inclined to do when he was nervous.

"Faye," he said, trying to hold her gaze, but failing. "I have to tell you something."

"Is everything okay?"

"No, not really."

"Well—"

He dropped her hand. "Just let me speak. Okay?"

Faye nodded.

"I'm having second thoughts." He hesitated, looking towards the window.

"About what?"

"About us."

"What? What do you mean? Second thoughts? We're married. Surely—" Her mouth was dry. The words came out as if she was being strangled.

"It's just that I thought I could, but . . ."

"But what's changed?"

He said nothing.

Faye leaned forward, turning her head so that she could look into his eyes. He looked away.

"I know I've been distracted," she said. "Work's been crazy. You know that. But the launch is over now. Things will be better. I'm sorry. I'll be around more. I'll make it up to you."

He put his head in his hands.

"I'll take leave. We can go away for a bit. I don't understand. What have I done? What's gone wrong? I thought we were—"

"Stop it!" He stood and walked to the window. "Stop begging. It's not that. It's . . . it's . . ."

Faye was crying. He stared at her.

"Stop it. Listen, I'll grab some things. I'll go and stay—"

"No!"

"I'll go and stay in a hotel for a bit. Until we can discuss this sensibly. Okay?"

"But what happened? I don't understand. What changed, Derek?"

"Nothing changed," he said, quietly. "Not for me, at least."

"But then . . ." She couldn't stop crying. Her world had collapsed.

Derek threw some clothes in a bag and left. Faye called in sick and spent the next three days at home. On the evening of the third day, she was in the kitchen making herself an omelette when Derek returned. She met him at the door. His eyes were bloodshot and his shoulders slumped.

"I'm home," he said. "I was wrong."

"About what?" she asked, holding herself rigid.

He looked down. "About not believing in our marriage."

"But why—"

"Please, Faye, is it not enough that I am here?"

She looked at him and saw despair. His head was bowed, his eyes red-rimmed and his arms hung limply at his sides. She'd never seen him look so broken. She wanted to comfort him. He'd made a mistake. He deserved another chance. Faye put her arms around him and held him while he cried.

A few days later, Diane arrived to return a pressure cooker she'd borrowed from Faye. Derek wasn't yet home from work and, after the women had had tea, Faye walked Diane to her car.

Diane turned to her as she opened her car door. "So I guess you heard about Michelle's latest drama?"

"No. What?"

"Pfft. She left Geoffrey when he refused to obey her wishes to give up his idea of leaving the bank."

"What?"

"He's starting a garden business."

"Oh?"

Diane laughed. "Yes, you can imagine how unimpressed madam is about that."

Faye said nothing.

"Anyway, she got over it and is back home with him again."

"Geoffrey's going ahead with his plans?"

"Apparently."

Later, as she handed him a beer, Faye asked Derek if he'd heard about Geoffrey's planned resignation from the bank. He grunted his acknowledgement.

"Who told you?" he asked.

"Diane was here earlier."

"What else did she gossip about?"

Faye glanced at him, surprised by his sanctimonious tone. He was generally loyal to Diane.

"Uh, nothing really. Just that Michelle wasn't very happy about the decision. Initially, anyway."

"Oh? And she's happy now? Di said she's happy?"

"Not in so many words, but I guessed so."

"Geez, Faye, of course she's not happy. How could she be?"

Derek tossed the last mouthful of beer into his mouth and left the room.

Faye leaned on her walking stick and looked into the reeds, watching as a long, slender stick insect blew its camouflage by creeping to the edge of a leaf and twitching its antennae.

The coinciding of Derek and Michelle's sojourns from their marriages more than twenty years ago hadn't occurred to her—until now. Was it possible? Had her husband and Michelle been together at that time? Was Clare the result? Or did Derek believe or hope that she was his daughter? That would explain his unusual interest in her. Had Derek returned to Faye all those years ago because Michelle had decided to forgive Geoffrey? Had Faye mistaken Derek's heartbreak about Michelle for remorse about having left her? Had she been a fool even then?

Faye's mind was still swirling as she forced herself to walk on. She thought fleetingly of the pair of duikers she'd seen disappearing into the bush earlier, how freely they'd run.

Derek was standing where he had been when she'd left the river earlier. He was once more bent at the hips, hands on his knees. But where was Geoffrey? Faye leaned forward and looked upriver. His red cap bobbed up and down as he jogged away towards the cabin. Her husband, chest heaving but quiet now, was also watching their friend leave.

Faye cupped her hands around her mouth.

"Derek!" she shouted.

He turned his head to look at her, his eyes registering neither surprise nor relief. Did he know she'd return?

Twenty-Two

It was Diane who told Derek that Michelle was pregnant. The fact that she had not called him herself with the news assured Derek that the baby was his. He drove to her office immediately and waited for her in the parking garage.

Michelle scowled when she saw him. "What are you doing here?"

"Did you think I wouldn't find out?"

"Of course not. I wasn't sure—"

"You weren't sure whether I would want to know I was going to have a kid?"

"What? Derek! No! This is not *yours*!" She gestured towards her flat belly. "My God! Is that why you're here?"

"I'm not completely stupid, Mich. Neither is the maths that difficult."

She flung her bag on the bonnet of her car and glared at him. "Maths? What are you talking about? Do you even know how far along I am?"

He hesitated.

"No, you don't! The reason I didn't tell you yet is because I," she pursed her lips and looked away, ". . . I still feel weird about what happened . . . between us. It was so foolish of me and I didn't think you'd want to hear from me for a while."

It was true that they hadn't spoken since Michelle had pleaded with Derek to stop calling after they'd been together at the hotel. But for her to imagine he didn't want to hear from her, under any circumstance, was ludicrous.

"So, what are you going to do?" he asked.

"What do you mean? I'm going to have Geoffrey's baby and he and I are going to raise it. Perhaps have another one or two in a few years."

"You're going to pretend it's his?"

"It *is* his, Derek. There is no doubt of that. Accept that, now and forever."

"But—"

Michelle snatched her bag and opened the car door. "Listen to me. This is my body. I know it, its rhythms, when I ovulate and when this child was conceived. The baby is *not* yours. Get it? I don't want to have this discussion with you, not now and not ever again."

"What about what I want?"

She flung the bag into the car, spun around and glared at him. "Ok! Let's talk about what you want. Shall we tell Geoffrey and Faye about our idiotic little liaison? When I was behaving like a teenager who couldn't get her best friend to do what she wanted so she pretended she had another best friend for a few days? Shall we then have a paternity test to prove to you that Geoffrey is the father? What else would you like? Have I missed anything?"

Derek felt winded. His mouth was dry. He swallowed. "You're heartless."

Michelle sighed and reached out to touch his forearm. He moved away.

"No, I'm not, Derek. I'm really sorry I gave you reason to think there was anything more than friendship for us. I messed up, badly. I've acknowledged that. And apologised. Several times. But that's where it ends."

As he walked away, his thoughts were not about the baby but about how Michelle had broken his heart—again.

By the time Clare was born, Faye was pregnant with Zach. When they discovered they were expecting a boy, Derek was disappointed. He wanted a daughter too, imagining it might somehow even things out. Every time he saw Clare, as a baby, toddler, adolescent and teenager, he imagined she and he shared characteristics. The length of their limbs. The sharpness of their features. He'd calculated the months, weeks and days to her birth and continued to believe Clare could be his daughter. Sometimes, often even, when life disappointed him, he fantasised how one day Michelle would stop denying the girl's paternity and her love for him. But, unable to dismiss the painful memory of having twice been seduced and then rejected by Michelle, he didn't challenge her about it again until Clare came back to town after her first year at university.

❧

Derek learned about the girl's illness when he overheard Faye and Zach in the kitchen one morning. He was eating muesli while his son, home for the holidays, and Faye were whisking eggs for their breakfast.

"You won't recognise her," said Zach.

"Really? Did you talk to her?" asked Faye.

"No. Just said hello. Angus was ready to go, so we left right away."

The mention of Michelle's son's name got Derek's attention. "Who are you talking about?"

"Clare," said Zach. "She's anorexic. So skinny. It's . . . it's really shocking."

"What? Anorexic? Since when? What the hell happened?"

Faye and Zach looked at him across the kitchen in surprise. He'd spoken loudly.

"Well?" he said, raising his brows at his son.

"I only know the little Angus told me. She hasn't been home since uni started and, it seems, hasn't eaten—well, not much anyway, while she's been away."

"But what happened?"

"What do you mean? To stop her eating? I don't know." Zach turned to his mother. "Does something happen to trigger it?"

Faye lifted her shoulders. "I don't think so. It's—"

"Something must have happened." Derek stood up. "A person doesn't simply stop eating."

His wife and son were silent as he left the room.

He dialled Michelle's cellphone number shortly afterwards.

"Do you have an hour to meet an old friend sometime in the next day or so?"

"Derek? Are you okay?"

"Yes. Just something I need to talk to you about."

"Okay. I'm listening."

He waited a beat. "I'd rather do it in person. Can we meet? Have a cup of coffee?"

Michelle named a coffee shop near court and they agreed on a time the next day. He arrived early and watched her walk in, spot him and wave to several people as she made her way across the room. Wearing a black and white dress that folded across her breasts and skimmed her hips, with her black gown slung over her arm, she was, he thought, more beautiful than he remembered. His were not the only eyes that followed her.

"So," she said, as the waiter placed their coffee in front of them and walked away. "It sounded serious. What's up?"

"I hear Clare's home?"

She peered over her cup at him. "Yes. Zach, too. I saw him briefly the other day."

Derek nodded, suddenly uncertain how to proceed. Michelle glanced at her watch.

"I have to be back in my rooms at half ten, so do you want to cut to the chase?" she said, smiling.

"What happened to her?"

Her smile disappeared and Michelle put down her cup. "Is that what this is about? Clare?"

"Zach says she has anorexia."

"Yes."

"I'm worried about her. Of course I am. You understand that, don't you? What happened?"

"Understand?"

"I know you said she's not mine and I—"

Michelle bowed her head for a moment and then looked up. "Derek, I appreciate your concern. We're—that is, Geoffrey and I and Clare—are handling it. Thank you. She's struggling but we'll—"

"Did you get to the bottom of it?"

"The bottom of it?"

"What happened to make her stop eating?"

She swallowed the last of her coffee before leaning forward and fixing Derek's eyes with hers. "It's a complicated illness. Geoffrey and I are giving her all the support we can."

"Like what? What are you doing? Have you contacted the university to find out what happened to her?"

"Happened?"

"Yes. Don't you want to know what caused this? I know I do. We have to—'

"That's enough, Derek. I have to go. Thanks for the coffee."

"What do you mean, 'that's enough'? I'm not going to stand by as my daughter fades away while you and gardener guy watch. Zach says she's unrecognisable. I want to know—"

Michelle stood up, glaring at him. "My God! You are impossible," she hissed. "She is not your daughter. I cannot believe that you are still holding on to that fallacy after all these years! Listen to me, Derek. For the final time. Clare is not your daughter and this is none of your business. If you want to be a friend, then you will stop behaving like an idiot and give us the space and respect we need to deal with this."

"I want to help—"

"Then back off, Derek. Back off, butt out and accept that Geoffrey is Clare's father, in every way."

He did back off. Derek didn't speak to Michelle about Clare again. He and Faye didn't see much of her and Geoffrey for a while after the meeting at the coffee shop. Whether that was by design or coincidence, he couldn't be sure but, by the time the group met up again, Clare was back at university. Derek, who had seen for himself how skeletal she'd become when he'd parked his car near their house and waited for her to run by one Saturday evening, was appalled that Michelle and Geoffrey had allowed her to return. He immediately began planning a business trip to Port Elizabeth so he could drive to the university and visit her.

As the day approached, Derek imagined Clare's relief as he urged her to confide in him and tell him about her ordeal with, he imagined, someone—another student or a lecturer, perhaps—whose abuse had so traumatised her it had rendered her unable or unwilling to eat. He saw himself confronting the person and meting out justice, which would free Clare from the trauma and allow her to recover. He'd be her knight-in-shining-armour and, with the girl and her mother so grateful for his intervention, he told himself that the time would be right for Michelle to tell Clare that Derek was her biological father. Even when he acknowledged how far-fetched his fantasy was, Derek felt that his concern for Clare was warranted. He couldn't let her fade away without trying to help.

His visit to campus and the ensuing lunch were disastrous. Derek hadn't anticipated she might imagine that he'd come to deliver bad news to her about Geoffrey and Michelle. He was thrown by how relieved she was when he told her they were fine. It hadn't ended there.

Clare didn't want to talk about her illness. She was embarrassed and looked like a cornered rabbit who would flee as soon as the chance presented itself. Her concern was not about herself but about Geoffrey and the pain she'd caused him. Derek left, humiliated and deflated. He was also worried Clare would tell her mother about his visit, and that Michelle would eliminate him from her life for good. As the months passed though, he realised Clare hadn't even found his visit consequential enough to mention. He knew he should be relieved, but it hurt.

Almost two years had passed and Derek had seen very little of Clare while she completed her degree. Michelle and Geoffrey were economical in their responses about her well-being when their friends asked after her. The general narrative was that she was picking up weight, albeit slowly and that, although she wasn't as sociable as she had been, neither was she depressed. She continued to run and was doing exceptionally well in her studies. Derek, cowed by Clare's response when he visited her, was no longer sure exactly what he would have done if he'd found out who had caused the girl's trauma. Even so, he hung onto the idea that he could have helped her recover completely if she'd given him the chance.

When he heard Clare would join the group on the hike in place of her mother, Derek was disappointed. Despite having been repeatedly spurned by Michelle, Derek still loved her. He loved her wit and energy, and felt challenged to be smarter and funnier when she was around. More alive. The group seemed lighter and their conversation more engaging when Michelle was with them. He consoled himself with the idea that Michelle's absence would be a good opportunity for him to get to know Clare better.

He hadn't planned to tell Diane that he believed Clare was his daughter during the hours after they'd crossed the Bloukrans, and it came as something of a surprise to himself when he realised just how convinced he was of the fact in that moment. But Derek's recklessness, if that's what it was, wasn't only due to the combination of shock, agony, painkillers and whiskey. It was sparked by the few minutes that he and Diane were pressed up against one another with only a rope between them and the raging river. It wasn't so much that he'd seen his life flash before his eyes, but more that he saw that, if he survived, he needed to live with more urgency.

Derek had loved Michelle from the moment she had put forward the conditions of her friendship when they lined up outside their grade one classroom. Despite what she said, he believed they belonged together. They had been together. It was good. They should be together again. Before it was too late. And if the only way to get Michelle to that point was to force her to tell Geoffrey about Clare's paternity, then so be it. He couldn't wait any longer.

Diane's reaction to his claim about Clare made him believe that Michelle had confided in her about their affair and the girl's paternity. Why would Diane be so angry by his disclosure if it wasn't true? Her coldness towards him, followed by her rummaging in his bag for the whiskey the next day and her threat were further evidence of this. Diane, Derek believed, had been sworn to secrecy by Mich and was determined to protect her friend. He was excited by the idea of the three of them being tied together by the secret.

"The Three Musketeers," his mother had once tagged them. "All for one and one for all."

⋘⋙

Derek wished he had insisted that Geoffrey go with the others when they left Grootkloof to find help. There had been no reason for him to stay, and his hovering annoyed Derek. Spaced-out on painkillers and whiskey, he had bristled every time Geoffrey poked his red-capped head around the door, found Derek awake and felt compelled to engage in inane conversation. Derek wanted to be left alone with his blurry thoughts.

Having somewhat tipped his hand by telling Diane about Clare, Derek's mind oscillated between two possible extreme outcomes. The appealing one was that Michelle would finally acknowledge their destiny—to be together. The other outcome was that Derek had taken a final step into lunacy and would be cast into the wilderness by his friends, including Michelle. He tried to assure himself he was willing to chance the latter because of the lure of the former.

On the second morning, after Geoffrey had enquired about his health (wasn't it obvious he was in agony?), offered his wishy-washy opinion about whether or not they would be rescued that day and finally wandered off towards the river, Derek washed down the last of the painkillers (three worked better than two) with the remains of the whiskey. He stood on the deck of cabin, staring at the cold grey mountains as he waited for the pain to subside and the buzz to begin. When it kicked in, he found himself hobbling down the track towards the river.

Mismatched and messy, the trees on either side of the roadway seemed at odds with one another. What had once been a pine plantation had been invaded by indigenous plants. The spindly conifers that remained looked like gawky teens at a toddler's birthday party— out of place and desperate to be among their own. While the native vegetation was largely confined to the understory of the forest, it was dense and robust. The ungainly teens, thought Derek, would soon be consumed by the hungry toddlers.

The sight of the river, swollen and fast, didn't alarm him. He stood for a moment, staring indifferently at the muddy mass swirling by until he heard voices. Turning his head, he saw Geoffrey on the bank downstream. But who was he talking to? Derek limped towards them and, as he approached, recognised Faye on the other side of the river.

Faye. His wife. Where had she been? Why had she come? Derek was as much surprised by seeing her as he was by the realisation he'd barely thought about her over the past forty-eight hours. How life had changed, he thought, trying to round up the scattered feelings, memories and images that seemed to flow through his mind. His thoughts spun, as opaque and transient as the river. There might have been more whiskey left in the flask than he'd thought.

Derek looked at Faye, feeling a stab of exasperation when he noticed her boots in the water. Was it necessary to ruin them? Had she forgotten how expensive they were? Her neck and blouse were a bloody mess. What had happened to her? Why was she shouting?

He tried to make sense of her words. Nothing she said added up. She was bloody, but fine. Geoff needed a helicopter. She had to go. So did he. Where were they going? The words bounced back and forth across the water, too quickly for Derek to grasp. All that stuck was that Clare was injured, critically so.

The pain of his powerlessness was intense. Geoff was to hurry for help. Faye was to rush back to the girl's side. What about him? What about Derek? He should be there. Clare needed to know he was her father and he would make everything right for her. He also needed Michelle to understand he was devoted to her and her daughter. But neither Faye nor Geoff would listen.

He tried to give his wife a message for Clare but she walked away. He told Geoff about his and Michelle's relationship and that Clare was his daughter, not the gardener's. If Derek couldn't convey the message to Clare, Geoff should do it. Geoff looked at him, eyes blinking with bafflement and doubt, asked a few questions until, with a final pitying glance, he too, hurried away.

It was, thought Derek, as if he was stuck in a nightmare. One of those in which no one would listen to him and he couldn't move. His back ached and his head throbbed. He was disgusted by his impotence. Why did no one believe him? Why was he of so little consequence to everyone? Was his father right when he told Derek, "You'll never amount to anything"?

No! He had to prove otherwise. He had to get to Clare.

"Derek!"

He looked up. Faye had returned. She stood, panting as she stared at him from the other side of the river. Thank God! Faye would listen to him this time. Like she always had. It was why he'd chosen her, married her, despite her shortcomings. Faye, the Holy Saint of Altruism. The woman who always saw the good in others, even when their malice threw a shadow across the sun. She was the only person he knew who disproved the notion that anger was easy and kind was hard. For her, kind was easy and anger unknown. Faye, the one who loved him and knew his worth, and whose loyalty was unshakable. She'd help him across the water and take him to Clare.

Twenty-Three

Faye made her way up the ravine in something of a daze. She hadn't eaten since the crackers and cheese she'd had at Heuningbos the previous day while waiting for Clare. Her blood sugar was low, her head cried for coffee and the hours on her feet were taking their toll.

It was the dislodged boulder, clotted with mud and leaning as if pointing at the thorn bush where she'd landed earlier, that made her realise how far she had come. She stepped over it to examine the broken branches. Distracted by the thorns she'd removed from her flesh, she hadn't noticed how pretty the plant was with its waxy green leaves and star-shaped white flowers.

A call, *kewee-kewee-kewee,* made her look upwards. Faye recognised the bars and blotches of black on white on the crown eagle's breast and belly as it performed an elaborate display of rise-and-fall manoeuvres directly above her. With a few wing-flaps at the top of each climb, the large bird undertook a series of steep dives and ascents, finishing each with circle or a figure of eight.

The clouds were all but gone and Faye speculated whether the eagle, vociferous in his exploits, was making the most of the clear skies to warn interlopers against entering his airspace. She watched as the bird was joined by his mate. With a lower *kooee-kooee-kooee* call, the female flew towards him before plummeting earthwards.

The male threw back his head and, with a shrill call, followed her. The birds swooped and soared, performing a striking mid-air dance, until they disappeared into the valley together. Were they, she wondered, among the eagles Clare said were monogamous?

Revived by the break and prodded by thoughts of the girl in the forest, Faye walked on. Her mind had cleared. There was much to think about and yet, she felt calm.

She thought about how life would be without Derek. Their friends were his before they became hers. Would her relationships with them survive? She'd lost touch with those she'd socialised with before she met Derek. He hadn't liked her friends and she'd given them up for him. She was ashamed of it. But Faye was not afraid of being alone. She'd look for work. Something to give her purpose, direction. She'd get a dog. At last. The idea of a dog at her side made her steps seem lighter.

❦

There had never been a time in her childhood that Faye's family hadn't included a dog. Her first memories were of a gentle, tan and black German shepherd called Trixie Belle. One of her parents' wedding presents, Trixie was old by the time Faye was big enough to hold onto the dog for support as she took her first steps. She could still smell the grassy, damp scent of Trixie's long fur as she climbed onto her back and snuggled into her neck. She remembered Veronica's words of caution.

"Don't pull Trixie's ears, Faye. She's patient but if you hurt her, she might snap at you. That's what dogs do if you don't respect them, even angelic ones like Trixie."

Trixie never snapped or even growled at Faye, but the little girl had seen the magnitude of her teeth and sniffed her rancid dog-breath often enough to understand what might happen if she overstepped the mark.

The family's next dog was Dingo Rue, brought home by Veronica when she found the famished, worm-infested mongrel puppy— perhaps, the family speculated, with some mastiff and boxer in her—

in a gutter outside a grocery shop. What she lacked in elegance and etiquette, Dingo made up for in personality. Even as an old dog, she was playful and her tail-wagging greetings were unprecedented, sometimes even bruising.

Dingo was joined in her latter days by another of Veronica's rescues. Wallis Simpson was a lively and much-indulged terrier of sorts and the only one of the family's dogs who was still around when Derek came onto the scene. Faye remembered making the introduction.

"This is Wallis, Wallis Simpson," she said, bending to pat the wriggling pooch.

Derek didn't attempt to touch Wallis. "A dog with two names? Why?"

"I don't know. All of our dogs have had two names. Why not? Many people have three."

"Seems excessive. For a dog."

"You don't like dogs?"

"I love dogs. Why would you ask that?"

Veronica had walked into the room and the dog discussion had ended. From that day on, whenever Derek arrived at the family home, he made a point of greeting Wallis, though still, he never patted her.

"Hello, dog with two names. How are you, Wallis Simpson?"

After they were married, Faye and Derek moved into a house with a small garden.

"Perfect," she said, as they stood on a patch of lawn in the backyard. "The ideal size for something with terrier or Staffie in it. Will you come to the rescue centre with me?"

"Absolutely not," replied Derek, folding his arms over his chest. "Nor will you go alone."

"What? But why?"

"Faye, you know how I feel about pets."

"No. I mean, you said you liked dogs. I remember the—"

"I *like* dogs?" He scoffed. "You must be confusing me with one of your other men. I've never liked dogs."

"But when we met and I—"

"I've always disliked dogs. Any pet, for that matter. You knew that."

"But Wallis?"

He grimaced. "Did I have a choice when it came to Wallis?"

She stared at him, baffled. How could she have got something so significant so wrong?

"It looks like you doubt me?" he said, tilting his head. "I do know my own likes and dislikes, you know."

So it was that Faye had lived without a dog for more than twenty years, but that would change now. If she had a dog, she wouldn't be lonely. Perhaps she could also rekindle some of the relationships that she'd allowed to lapse to appease him. If she were able to find her old friend, would Eva forgive her?

Faye and Eva had been friends since their early teens when Eva's family moved into the neighbourhood. Although they attended different schools, their schedules were similar and, before long, Eva regularly met Faye at her gate and they walked Dingo, Wallis and Eva's nervous Maltese poodle, Frank. Faye helped Eva with her maths and Eva designed and drew graphs for Faye's projects. They went shopping and to the movies together on weekends, read the same books and discussed them at length. The girls shared their dreams and imagined their lives forever intertwined.

Eva cried in Faye's arms when her mother died suddenly and agreed to go on holiday with Faye and her family when, months later, she still couldn't see beyond her grief. When they returned, tanned and calm, Eva presented the family with a painting she'd done of Faye on the beach, accompanied by a card on which she'd written, "To the kindest person I know and her equally caring family, thank you for helping me see that the sun still shines and that its rays can reach me." Although she'd never hung it in the places she'd shared with Derek, Faye still had the painting. She'd hang it soon, when she had a place of her own.

When Faye went to university, Eva enrolled at art school, planning a career in graphic design. In the evenings and over weekends, they compared stories about their courses, lecturers and new friends. Faye introduced Eva to Derek when they met for coffee in town one Saturday morning.

"She's rather dull for someone who fancies herself an artist, isn't she?" said Derek when Eva left.

"Dull? No, Eva's not dull," Faye replied, admitting to herself though, that her friend had seemed subdued that morning. "She has a lot on her mind at the moment. Her class is preparing for an exhibition."

Derek gave a dismissive wave. "I don't care. She's your friend, not mine."

"What did you think about him?" asked Faye on the phone to her friend that evening.

"He's handsome," said Eva.

There was a long pause.

"Eva? Are you still there?"

"Yes."

"Is that all you have to say about him? Is he so handsome that you were unable to form any other opinions of him?"

"I guess so!" They laughed and changed the subject.

Some weeks later, Faye convinced Eva to come to a house party with her at the commune shared by Diane, Michelle and several other students. After the introductions, they stood in the kitchen, drinking beer out of plastic cups and chatting. An hour or so later, Faye and Derek were dancing when Eva touched her shoulder. She had a headache, she said, and was going home. She resisted when Faye offered to accompany her, insisting she'd be fine.

When Faye stopped by the next day to see how she was, Eva opened the door without a word.

"Are you still feeling ill?" asked Faye, following her friend into the house.

Eva shook her head.

"What's wrong?"

"Would you like some coffee?"

"Yes, please."

Eva prepared the coffee, still silent. It wasn't like her to be sullen. They sat opposite one another at the kitchen table.

"Eva?"

"I don't know how to tell you this without sounding like an insecure, possessive friend," she said, looking into her cup.

"What?"

"Derek, he's, well, he isn't a kind person."

"What do you mean? What has he done? Did he say something to you?"

Faye thought about Derek's comment at the coffee shop. Surely he would not have repeated it to Eva. She felt herself redden.

Eva looked at her. "You know it yourself, don't you?"

"No. I don't know what you mean. What did he say?"

"You mean aside from the comment that if I smiled more, his friends might be brave enough to ask me to dance?"

"What? Oh, Eva, I'm sorry. He was joking, I'm sure. He doesn't mean—"

"Sure. It's not just that. He . . . he's smug and patronising. And Faye, don't you see how, well, the way he says things as if they're jokes, but there's something deeper to it."

"Something deeper? Like what?"

"I don't know. He doesn't seem to care about trampling on people's feelings. It's just that I don't trust him and I—"

"You don't trust him? What do you think he's going to do, Eva? Steal the family silver? Ha! Good luck with finding *that* in our home."

Eva stared at her, biting her lower lip.

"What?" asked Faye, rattled.

Her friend exhaled. "It's just . . . well, you're starting to sound like him."

Faye put her mug down and stood up. She was cross.

"You know what, Eva? You do sound insecure. And possessive. I'm going. Let me know when you feel better."

Still upset the next day, Faye told Derek what Eva had said, her voice trembling. He took her in his arms and held her close.

"Don't cry. You don't need that kind of envy in your life. If she was a real friend, she'd celebrate your happiness. She's uninteresting, jealous and needy. You don't need her; you have me now."

When she arrived home, she found a letter from Eva in the post box. She tore it up without reading it.

A few days later, Faye's mother came into her room while she was studying.

"Eva was here earlier," she said, sitting on the bed. "She said you two have fallen out."

"Yes."

"What evil could she have done that you will not even let her apologise?"

"Some things cannot be unsaid. She's not who I thought she was."

Veronica raised her brows. "Is it possible you feel that way because you want to defend Derek?"

"Oh! So she did tell you what happened."

"She said she'd criticised Derek."

"And she wanted to apologise for that? For being wrong about him?"

"I think she wanted to apologise for upsetting you." Veronica stood up. "You're best friends, Faye. Don't turn your back on her. If you believe her criticism of Derek is wrong, let her get to know him and find out for herself."

Faye never spoke to Eva again. Was it because she subconsciously knew Eva was right about Derek? And that if her friend and boyfriend spent time together, Faye would recognise that Eva was right?

Now she would ask Zach to show her how to use Facebook. Perhaps she'd be able to reconnect with Eva there. Even if it was too late to rebuild their friendship, she wanted to apologise for being so naïve, and for setting their friendship aside so easily.

As the trail crested the ravine, Faye paused to catch her breath. She wondered where Geoffrey was. With little knowledge of the route he'd have to take, it was impossible to know how long it would be before he could raise the alarm and a helicopter would be dispatched. Faye hoped her description of where Clare was waiting would be enough for Geoffrey to convey an accurate description. Would they find her easily?

She'd been gone from Clare's side for almost six hours and, although the weather had cleared, she worried about having to nurse Clare through another night in the forest. If she had indeed punctured a lung, another night without proper medical attention could be critical. Faye hoped the girl had stayed calm in her absence. Thank goodness she was so brave about being in the wilderness. Faye couldn't imagine Zach being as composed as Clare about staying alone in the bush. Geoffrey had told Faye years ago that his mother had taught him to love and understand the bush. He, it seemed, had passed that on to Clare. Even so, all that time alone might have unsettled her.

She worried, too, whether she'd done the right thing by promising Geoffrey she would stay with Clare until help arrived. What if the rangers were at Heuningbos and, having not yet spoken to the others, had left oblivious of the fact she and Clare needed their help? There was nothing there to alert them that any of the hikers were still in the vicinity. She wished she'd thought to leave a note before she went looking for Clare. Should she go there tonight?

Her legs were stiff and tired, and she longed to rest. It wasn't just that she'd been hiking all day; she was hungry and sore.

"But you are not afraid, Faye," she said quietly.

Then, as if responding to herself, she called out, "No, I am not afraid and I never was—I just didn't know it until now!"

As the path levelled out and widened, she looked towards the mountains. The sun had already slipped behind the tallest peak. She had to face it; it was unlikely that anyone would come for Clare today. It was late and from what she'd understood, Geoffrey had a significant distance to cover. It was going to be a long night in the forest but, provided the girl was strong enough, that would be okay. What was there to be afraid of in this place where everything was as you saw it—naked and enduring because it knew no other way? The stars shine. The plants grow. The sun shines. The rain falls. The insects crawl. The animals roam. They ask for nothing but expect it all.

Was it this inevitability, the simplicity of the light, the dark, the day, the night that had brought Faye to back herself? She wasn't sure, but she was glad it was over. Today, as she'd walked to the river, she reached the end of a journey she only recently realised she'd begun.

Twenty-four

She may have slept again, but she wasn't sure. Her thoughts were muddled and her head fuzzy, as if on the other side of another migraine. It was as if someone had lit a fire in her chest and, as the flames flared, they licked at her rib cage. She lay motionless, moving only her eyes as she looked up into the branches, searching for the shiny scales of the skink. Now that she knew it wasn't a snake, Clare liked the idea of the reptile being there. She welcomed the distraction from her pain. She and the lizard could keep one another company. But she saw only dying leaves and desiccated bark.

Perhaps, she thought, looking out into the trees where the leaves were fresh and green, she should imagine she was engaging in shinrin-yoku.

"Is that like karate?" she'd asked when, years earlier, her father mentioned one of his clients had gone to Japan to learn about it.

He had laughed. "I'm glad I'm not the only one who didn't know what it is. I nearly asked her if it was a kind of sushi. No, not karate. It means 'forest bathing.' It's when you go into the forest or somewhere else in the nature to relax and enjoy the wild."

"Like when we go for a hike in Newlands Forest? You have to go to Japan to learn about it?"

"I guess it's similar to our hikes. But it's . . . it's more deliberate than that. You go to the forest specifically to meditate and consciously relax."

"Is that new to the Japanese? Being in the forest, I mean?"

"Hmm, I don't know. Perhaps it's just become more popular as more people work and live in tiny spaces in big cities with their noses pressed up against computer screens. It's not as easy for everyone to get into nature as it is for us."

"How do you say it again?"

"Shinrin-yoku," said her father.

"Shinrin-yoku," repeated Clare.

She'd googled it later that evening when she was meant to be writing an Afrikaans essay about the work of author André Brink. The photographs that popped up of Japanese forests and cherry trees in blossom convinced her shinrin-yoku was different from hiking in the trees around Cape Town. She would, she decided, like to try it one day. Perhaps her father would go with her. He'd be fascinated by Japanese gardens.

For years, she hadn't thought about her childhood dream of travelling to Japan with him. She couldn't recall whether she'd ever proposed the idea to her father. Now, as she lay alone and immobile in the trees in the Tsitsikamma thinking about forest bathing, Clare vowed to do it; she'd recover from her injury and anorexia and one day, she and her dad would shinrin-yoku in Japan.

The sun had moved behind the shelter and the birds were already quieter. The novelty of the rainless day had long since worn off for them. She wasn't sure how late it was and didn't dare move her arm to look at her watch for fear of pain. Was it so late the birds were already roosting? Or did they, like Gran and other animals, know the value of napping in the afternoon?

"A ten- to twenty-minute snooze puts the zing back into your day," she'd told Clare and her siblings when they'd asked why she typically disappeared after lunch each day. "If humans hadn't stopped listening to their bodies millions of years ago, we would all sleep for bit during the day. Animals know it works. Watch how dogs and cats slow down during the warmest part of the day and sleep to replenish their energy. Later, when it's cooler, they come alive again, revitalised. We should learn from them."

It was true. When Gran reappeared in the afternoon, it was as if she'd been recharged. Her steps were quicker, her focus sharper and her purpose apparent. If the weather was good, she'd work in her garden until the shadows grew long and it was time for her dogs' evening walk. If it was unpleasant outdoors, she'd spend the hours on one of her carpentry projects in her cramped garden shed. Even in her old age, she was one of the most active people Clare knew.

If I survive this, Gran, I will learn to listen to my body again, thought Clare. I will nap when I am tired, eat when I am hungry and go to Japan with Dad. I will be the woman you believed I would become. Help me get through this, Gran, wherever you are and I'll make it up to everyone I've disappointed. I'll talk to Dad about it, no matter how hard it might be. And Buhle and Maryanne. I'll ask them to listen to me, even if they don't think they'll understand. And Mark, who I know understands.

She tasted tears on her lips, salty and dusty. She typically hated crying. She was afraid if she started, she'd never stop. Now though, it didn't matter. She didn't have the energy, courage or will to wipe her eyes or stop crying. There was no one around. She didn't have to pretend to be strong. It was okay to wallow and give in to helplessness. She'd fight again when Faye returned.

A flash of wing bar and a shudder of leaves high in the canopy warned Clare that something was moving in the forest. She narrowed her eyes and tried to still her wheezing so that she could focus her senses. The sound came, *choof, choof, choof.* Heavy footsteps, approaching. Just two. Then they stopped.

"Clare?" Faye's head and torso filled the opening of the shelter. "Are you awake?"

"Ye-es." She was unable to disguise the tremble in her voice.

Faye crawled under the branches and knelt alongside her. "How are you feeling?"

"Still can't move. It's crazy how it hurts and how tired I am. It's as if I've run too far on too little."

Faye pressed her lips together. Clare recognised a flicker of concern in her eyes. It was an expression she'd seen on her parents' faces often in recent years. She glanced down and saw that Faye's neck and the exposed part of her chest were streaked with deep scratches, some of them oozing. The front of her pale green shirt was bloody. Her neck and chest were scratched raw, as if someone had clawed at her with their fingernails.

"What happened? You're—"

"It's okay. Looks worse than it is. Let's just say the thorn bush wasn't as welcoming as I hoped it would be when I tried to embrace it."

"But—"

"Really. I'm okay."

"Did you find my father? Is he—"

"Yes. He's gone to find help. He'll come . . . send help."

"They were still at Grootkloof Cabin? You managed to cross the river and get to them?"

"Yes and no. Your father and Derek were still there. Derek hurt his back during the crossing two days ago. He couldn't go on. Your dad stayed with him. The others went to find help, and us, they hoped, yesterday. As luck would have it—God, that was lucky—your dad happened to be at the river—it's still in flood—when I arrived. He's gone to get help for us."

"There was no way he could cross the river . . . come to . . . with you?"

"No, it's still too full. Raging. An escape route is the only way out. Even if it wasn't, it's quicker for your dad to find help from that side."

"How will they get to us? Do you know?"

"A helicopter."

"Really?"

Clare had accepted she was badly injured. Even so, the idea of being rescued by helicopter embarrassed her. She'd joined her father and his friends on the hike at the last minute hoping for a low-key, peaceful time. Instead, she was the centre of attention and the subject of a rescue mission.

"It's the only way. I made a large cross in the veld using rocks and branches to create arrows pointing this way so they can easily find us."

"When do you think they will come?"

"Tomorrow. I hope."

They were quiet for a moment. Clare thought about the previous night. How she'd slept for the first part and then lain awake, desperate to move but even more so to remain still.

"Just one more night," said Faye, as if reading her thoughts.

"What about Derek?" asked Clare, not wanting to wallow. "Is he okay?"

"Don't worry about the others. They'll be fine."

Clare exhaled, closing her eyes as if to shut out the pain. Faye picked up the tablets from the spot where she'd left them that morning. The food and water hadn't been touched either.

"Let's get these down you and, if you can, you should eat," she said, tipping two of the pills into her hand. "I'll tell you everything when that's done. Here."

Clare glanced at the tablets and the scratches on Faye's neck. "We should share them."

Faye shook her head with a small smile. "I'll be fine. If all I have is a few scratches to trade for everything to work out for us, I'll gratefully accept them."

When, after she'd given her the pills and fed Clare, Faye lay down with a noisy sigh, it dawned on the young woman how exhausted her companion must be.

"How was the hike? Difficult?" she asked.

"Not really. Long though. It'll be dark soon."

"I'm sorry."

"For what?"

"Everything I've put you through," she said. "Talk about a dream hike being hijacked by someone who wasn't even meant to be part of it."

Faye placed her hand lightly on Clare's arm. "It hasn't gone as planned for anyone. You recover and I'll tell you the subplot about this trip."

"Subplot? What do you mean?"

"Let's just say I've learned some things about myself over the past two days."

"Oh?"

Faye was silent.

"I've learned some stuff about myself, too," said Clare.

"Good things? Helpful things?"

"Hmm. Perhaps. Surprising things, for sure."

"Such as?"

"Such as, it might be useful to be able to be alone, but it's not necessarily preferable."

"Ah. That's significant. Are you thinking of anyone in particular?"

"Possibly. Though I've probably blown that chance."

"How so?"

"I have, or rather, I had a friend, a running friend. Mark. We ran together for almost two years at uni. Every day almost. We talked a lot. At first, he talked and I listened. Then I also talked. We ran and talked."

"That's impressive. Running *and* talking."

"The thing is, I could talk to Mark about anything. When you run and talk, you don't look at one another. It makes it easier." Clare thought, but didn't say, *like it is for us now; lying here, looking up into the leaves and branches, not at one another.*

"I know what you mean," said Faye. "Talking while you're doing something together is easier. Zach and I have the best conversations when we're cooking together. Usually breakfast. There is something more natural about talking while you're busy than when you're sitting staring at one another in an intense, dedicated kind of conversation set-up."

"Yes. It was like that for me and Mark. We talked. I talked about myself and my anorexia. He made me laugh at myself. He never lectured or judged me. I almost felt normal. No, I *did* feel normal with Mark." She was quiet for a moment, as if registering the full significance of what she'd said. "I love running. I always feel good after a run. But after running with Mark, I felt good *and* normal. Does that make sense?"

"Yes."

"Mark's sister was anorexic, but it wasn't just that he understood the condition. He seemed to get me. Why I like running. Why I need to prove I can get better on my own—by controlling the illness."

"He sounds like a good person. What makes you think you've blown it with him?"

"We stopped running. He lives somewhere else now. It's probably silly of me to think about him. I don't want to be alone all the time but that doesn't mean I have to be with Mark. I mean it generally. I've been by myself a lot over the past three years. I think I'd like to try having friends again, people."

"Well, yes. I'm sure Mark isn't the only person who will get you, appreciate you, but he does sound important to you."

Clare ignored her. "Also, I need to learn how to accept help," she said.

Faye patted her arm. "I like that."

"More than the idea of not being alone?"

"No. I mean, yes. It's good that you don't necessarily want to be alone. It's just, well, it's sort of contrary to what I've been thinking about recently."

"Oh?"

"Pfft. I don't want to bore you with my middle-aged ramblings. The thing is, Clare, you're young. You have your whole life ahead. Don't waste time thinking you can't rectify the mistakes you've made. You don't have to pay the price forever for making bad decisions. Also, the longer you allow your mistakes to go on, the harder it is to make amends, to fix them."

A light breeze ruffled the leaves in the tallest trees, passing by like a sigh. The earthy scent of rotting wood was familiar now and, without the rain and with Faye at her side, Clare felt comforted, pain notwithstanding.

"That's my experience, anyway," said Faye.

"I can't imagine you making mistakes. You're always so calm. So together. I mean, look at how you've managed this. I can't picture my mother in these circumstances—where there's no one to do things for her and follow her instructions."

Faye chuckled. "I've made mistakes. The worst of it is that people who knew me best warned me, tried to help, but I wouldn't hear it. Don't be like me, Clare. Listen. Accept help. Don't leave it too late."

"I'm sorry." Clare stifled a yawn, wincing with the effort.

"Are you okay? Rest for a bit."

"It's strange how I've known you and Derek all my life and yet, I don't . . . don't really know you at all."

"Hmm."

"I realised that when he came and saw me on campus, it was awkward. I guess it's a generational thing. But I do feel like I know you better now, after all this."

"It was awkward with Derek?"

"Terribly." She sighed. "I'm sorry. He obviously thought he was doing Mom and Dad a favour by visiting me and checking up on me. But I was so embarrassed by the idea of talking to him about my anorexia, and I made it very difficult for him. Surely he told you how awful it was?"

"He wanted to discuss your anorexia?"

"Well, it seemed like it. He asked me what had happened. As if he imagined some kind of traumatic event must've caused it."

"Ouch. I'm sorry. He didn't . . . he doesn't get it."

"No, no. Don't apologise. I guess he was trying to help my folks. I should've thanked him at least. I mean, for trying. I'll do it when I see him next."

Faye didn't reply. She was asleep.

Twenty-five

It felt wrong to be walking away from his daughter and not towards her, but Geoffrey pushed hard up the trackless ridge leading to the road. Steep and irregular, the off-trail path traversed several patches of shingle and clusters of large boulders that were loosely connected by scatterings of spikey shrubs and grass.

It was a scramble rather than a hike, and Geoffrey found it impossible to get into any kind of rhythm. He was impatient to get to the top before nightfall, but knew being too hasty was risky. If he slipped, lost his footing, twisted an ankle or injured himself some other way, he could exacerbate an already worrying situation. Without a clear pathway, the route wasn't always obvious. He was reassured by the occasional boot print, presumably that of Diane, Bruce, Bev or Helen, in some of the sandy spots. The marks confirmed that he was on track, he'd find his friends and the rangers, and get help for Clare.

As he climbed, Geoffrey tried to push aside disquieting thoughts that nudged for his attention like an overly eager shop assistant. He stopped for a moment to look at a thick-stemmed, bushy king protea plant. The dark green of its leathery, paddle-shaped leaves provided a muted backdrop for six large, bowl-shaped flower heads. The flowers, their dusky pink petals assembled around the florets like a crown held towards the sun for admiration, were Michelle's favourite blooms. She'd included one in her bridal bouquet and asked Geoffrey to plant some in their garden.

It made sense that she loved the flower, thought Geoffrey. Michelle was as vibrant, robust and commanding as a king protea. He walked on, imagining how it would have been if his wife had been with him on the hike as planned. What would she have done? Of course, if Michelle had come, Clare wouldn't have been there and he wouldn't be climbing a mountain looking for help for their daughter. Even so, he pictured his wife at the Bloukrans River as the group prepared to cross it two days earlier. Would she have tried to convince them otherwise? Probably not. She wouldn't, as they hadn't, have known that it had rained heavily in one of the river's catchment areas before it reached them. Michelle would have had no idea the river would flood at the precise moment they were crossing it—when Diane was midway across.

Geoffrey felt ill as he thought again of what could've happened if Diane hadn't had the strength to hold onto the ropes or if Derek hadn't got to her in time. He recalled how the colour had drained from Bruce's face and how his friend had whimpered with frustration as they'd wrestled to free the tree entangled in the rope. Geoffrey was frantic with panic; he could only imagine how Bruce felt. He thought about how he would've reacted if Michelle had been trapped in the deluge of water and debris.

Others thought it—some had even said it—and Geoffrey knew it: he and Michelle were an unlikely couple. She was the lion who roared and ruled. He was the elephant who could have, but didn't care to reign.

Michelle was self-assured and ambitious to the point of sometimes being ruthless. She didn't enrol at university to become a lawyer; she signed up so that she could become a high court judge. And she did. Geoffrey, on the other hand, went because he got excellent grades at school and his father thought getting a degree was a good idea. The boy was grateful for his father's encouragement and didn't want to let him down. He studied hard and graduated, but his best memories about being at university were watching the seasons change in the trees, chatting to the gardeners on campus and discovering that Michelle Lowe was interested in him.

He had been surprised and flattered by Michelle's attention.

"She told Diane she's 'intrigued' by you," said Bruce. "Diane insists that in 'Michelle-language,' that means she has a major crush on you."

"Crush?" said Geoffrey, hoping his friend hadn't noticed that he was blushing. "She doesn't seem like the kind of girl who has crushes."

Bruce gave him light punch. "Exactly. That's why she's 'intrigued.' The question is, what are you going to do about it?"

Geoffrey didn't know Michelle beyond having been introduced to her by Bruce and Diane in the canteen. They'd chatted briefly a few times since. He'd seen enough to know she was interesting and beautiful, and felt he should show his gratitude for her "intrigue" by asking her out. He didn't imagine anything would come of it; least of all, that he'd fall in love with a woman whose star shone so brightly— and who wasn't coy about regularly polishing said star herself. But he did, and was even more surprised when she fell in love with him.

Marriage and work didn't change how different they were. Michelle worked late and over the weekends, and spoke more about law than anything else. Geoffrey left all thoughts of work on his desk the instant he closed his office door and, because he never thought of it when he was elsewhere, he never spoke about the bank or what he did there when he wasn't at work.

Michelle noticed what cars people drove and where they lived. Geoffrey noticed when people were sad and if they looked hungry. She was heads. He was tails. Geoffrey didn't compete with her on any level. It was one of the reasons Michelle loved him. His indifference to wealth and status only bothered her because of what it might mean to their future as a family. But she'd always believed when they were married, she'd be able to shore up his ambition. As such, Michelle was shocked when he told her he wanted to give up his job.

She was used to getting her own way and, when she fought

against his plan, Michelle was astounded he didn't give in to her demands. She left him for a few days, which Geoffrey hated. But he didn't capitulate. He disliked arguing and wanted peace, but he knew that if he didn't stand his ground, not only would he be an unhappy banker, but he'd also be an unhappy spouse.

It was a critical time in their relationship, but Geoffrey believed the outcome sealed things for them. His love for Michelle never wavered and he was sure that his not giving in to her demands helped her finally accept exactly who he was. The years that followed confirmed to him that not only did the incident compel Michelle to recognise and accept him and his modest ambitions, but it also deepened her love for him. Geoffrey had never imagined, until that morning at the river, that the few days, all those years ago, when he and Michelle were at an impasse regarding his decision to leave the bank, might've spawned any drama other than the one that involved the two of them at the time.

Climbing, perspiring and breathing hard, he paused and looked up. There was nothing but sky above, but already the slanting rays of the sun were casting long shadows on the earth and creating an orange tinge overhead. It was unlikely he'd make the road before nightfall, but Geoffrey was determined to reach the plateau. That way, come first light, he'd be on the highland and able to move quickly towards the track. He looked down to where the trees and bush created a cover so dense it was hard to imagine hiking through it. Beyond the forest, the crevices and folds of the mountains suggested another land and other lives. He couldn't see the river. It was just as well; he didn't want to think about being there. He turned and walked on.

It was dusk when he reached the final summit, which required scrambling over a knobbly mound of boulders, edging through a bushy ravine and clambering up several metres of vertical rock. As he turned sideways and squeezed himself into a chute, hooking his fingers onto a ledge and inching his way up, Geoffrey wondered how the others had managed it. The crevasse was too narrow to accommodate more than one person at a time so it wouldn't have been possible for them to help one another. He was wiry and strong from lifting and carrying gardening equipment, but still found making his way up the fissure difficult. It was possible that Helen, Bev, Bruce and Diane would've had to find a route around it.

By the time he pulled himself out of the cleft, Geoffrey was exhausted. He lay on his back in the sand to recover his strength. It was nearly dark and although he was tempted to continue, he didn't want to risk getting disorientated and lost.

He stared at the sky until the first stars appeared, his mind on Clare. He wished he'd told her how much he loved her when they'd said goodbye at Heuningbos. He'd tell her the moment he saw her again. He'd also say how proud he was of her, and how important it was to him that she recover. He would tread less cautiously about expressing his love. He wouldn't wait until she was better and stronger. It didn't matter. All that mattered was that Clare knew that no matter what, her father loved her.

He moved closer to a large boulder that would provide shelter, took his space blanket from his backpack and settled to sleep. Everything would be okay, he told himself. They'd get Clare to the hospital. She'd recover and they'd go home to Michelle, where they'd stare at one another, shake their heads and marvel at the madness of the hike. He'd go to work, turn the earth, plant flowers and come home with dirty hands. Michelle would slip her high heels on every morning and head to court. Clare would recover and come to Sunday lunch with Angus and Linda. They'd joke, laugh and life would go on. They'd be a family and everything would be okay.

Twenty-Six

"Did you notice the claw prints on the tree?" whispered Clare.

"Claw prints?" said Faye, surprised by how lucid the girl sounded.

After accidentally falling asleep for a short time the previous evening, Faye had forced herself to stay awake throughout the night. She'd pulled herself into a sitting position, pushed her lower back against a knobbly branch to help keep herself alert and listened to Clare's wheezing and moaning. At times, when the girl's chest rattled like a biscuit tin of buttons during an earthquake, Faye wished she'd kept the faith she knew briefly as a child when her aunt had convinced her God would look over her if she believed and prayed enough. How helpful it would be to believe all would be well.

Instead, as if playing a movie in her head, she recalled what she'd learned about first aid at school, going through the seven steps of CPR. She needed to be ready, and listened for the tell-tale clue of a change in breathing pattern. A hospice nurse caring for Veronica during her last days had told Faye how, when approaching death, a person's breathing rate changed from a normal rhythm to a pattern of several rapid breaths, followed by a period of no breathing. Although Clare's breathing was shallow and irregular, it didn't stop. But for much of the night, Faye was uncertain whether the girl was asleep or swimming in painful semi-consciousness. By the time the first signs of morning glowed lightly across the horizon, Faye felt weak from exhaustion and after being taut with worry for so many hours.

"Halfway up the tree," said Clare, her eyes still closed and her mouth barely moving. "Leopards stand on their hind legs and scratch to clean their claws—only on certain trees, which they return to time and again—also to spread their scent and mark their territory."

"Leopards? Territory?" Faye glanced outside to where the morning light seemed to creep through the trees towards them. "You're kidding?"

Clare opened her eyes, blinking. Had she been talking in her sleep? Delirious? Faye placed the back of her fingers on the girl's forehead. She was cool and clammy. Even in the faint light, she could see that the skin around her lips was blue.

"Were you dreaming about leopards? Trees?"

"I don't think so. Why do you ask?"

"No reason," she said, tucking the space blanket behind Clare's shoulders. Her eyes were closed again. Faye placed her fingers over the girl's hand. Had it always been so tiny?

"Are you awake?" she asked.

"Hmm? Yes."

"Is the pain any better? Worse?"

"I don't know. I feel so tired." Clare gave a tiny yawn as if too exhausted to open her mouth fully. "Why would I be tired? I haven't moved for days."

Because your organs are starved of oxygen, thought Faye. She lifted the water bottle.

"Will you try and drink?"

Clare managed a few sips.

During the night, Faye had debated leaving Clare for a few hours the next morning and going to the cabin to get food and a sleeping bag. She was lightheaded from not eating and wanted to get a sleeping bag to keep Clare warmer. She would also, she'd thought, leave a note at the cabin. She wanted to ensure that anyone who arrived at Heuningbos would know that she and Clare were little under two hours hike away, increasingly desperate for help. She had no idea whether Geoffrey had been able to alert anyone yet. Now though, with the soft light of morning giving face to Clare's condition, Faye knew she couldn't leave the girl, not even briefly. They'd have to make do until help arrived. Let that be soon, she thought. She sat up, unzipped her jacket, took it off and laid it over Clare.

"Faye?"

"Yes."

"How many days have we been here?"

"This will be our third. Only two nights though."

"When I first lay . . . sat here, I couldn't imagine ever getting comfortable." Clare paused to catch her breath. Her chest rattled. "Now I can't imagine leaving. I could just stay."

Faye's eyes prickled. She looked away. "Well, that's not an option. Our reservation was only for two nights. It's too expensive an establishment to stay any longer. We leave today."

"Okay. Well, I do want to talk to my father. And apologise to Derek for being so rude to him when he visited me at university."

"Talking to your father will be good, but I don't think you need to worry about Derek."

Clare was silent. Faye thought she'd fallen asleep once more. Then she felt her fingers move beneath her hand.

"Did you know that the rosettes or spots on every leopard are unique?" said the girl.

"I didn't."

"Also, each leopard has its own identifiable sound."

"Really? How do you know so much—"

"They sound something like someone sawing wood. But every one of them is different. So they can tell one another apart—know whether there's a stranger in their territory or a possible mate."

"Did you hear a leopard? Here?"

The girl was quiet for a moment.

"How did you know you wanted to, erm, marry Derek?"

Faye smiled, amused by how Clare's thoughts meandered from Geoffrey and Derek to leopards and returned to Derek. She'd rather hear more about leopards.

"Pfft. It's so long ago, I can't really recall."

It wasn't true; she remembered well. Faye had been thrilled when Derek proposed. She hadn't thought about the possibility until, a few days after Geoffrey and Michelle announced their engagement at the get-together at Michelle's parents' home, she bumped into Diane at the supermarket.

"So, I guess you and Derek will be next," said Diane, as they walked towards the tills together.

Faye stared at her. "Gosh, I hadn't thought about it."

"You're the only woman I know who I actually believe when she says that. Don't you want to get married? Or just not to Derek?"

"I think so."

Diane laughed and they went their separate ways, Faye thinking for the first time about marrying Derek. She hadn't thought about it because it hadn't seemed possible. Even though she was in love with him and being with him had opened a new world to her, it wasn't her world. Derek and his friends went places and did things she'd only dreamt of. They were welcomed at the trendiest clubs and invited to the best parties. Then it occurred to her; if they did get married, Faye would, for the first time in her life, maybe feel as if she was in the inner circle.

It wasn't as if she'd had a deprived childhood, but rather that her family was more accustomed to living on the outside, looking in. Hotels were places others checked into during the holidays, while Faye's family camped at the beach or stayed with grandparents. The only restaurant she'd eaten at before she met Derek, was the pizza place the family frequented every first Friday of the month.

It wasn't just that Derek and his friends' families were wealthier than Faye's; they also took for granted they'd be welcome wherever they wanted to go whenever it suited them. For a while, when Faye first began going out with Derek, she would look around waiting for the moment someone would tell her she wasn't authorised to be there. It didn't happen, but it never occurred to her that it was because she deserved to be there as much as they did. She always felt that she was there because of them. Perhaps, she thought, if she married Derek, she would learn to belong. Still, it came as a surprise to her when, just a few days later, Derek proposed.

He was waiting for her when she left work.

"This is nice," said Faye, as they got into his car. "Always a treat not to have to catch the train."

"I thought we could drive to Mouille Point and go for a walk on the promenade," he said.

"Sounds lovely."

They hadn't walked far when, without looking at her, Derek took her hand and said, "Do you want to get married?"

Faye stopped. So did he. When she didn't say anything, he turned to her. "Well?"

"Are you asking me if it's something I want to do in general, or if—"

"Of course not."

She stared at him.

Derek smiled and took her hands in his. "Faye, will you marry me?"

"Really?"

He cocked his head, still smiling. "Everyone's doing it."

"Yes."

"Yes?"

"Yes, they are and . . . yes, I'll marry you."

She didn't remember much more of the afternoon. It was only at lunch with her mother a few days later, when Veronica made reference to how "biting" Derek's comments could be, that Faye realised how muted her mother and father had been in their congratulations when she told them her news.

Faye saw Derek in a new light during their engagement. She had never thought about spending the rest of her life with him, and now that she'd said she would, she imagined being with him all the time and realised how different that would be from dating him. She noticed Derek was often impatient and intolerant with others. He believed most people who didn't agree with him were foolish and those who changed their minds, weak. When Bruce, newly married to Diane, told his friends that he wasn't coping with the stresses of being a medical doctor and had decided to retrain as a pharmacist, Derek emitted a scornful laugh.

"That's ridiculous! What a waste of time and money," he said.

"What do you want him to do, Derek?" bristled Diane. "Be miserable for the rest of his life?"

"Of course not. Make it work for you, man. Choose a specialisation that doesn't . . . I don't know . . . cause you stress. Or whatever it is you're experiencing."

Faye was shocked Derek wasn't more sympathetic towards Bruce. She lay awake that night worrying about it. She wished there was someone she could talk to about her concerns. The problem was that her new friends were Derek's old friends. Even though Michelle and Diane knew Derek better than anyone, they wouldn't be objective and it would be weird to expect them to offer their opinions. Faye knew her mother would be honest but, perhaps because she didn't want to face what Veronica saw in Derek, she didn't want to raise the subject with her. The next morning, she convinced herself everyone had their faults and that when they were married, she and Derek would help one another become better people.

Besides, the wedding plans were well underway.

"What I do know, though," said Faye, staring out of the shelter, "is that I didn't realise what an unknown thing marriage is. The problem is you can't change that; you have to experience marriage to find out."

Clare didn't respond.

The sun had reached the forest, etching the edges of the leaves with its light and casting long shadows across the ground. The trees around the shelter had grown familiar to Faye and, as one might acknowledge a friendly neighbour, she almost felt compelled to greet them. She remembered the disquiet she'd experienced before she spotted the wild pigs watching her. It was as if she was a different person.

"The pigs are elsewhere this morning, it seems," she said.

"Uh-huh."

Clare's eyes were closed once more and her breathing ragged. Faye stroked her hand, her own felt clammy. She was afraid. What if help didn't come soon enough? How would she face Geoffrey and Michelle?

She gazed into the trees, trying to still her heart. It wouldn't help to panic. She needed to be calm and stay pragmatic. She'd get Clare to drink a little. Keep her hydrated and warm. There was nothing else she could do.

The sounds of the forest were changing as if, as the sun rose, the volume dial was turned up. Faye listened as the bird calls became louder and more diverse, and the insects buzzed with increasing intent. She also heard a knocking sound, a patter. Her heart sped up again. Was it the sound of a helicopter approaching? Then it stopped. *Where had it gone?* A few moments later she heard it again, *Tap, tap, tap.* Why wasn't the sound growing louder? Was it going in the wrong direction? She looked as high into the trees as she could. *'Tap, tap, tap.'*

"It's a cardinal woodpecker."

"What?" she asked, turning to Clare. Her eyes were open and she lifted a finger. Faye looked toward where she pointed and saw the red crown of a bird rocking against an old tree that had collapsed and fallen against another. The compact bird, with its olive-coloured back marked with dots and paler bands and its white and black underparts, was pecking at the rotting bark. A bird. Not a plane. Faye sighed. She had to stay calm.

"No pigs today," murmured Clare, "just a pecker."

Faye laughed softly. Where there was wit, there was life.

Twenty-Seven

Awake well before dawn, Geoffrey sat on the boulder he'd sheltered alongside overnight and watched the light caress the mountains in the distance until, gradually drawing closer, it swathed everything before it in soothing lavender.

A movement on a ledge below caught his eye and he watched as a genet slipped between the rocks and sprung onto a branch, his furry, striped tail almost as long as his body. Silhouetted against the pastel sky, the animal crouched for a moment, cat-like with his head low and ears curved forward. His pounce was quick and light, and when he lifted his head, the genet revealed the full measure of his agility; he had a mouse in his mouth. Geoffrey wanted to applaud.

Once he could make out the veld behind him, he stood and slung his bag on his back. Waist-high swards of grass and fynbos lay between him and the track, and by the time his boots met the roadway, which was no more than two narrow tracks in the veld, it was afternoon. The clear route meant he could walk faster and was able to examine the sandy sections for tyre tracks. There were no tracks to indicate a vehicle had passed by recently. It would, thought Geoffrey, be a good sign if it meant the rangers were still on their way; he hadn't missed them. But if it was because the rivers were still too high for the rangers to easily move around, it would be unfortunate.

Which was it, he wondered?

The answer came quickly as he saw a Land Cruiser navigating the bumpy track towards him. Geoffrey whooped and began running. The car stopped and the passenger doors opened. Bruce stepped out, followed by Diane. The driver was slower to exit.

"Hey!" said Bruce, smiling. "You grew impatient and came looking for us?"

Diane was more perceptive. "What happened? What's wrong? Is it Derek?"

The driver, a tall young man in the ranger uniform of olive green shirt and pants, shiny boots and cap with the national park's logo embroidered on it, held back, raising his hand in a cautious wave when Geoffrey caught his eye.

"It's Clare. She fell. Faye thinks she might have perforated a lung. She's not doing well."

"Oh, my God," said Diane.

The young man came forward, his dark eyes concerned. "Where is she?"

Geoffrey explained what Faye had told him at the river.

Diane looked at the ranger. "What do we do?"

"I'll radio the office." He looked at Geoffrey. "Come, meneer. Sit with me while I make the call. You can clarify if necessary."

Geoffrey nodded and held out his hand. They shook. "Thank you. I'm Geoffrey."

"Simon. Come."

The radio call to the office was quick. There wasn't a great deal of information to impart. It was agreed a helicopter rescue would be necessary. Geoffrey was relieved and wanted to ask how soon it would be there, but didn't. It was clear from the conversation that all parties accepted it was an emergency. Geoffrey did, however, ask Simon when the radio was silent.

"It's hard to say. It depends on where the helicopter has to come from," he replied.

Geoffrey felt his chest tighten. "You don't have one in the park?"

"Not a rescue helicopter, no."

"But—"

"It'll come from one of the hospitals in the area. With medics. There's a procedure. It'll happen as fast as it can. I'll check in with them in an hour or so if we don't hear more. We should get going."

Diane put a hand on Geoffrey's shoulder from the seat behind. He didn't notice.

"Where? Where are we going? Can we try and get to her?" he asked.

Simon started the engine and drove forward. "No. I'm sorry. That's not possible. Not today. Perhaps tomorrow. We can fetch your friend, though."

Derek. Geoffrey had forgotten about him. He turned to Bruce and Diane. "Where are Bev and Helen? Where did you stay last night?"

Bruce leaned forward. "We walked all the way to the main offices. Arrived late in the evening. They gave us a room there. Bev and Helen are still there."

"But it's impossible to get to Heuningbos? By road, I mean?"

"Yes. One of the bridges was washed away," said Bruce. "The flooding was unlike anything they've seen in years . . . particularly at this time of the year."

He glance down. Geoffrey noticed Diane looking at her husband, as if expecting him to say more, but Bruce was quiet.

She turned and looked at Geoffrey. "The park officials were shocked to see us. They thought we'd still be at Heuningbos Hut with our supplies, stranded for a few days but not in any danger."

"Huh? Why would they think that?"

"Because they told Derek before we left we should stay there if the weather looked dodgy in any way."

"What?"

Diane clenched her jaws and nodded. "Yes. He knew. They warned him about possible flooding in the catchment area . . . how dangerous it could be."

They didn't speak again as the truck bumped and rattled over the track across the highlands. Geoffrey felt ill. He wasn't sure whether he was angry or worried. He was certainly mad with himself. He should have checked before they left instead of being convinced by Derek's summation of the weather forecast for the next six days. He should have gone into the office with Derek when they registered for the hike.

"The one thing you have to remember about Derek is that what you see is not necessarily what you get, what he says is not necessarily what he means, and what he assures you is fact isn't necessarily so," said Michelle several years ago when Geoffrey expressed surprise their friend had not arrived at a charity event Geoffrey's company had sponsored.

"This is the guy who has been your closest friend since primary school?"

Michelle chuckled. "He's not all bad. You just have to take everything about him with a truckload of salt."

Geoffrey wished he'd heeded her advice.

Eventually, having steered the vehicle down a twisty, rocky track into the valley, Simon turned onto a smoother, sandy road that sliced through the trees. Grootkloof Cabin came into view. Framed by the shaggy forest and with the ragged mountains behind it, the view was picture-postcard perfect. Geoffrey wished again that Clare had seen it. Simon pulled up alongside the cabin.

"Will you radio the office to get an update?" asked Geoffrey.

Simon nodded. "Once we've found your friend. I want to let them know we have him and are on our way back first."

They climbed out of the vehicle, looking around. They expected Derek to appear. He didn't. Geoffrey followed Diane and Bruce into the cabin. Their friend's backpack lay on the floor, an empty blister pack of painkillers and a silver hip flask alongside it.

"Bloody hell," said Diane, rolling her eyes. "I'll check the lapa. You go to the bathroom."

They called for him but still, no Derek.

"Where did you last see him?" asked Simon.

"I left him at the river, but assumed he would have made his way back by now."

"He was walking okay?" asked Diane.

"Not easily or without pain, but he was mobile."

"One of you stay here in case he appears. We'll go to the river," said Simon.

Bruce sat on the stairs of the lapa as the others climbed back into the vehicle and drove off. There was no sign of him at the river either. Diane and Geoffrey walked downstream while Simon went the other way.

"Where could he be? Why would he go anywhere?" asked Diane.

"I don't know. He didn't move from the bed until yesterday. I was surprised to see him at the river."

"He didn't walk here with you?"

"No. When I asked him earlier, he declined. I guess he took the rest of the pills when I left and felt better. He seemed doped up when he arrived here."

"Doped up on painkillers and whiskey. Do you think he would have struggled to get back?"

"No. He would have made it. Slowly. I mean . . . I don't really know . . . it's possible he was feeling stronger than I imagined. But . . ."

He hesitated and looked over the water. Diane stared at him, brows raised.

"What? You don't think he somehow crossed the river and went with Faye do you?"

"No. Not with Faye. She left before I did. Also, I can't see how he could have got to the other side. I mean, look at it," he gestured to the river. "But, well, he was acting rather strangely."

"Strangely?"

"Yes."

"What do you mean?"

Geoffrey hesitated, took his cap off and scratched his head, looking across the river.

"He . . . he yelled to Faye to tell Clare that her father loves her." Diane swallowed.

"What? He's . . . he's . . . why would he? What did he mean? I mean, you—"

"That's what I asked him."

"What did he say?" she asked, her voice quiet now.

"He said Clare was his daughter."

He turned to look at Diane. She glanced away, lip wedged between her teeth.

"What . . . what did you do? Say to him?"

"I asked him how."

"Oh, God," said Diane under her breath.

Geoffrey took a step closer to her. "Is it true? Do you know?"

"No! God no, it's not true. Derek had been drinking and—" said Diane, placing her hand on Geoffrey's forearm.

"But you knew? About him and Michelle? What did you know? That they were lovers after we were married?"

"Geoffrey—"

"Around the time Clare was conceived?"

"No! God, Geoffrey. It wasn't then. Clare is your daughter. There is no question of that. Michelle . . . when you were fighting . . . about you starting your business. She . . . it was a short, stupid moment. She hated herself for it. Clare is your daughter. Look at her, Geoffrey. There's no doubt of that. How can you doubt it?"

He hung his head.

"Did Faye hear? Where was she?"

"No. She'd already left to get back to Clare."

The noise of river hung between them.

"What did you do to Derek, Geoffrey? Where is he?"

He pulled his cap back on his head. "Nothing. I did nothing. What could I do? He was acting like an idiot. I left. I needed to get help to Clare. That's all that mattered."

He looked up and down the river before turning and walking back towards the truck where Simon was waiting. Diane followed.

"Geoffrey! Wait!"

He stopped. She placed her hand on his arm again.

"It's not true," she said. "Derek is delusional. He's not himself. After the accident . . . it's not true. You have to believe me."

He nodded.

"We shouldn't talk about this, Geoffrey. Not to the others. At least until—"

Geoffrey stared at her, brow creased, bobbed his head and they walked on.

Twenty-Eight

With Clare drifting in and out of sleep, the hours passed slowly for Faye. She was entertained for a while by a pair of courting doves. Their foreplay began when they perched on a branch a short distance apart and preened themselves quietly. After a few minutes, the cock turned his head towards the hen and scooted a little closer to her, cooing as he did. She continued combing her feathers with her bill. Emboldened, he leaned towards her, pushing his beak at hers. At first, it seemed to Faye that the male was trying to engage his mate in an awkward first kiss but then, when the hen responded by placing her beak inside his, it became more of a feeding mimicry. The pecking motion continued until the hen fluttered down and landed on the ground. The cock followed and, continuing to flap his wings directly about the female, mounted her. Faye looked away out of respect for the birds' privacy.

She crawled out of the shelter to stretch her legs a few times, but never ventured far. For a while, she leaned against a mossy tree, which, while it had fallen and now rested on the forest floor, wasn't dead. Somehow, it had hung on to life by either growing new roots or sending those that had not been pulled from the earth deeper. Faye looked at its branches. They were verdant and strong, finding their way up to the light. Things are not always as they seem, she thought. Things that fall can rise again.

As she rested against the tree, Faye examined herself. In addition to the bloodstains, now a faded brown, her clothing was discoloured by mud and decaying vegetation. She imagined standing beneath a hot shower, washing the grime and tension from her body. How good, once Clare was safe, it would be to wash and eat. She glanced at the orange, the last of the food, lying next to Clare. Her stomach grumbled, but she knew she'd have to be okay without it.

When she noticed Clare's eyelids fluttering against her cheeks, Faye slid back into the shelter alongside the girl. With every hour that passed, Clare seemed to fade. Faye tried not to imagine what might be happening to her if, as she feared, her organs were being starved of oxygen. She had barely managed a few sips of water since sunrise and her breathing was increasingly laboured.

Faye had read somewhere that it was possible for a person to survive for about three weeks without food, provided they had shelter and water. But that was unlikely to be the case if they were injured and, as in Clare's case, if the injuries caused respiratory distress. Faye felt the panic rise again.

Stop it, she thought. We are not going to be here for much longer. Stay calm. Help is on its way. Focus on what you can do; what might help and inspire hope.

"Can I tell you what I've discovered about myself during the past two days? How you've helped me? Would you be interested in hearing my ramblings now?" she said.

The girl opened her eyes and blinked. Even that, it seemed, took effort. "Yes. Of course." Her words were quiet and interspersed with shallow breaths.

"Will you try and eat some orange while you listen?"

"Okay."

Faye peeled the orange. Its sweet citrus scent made her mouth water. She swallowed the saliva and spoke.

"For a long time, I bought into the belief—not mine, but one that was deftly sold to me—that I am a fearful person. I let it block me, stop me from being who I was and from becoming who I should be."

She fed Clare a segment. The girl chewed it slowly. Her eyes began to water.

"What is it?" asked Faye. "Is it painful?"

Clare gulped, her eyes closed. "Yes. But . . . don't . . . stop," she said. "I can do it if you keep talking and distract me."

"Are you sure?"

"Sure."

She opened her mouth and nodded. Faye popped another segment between her lips.

"Okay. Well, being with you, seeing how brave you are—I mean, starting with you choosing to sleep outside at Heuningbos that first night—and also having to go into the wilderness on my own has proved to me what I may have always known but couldn't acknowledge: I am not afraid. I am not a fearful woman. I can be alone and do things. I am capable and I am brave, brave enough to make some changes. You've shown me that."

Clare blinked. Faye gave her another piece of fruit. She chewed it slowly and closed her eyes as she swallowed it. Then she looked at Faye.

"I'm not brave, but thank you. What . . . what are you going to do? What will you change?"

"I'm going to live alone, find a job and get a dog."

"Oh? You're . . . you and Derek?"

"We won't be together. No."

They were still for a moment.

"I don't know if I should be happy about being the one who inspired you to, erm, leave Derek. I mean, it somehow doesn't—"

"It should have happened decades ago. I would say, Derek and I should never have married, but then I wouldn't have Zach and that is unthinkable."

Clare's mouth lifted in a tiny smile. "Then I am happy for you. But perhaps don't mention to anyone that you think I had anything to do with the decision. I've done enough to disappoint my folks."

"Ah, Clare, you've got to give up on that notion. About your folks and you disappointing them. But, fair enough, I won't lay the blame for my decision at your door."

Faye took the girl's hand. "Can I give you some advice now? I mean, I've reached an important point in my life on this trip and I'd like to think that things might change for you too. Can I?"

Clare gave a small nod.

"You spoke about Mark earlier and said how, after you'd been running with him and talking, you felt good. And normal. Well, I thought about it afterwards. About how determined you are to get through your illness on your own. I wondered if the feeling you had with Mark isn't a clue to how it might be for you if you *did* accept help. Do you understand what I mean?"

"I'm not sure."

"Well, what you had with Mark was a kind of therapy, wasn't it?" She didn't respond.

"He encouraged you to speak about yourself and your illness. It made you feel better. Perhaps you were even able to eat more after being with him?"

"Yes, sometimes."

"So maybe, if you think of therapy in terms of what you had with Mark, you might reconsider getting help to get better."

"But Mark was a friend, not a therapist."

"Yes, that's true. So perhaps you'll consider another related angle?" Faye glanced at Clare. Her eyes were closed.

"Shall I stop talking? Is it too much?"

"No," whispered the girl. "It's okay. Don't stop."

"Okay. The other angle; don't give up on your friendship with Mark. It's not only that he allows you to talk, but he also takes you out of yourself. You said he makes you laugh. You look forward to being with him. I don't know much about your illness, but I do know that, like other similar illnesses, it makes the sufferer very insular, inward-looking. When you care about someone else, that person crowds out some of those thoughts. Thoughts about others take up time and space and energy. Your own fears and worries have to make way. And sometimes that's not a bad thing."

She looked at Clare again. She hadn't opened her eyes. Had the talking tired her out completely? Faye was silent until she felt Clare's hand move under hers as if to say, "Go on."

"But maybe you came to that realisation yourself already?" said Faye. "That's what you mean about not wanting to be alone anymore, isn't it?"

"Yes. If I can . . . when I can . . . I'll call Mark. He's in Durban now, but still—"

Faye swallowed. There was lump in her throat.

"If he's the kind of friend I think he is, it doesn't matter where he is." She let out a shuddery breath. "We meet so many people in our lives. Many become friends, but only a few remain friends. When you come across remarkable people, people you imagine being friends forever, you should do whatever it takes to keep them in your life."

"Thanks, Faye."

"Hmm? For what?"

"Everything."

Twenty-Nine

Bev and Helen were sitting on a bench opposite the main rangers' office, the rays of the late afternoon sun on their backs, when Simon drove the big Land Cruiser into the parking area. Acknowledging the women with a quick wave, he and Geoffrey hurried into the office, closing the door behind them. The women stood to meet Diane and Bruce as they made their way across the dusty lawn.

"No sign of Derek then?" asked Bev.

"You heard?" said Bruce.

Bev nodded. "The rangers told us they've sent a team to the cabin to keep looking. They'll stay the night if necessary."

Bruce looked towards the road. "We passed them on the way here. Simon said there will be divers too, if necessary. Tomorrow. When the water subsides."

They were silent as the three women sat on the bench.

"And Clare?" asked Bruce, still looking into the distance. "Did you hear anything more about her? The helicopter?"

Bev ran her fingers through her hair. "Just that they were in touch with a few hospitals. Trying to arrange it. Before nightfall. Did you ... erm ... say anything to Geoffrey about Derek? I mean, his knowing about the storm?"

Diane glanced at Bruce, nodding. "He didn't say anything. He's
. . . he's worried about Clare."

A flock of Cape weavers, their nests hanging like grassy baubles
in a tree behind the main office, flitted and chatted noisily among
the branches as they prepared for the night. For a while, the group
watched the birds.

"What do you think? Where is Derek?" said Helen.

When there was no reply, she glanced at her friends. "Bruce?
Diane?"

Diane stared at her boots, giving her head a small shake.

"We've got to believe that he found a way to get across the river
and has gone to help Faye with Clare," said Bruce. "When the helicopter
arrives, they'll radio back and we'll hear that he's with them."

Diane glanced at her husband, but remained silent.

"You don't think so?" asked Helen, looking at her.

"I don't know what to think. I saw the river. It was impassable
today. I can't imagine him crossing it yesterday. It doesn't seem—"

Bruce cut her off. Even so, his voice was subdued, as if he wasn't
convinced by his own words. "He could have found another place—
somewhere that was easier to get across."

"Or he decided—who knows why—not to wait and is trying to
make his way to us, here," offered Helen. "Did Geoffrey say how he
was? I mean, was Derek feeling stronger? Up to taking on the escape
route?"

All eyes were on Diane. She was looking at her boots again. "He
didn't seem up to much," she muttered. "Geoffrey was surprised that
he got as far as the river."

"But that was yesterday," said Bruce. "It's possible he's feeling
better today."

"Oh God, I hope he's okay," said Bev, laying her head on Helen's
shoulder. "I hope they're all okay. Let this nightmare be over."

The office door opened and Geoffrey emerged. He paused
on the stair and looked around as if he'd stepped into a world he

didn't recognise. His eyes settled on his friends and he approached, shoulders hunched and feet dragging.

"The helicopter is on its way," he said, scratching his head. "It'll be there at any moment. We'll know if . . . have news soon, I hope."

"Thank God," said Bev.

"Will they take Faye, too? And . . . Derek? If he's with them? To the hospital, I mean?" asked Bruce.

"They don't know for certain but it's unlikely. I asked. It's a rescue helicopter. Only has space for the pilot, co-pilot, two medics and one patient. I'm sorry."

"How was Faye, Geoffrey? When you saw her at the river yesterday?" asked Bev.

"She seemed okay. She had some scratches from a bush but said she was okay. Worried about Clare. Very worried."

Helen stood, walked to Geoffrey and placed a hand on his shoulder. "They'll be okay. All of them. We have to believe that," she said. "Clare will get to hospital and recover. The others will make it to Heuningbos and wait until the vehicles can reach them there."

"Yes," said Geoffrey. "When Derek gets to Faye, she'll take care of him."

"When will you contact Michelle? To tell her about Clare?"

"When we know more. Simon will tell us."

Thirty

The sun was low and the forest lively with the sounds of birds roosting. Faye tried telling herself Clare would be strong enough to withstand another night without medical care, but she couldn't silence her doubt. Sometimes she thought she heard breaks in the girl's breathing, just as the hospice nurse had described. She'd lean forward and place her cheek close to Clare's mouth to feel her breath on her skin. It was light, but was there. Her chest barely moved but Faye told herself that it was because Clare was breathing as shallowly as possible to protect herself from the pain. Even so, the stillness was disconcerting.

With the water bottle almost empty—Faye had drunk most of it—and aware of how quickly it would grow dark, she was about to wake Clare and tell her she was going to try and find more water when she heard the distinctive *chuff, chuff, chuff* sound of a helicopter in the distance. She scrambled out of the shelter, clenching her jaw to prevent herself from calling out before she was certain. The sound grew louder and there was a noisy flutter as the birds fled the trees. Faye crouched in the entrance of the shelter and placed her hands around Clare's ankles. She barely opened her eyes.

"They're here!" said Faye, unable to stop her voice from trembling. Clare said nothing. Her eyes were closed again.

"I'm going to let them know where we are," said Faye, gently squeezing her legs. "You're going to be okay. Lie still. I'll be back."

Heart thumping loudly in her ears, Faye ran through the trees and into the opening towards the sound. The helicopter was hovering above the sandy patch: they'd seen the cross she'd made the day before using branches and rocks. She waved her arms frantically, her knees almost giving way when she saw two people wave back.

When the engine died and the rotor blade slowed, the door opened. A woman with a huge backpack, followed by a man carrying a stretcher, lit up the veld with their red and white overalls. They ran to Faye.

"You're okay?" said the woman.

"Yes, but Clare . . . my friend—"

"There are two of you?"

Faye turned. "Come. This way."

The paramedics followed her to the shelter. The woman—Faye heard her colleague address her as Gcina—knelt at Clare's side. The girl was motionless.

"Tell us what happened. What you know," she said, glancing at Faye and opening her bag.

Faye took a deep breath and explained. The paramedics asked her several questions and when the man bent to go into the shelter, too, Faye stumbled backwards and sat on the ground. For a moment, she imagined she might float away over the trees and out of sight. Then she felt a hand on her shoulder. Another person, the pilot, she assumed, was crouching alongside her.

"Are you okay?" he asked.

She nodded.

"When did you last eat?" called Gcina from the shelter, where she and her colleague were busy with Clare.

"I don't know," said Faye.

Gcina glanced at the pilot. "Tim, fetch the Tupperware container near my seat in the heli. There are some sandwiches in it."

"Mine is there, too," said her partner.

The pilot left. Faye leaned forward to try and see what they were doing, but the paramedics crouched over Clare, blocking the view.

"Is she okay?" she called.

Gcina glanced at her, but said nothing.

Tim returned, carrying a sandwich box and flask. Gcina beckoned him to her and spoke to him quietly. He nodded and went to Faye.

"Can you stand? Walk?"

"Yes."

He held out his hand and helped her up. "Come. Let's get out of the trees."

Faye looked towards Clare. Gcina caught her eye.

"Go with him," she said.

"But—"

Faye wanted to resist. She should stay with Clare. She promised Geoffrey she would. Why didn't they want her there? What were they doing to the girl? She stood her ground but Tim steered her forward.

"Please," he said. "Come. For your friend's sake."

She felt numb as she allowed herself to be guided away. Was it too late to save Clare? Was she already dead? She heard loud sobbing and it was only when Tim glanced at her that she realised it was coming from her.

They sat on the path on the edge of the forest. Tim handed her a sandwich. She ate, oblivious to what it tasted like. He poured tea from the flask. It was warm and sugary. She continued to cry, quietly now.

"What's happening?" she asked. "Is she . . . why couldn't I stay with Clare?"

"It's procedure," said Tim, not looking at her. "It makes it easier, less risk of upsetting the patient."

"Will she be okay?"

"Gcina and Vusi are incredible. They'll do everything they possibly can for her."

The co-pilot made his way to them from the helicopter and he and Tim stood aside, talking quietly. Without realising she was doing it, Faye ate another sandwich and drank more tea. The sun was all but gone, leaving the fynbos and trees bathed in purple and pink. How long had it been since the helicopter arrived? Why were Gcina and Vusi taking so long with Clare? Or were they? Faye had lost track of time.

She stared into the distance, trying to imagine how she'd felt when she first walked here four days before. Or was it five days? The sound of footsteps made her turn around.

The paramedics approached, carrying a stretcher between them. Faye stood up. Clare was covered, a transparent mask over her nose and mouth. She didn't move. The pilots ran towards the helicopter.

"Is she okay?" asked Faye, keeping pace with Gcina.

"We're doing our best," she replied. "Stay here. I'll come back to you when we have her safely in the cabin."

She watched from a distance as they got Clare inside. The four chatted a while before Gcina returned to Faye.

"Are you sure you are all right?" she asked, glancing at Faye's neck and dirty shirt.

"Yes, I'm certain. It was hunger . . . earlier, I mean."

Gcina nodded. "Listen, we have a bit of a problem. We—"

Faye's heart leapt. "But she—"

Gcina placed her hand on Faye's shoulder. "Listen to me. Your friend's lung has partially collapsed. She's in a bad way. We need to get her to the hospital quickly. But there's more."

"What?" Faye wasn't sure she wanted to hear the answer.

"We weren't told there were two of you. And, well, it's a small helicopter. We're at capacity with your friend."

"It's okay. Go," said Faye, relief flooding over her. She hadn't, she realised, imagined getting into the chopper herself at all.

Gcina squinted at her. "I could stay here with you until the others come back . . . probably tomorrow."

"No. You must go. You need to be with Clare. I'm fine. I'll walk to the hut."

"Hut?"

"The hikers' hut. Heuningbos. It's less than two hours from here. Easy hike. I know the way. There's food there, dry clothes. I'll go and wait until the rangers get to me tomorrow. Or whenever."

"Are you sure?"

"Yes. I've eaten now. I'll be okay. Please. Don't delay. Take Clare."

Gcina looked uncertain. She glanced at the purpling sky. "Do you have a torch?"

"Not with me."

There was a whining sound as the helicopter started up behind them. Gcina trotted back and spoke to the men.

"You're a brave woman," she said when she returned to Faye and handed her a small torch. "You're sure there's food there?"

"Thanks. I'll be fine."

"Tim has radioed the rangers' office. They know you'll be there so hopefully will arrive early tomorrow."

"Thank you. Just one thing. Do you know about the others? Are they all okay?"

"I'm sorry. We came directly from town. Given this location and told to collect one injured patient. Nothing more. We could radio now."

"No. Don't worry. It's okay. You must get going. I'll find out tomorrow."

The rotor was spinning. Gcina seemed reluctant to go.

"Can I give you a quick hug?" she asked Faye.

The women embraced briefly and Faye followed her closer to the helicopter, crouching and peering in at Clare, who lay facing the door. Her eyes were closed, her face pale and translucent. She showed no sign of life.

Thirty-One

The narrow wall outside the cottage the friends had been allocated near the rangers' office was just large enough for them to sit on. Bruce had finally convinced Geoffrey to eat and drink something by the time they saw Simon approaching, his head bowed. The group straightened their backs as one. They stared at him, trying to read his posture.

He looked up and said, "She's on her way to hospital in Mossel Bay. They'll let us know as soon as the doctors have had a chance to examine her."

"But she's okay? Stable?" asked Geoffrey, getting to his feet.

"The paramedics did what they could on site. They're unable to say anything more at this stage."

"Did they have to . . . to intubate her?"

Simon nodded.

Geoffrey walked backwards, leaned against the wall and placed his head in his hands. Bruce put a hand on his shoulder. "She'll be okay, Geoffrey. They got there in time."

"What about Faye?" asked Diane. "Is she with them?"

"No. No room on the helicopter. Apparently she was okay. She's walking back to Heuningbos," said Simon. "We'll find a way to get to her tomorrow."

"No word about Derek then?" asked Bruce. "At Grootkloof or with Faye?"

"No. No sign of him. The medics didn't see him but neither did they ask Faye about him. They didn't know to ask. I'm sorry. It's all been a bit confusing and rushed. We'll resume the search for him tomorrow. We're in touch with the team at Grootkloof. They'll let us know immediately if he pitches up."

The group was quiet.

Simon addressed Geoffrey. "Do you want to call your wife now?"

The friends watched as the two men walked away. As the door closed, Helen placed her hands on her head as if in surrender.

"It's not good news, is it? Not about Clare or Derek," said Bev.

Bruce sighed. "She'll be okay. She has to be. Derek? He might still be on his way. He'd walk slowly. Or he's realised he can't go on and is waiting somewhere on the trail. The ravine from the river is steep, slow going. They'll find him tomorrow. He—"

"I'll go to the hospital with Geoffrey," said Diane, as if to herself.

Her husband looked at her, his forehead creased. "What? Well—"

"He's finished, exhausted. Someone has to go with him—to drive."

"We don't know that he's going to want to go tonight. It's a long drive. Let's see what—"

"He will want to go tonight. And he should. He needs to be with Clare," said Diane, looking into the distance.

"I'll go with him," said Bruce, taking her hand. "You're knackered, too. It's been a tough few days for us all."

She shuddered. "God! And it's not over yet. Okay. You go. I'll need to be here for Faye."

"And Derek," said Bruce.

The women said nothing.

Thirty-Two

Faye stood, rooted to the spot, as the helicopter disappeared into the sky. It flew over the Bloukrans and, quite possibly, directly above the spot where Clare had fallen. How Faye had longed for the paramedics to tell her everything was fine. To say she had done an excellent job taking care of Clare and that she would recover without complications. During the day, as she'd waited for the rescue, she'd imagined her relief when Clare was on her way to hospital. Instead, she felt bereft. Like a child might if she woke to find no gifts on Christmas morning. It was hard to be hopeful in the wake of Gcina and Vusi's worried faces.

With the machine gone, the silence of the wilderness was restored. Faye looked around the field of fynbos. To her left, tufts of copper-tipped reeds bent with the weight of their knobbly brown seeds. Behind them, a family of squat protea trees, heavy with pine cone-like fruit, stood solid in the windless evening. She looked towards the mountains and felt her heart swell. The wilderness was not without, but within her. She thought about what Clare had said about not wanting to leave. She felt the same. How was it possible to stand in the middle of nowhere and yet, feel at home?

The light was fading and she knew she should get going. As she walked through the trees to pack her backpack, she silently thanked them. It seemed that they—the tall and straight, thick and gnarly, thin and supple and every tree in between—had not only sheltered her and Clare, but also revealed to her a sanctuary she'd take away and keep forever. The Faye leaving the forest wasn't the Faye who'd arrived there.

She slid her arms through the straps and settled the bag on her back. The cavern beneath the branch seemed large and chilly without Clare in it. Faye wondered what animals might come by and whether they'd venture in, curious about the shape and scent of the place. She unwound the cable of ivy she'd used to tie back the branch responsible for funnelling the water into the shelter when she built it. The branch slowly swung back to where it had been with, Faye imagined, a sigh and a dirty look.

"Sorry, but thanks," she said.

Faye was almost at the path when she saw the scarred tree. At first, she thought the series of strange stripes on its bark were lichen. As she drew closer, she saw that it was as if someone had taken an axe to the tree, striking it in several groups of four or five longitudinal, parallel blows halfway up the tree. Halfway up the tree? Wasn't that where Clare said leopards clawed tree trunks? She peered closer. Yes. Claw marks. They were the claw marks of the leopard Clare had spoken of. Faye's heart raced as if she'd drunk too much coffee. She looked around. The forest was still but the shadows were long and the light dimming.

"I am not a fearful woman. I can be alone and do things. I am capable and I am brave," she said, almost running from the trees.

Once out of the forest and in the open, where the shadows were shorter and fewer, Faye felt calmer. It was, she thought, an evening as still and clear as the first night the group had spent on the trail. She thought about that night and how she'd sat outside, alone, after Derek had gone to bed, annoyed with her for reasons she'd forgotten. How she'd envied Clare's bravery. She'd almost come full circle. No. She'd gone much further than that. She'd reached a place she didn't know existed.

The path to Heuningbos was familiar and, even by night, she could anticipate the rise and fall of the earth beneath her feet, when the surface went from smooth to rough, where the large boulders were and at what point the grass and shrubs would brush against her legs. She looked across the veld and felt the thuds of her boots beating to the rhythm of her heart. She couldn't remember ever having felt as connected to the world. The hours of isolation and the time she'd spent with Clare had altered her. The wilderness, which at first had frightened her, had become her ally.

There was no moon to light the way, but Faye didn't use the torch Gcina had given her. Instead, she kept her eyes on the path which unfolded before her like a sandy ribbon. The night air was rich with the minty scent of wild rosemary. Rosemary. Faye remembered Zach chopping fresh rosemary from the garden as he helped her prepare Sunday lunch.

"It'll add a lemony-pine taste," he'd explained, sprinkling the herbs over the potatoes, which were ready for roasting.

She felt a tug at her chest and imagined her son's strong, welcoming embrace. She knew she could rely on him.

Faye was still thinking about Zach when she saw a large shadow move towards a bush a few metres away from the path. She froze. It had disappeared but she could hear the *tip-tip-tip* sound of something walking. She stared towards the dark vegetation. Was something stalking her? The leopard? Should she use the torch? She slowly reached into her pocket to remove it. The animal stepped into a space between the plants and paused.

She noticed its ears first. They were rabbit-like but longer, narrower and stood erect, pointing high above its rounded back. The animal had a long, pig-like snout and a strange kangaroo-shaped tale. An aardvark. Nocturnal vacuumer of termites. Faye and the aardvark looked at one another for several seconds and then, without undue hurry, the animal continued walking. Faye, breathing once more, watched it go.

"Nice to meet you," she whispered into the night.

Faye imagined telling Clare about the aardvark and how she'd believed that it might be a leopard.

"Please, make that possible," she said.

She pictured how they'd laugh—Clare able to do so without restraint by then—as they agreed how far she had come since fleeing from the pigs just a few days earlier. How incredible it was that she, the woman who had panicked at the sight of a few wild pigs, had seen baboons, Knysna loeries, eagles, duiker, aardvark and the claw marks of a leopard, and had lived to love to tell the tale. How was it possible so much had changed for her in so short a time, when it had taken so long for her to see the truth that lay between her and Derek? How was it possible that putting the wilderness between them would bring such clarity?

She remembered the look on her husband's face when she'd called his name at the river. For a moment, she'd thought he was pleased to see she had returned and her anger had subsided. He limped to the bank and called across to her.

"Thank God you've come back," he shouted. "Help me get across so that I can get to Clare."

"What? Don't be ridiculous. You cannot cross." She felt the anger rise again like bile.

"I can. At the rope." He gestured upstream. "I did it two days ago. Even rescued Di."

"I'm not going to help you cross, Derek. I want to—"

"Then why did you return? What are you doing here? Oh, I get it. You don't want me near Clare. You're jealous and insecure—"

"Stop it! I don't know what's going on and why you would tell Geoffrey that Clare was your daughter—"

He froze for moment. "Because she—"

"No! I don't want to hear it. I don't care about that now." Faye was shouting, her hands over her ears.

"What? I don't—"

"Shut up and listen to me, Derek. I came back to tell you that I no longer want to be married to you. I want a divorce."

"Have you gone mad, woman? How—"

"No, I have finally come to my senses. There's no time now to discuss the details but that's my decision and I wanted you to know it today. Here. Now. So that I can celebrate my release in the wild."

"The wild? What are you—"

"I am sure you will do your level best to make this difficult for me, but you're that side and I am this side and I am going to walk away now and picture my life without you."

"No! Faye! You're insane." He started laughing. The pitch was unusually high for Derek. There was a hysteria to it that made her realise there was something more to his behaviour.

He gasped and shouted, "Go to the rope and help me across."

"Have you been drinking? What else have you taken?"

He ignored her, hobbling upstream to where the ropes bounced on the water, and then inching his way down the bank towards the water.

"Derek! Don't be stupid!"

The water, reeds and large boulders made it difficult for Faye to walk upstream. By the time she got to the rope, Derek had waded into the water up to his thighs and was holding onto the rope with two hands.

"Get out!" she screamed, grabbing onto the other side of the cable.

He stopped, stared into the water and then raised his eyes to meet hers. His were hooded, glassy-looking.

"I can make it," he said, his voice shrill now. "Get to her before Geoff. Rescue her."

"Don't be an idiot. Get out of the water and go to the cabin. Sleep off whatever you have in your system. Wait for the rangers. I have to get back to Clare."

"No! I'm coming with you!"

He took another step into the water, lost his footing and stumbled, sinking to his chest.

"Derek!" she screamed.

He pulled himself up using the rope, and began laughing again.

"Get out!" she shouted, angrier than ever. "If you don't turn around and get out of the river, I will tell everyone how you ignored the rangers' warnings about the rain and created this whole mess."

He stared at her.

"You're pathetic, Faye. 'I will tell everyone . . .' What are you, three?"

"Get out of the river."

Derek loosely held onto the rope with one hand. Despite having stumbled, he ignored the fact that if he slipped or if the rope jerked suddenly and he was unable to hold onto it, he'd be swept downstream and almost certainly drown. Faye held onto the rope from the other side, as if it might help. He looked at her, his mouth twisted in a sneer.

"Get out of the river," she repeated.

He ignored her. "And you know what the most pathetic thing is? You don't have the guts to say anything. You'll *never* say a word against me. You don't have it in you."

Fury flowed through her like a fire fanned free.

With the smooth, sandy path becoming increasingly rocky and twisty, Faye slowed down and began the steep descent towards the stream. As the single track followed the curve of the hill, she noticed a dim light in the distance. She held still, trying to place it. The river was below, the bridge slightly to the right and Heuningbos a few hundred metres behind on the other hillside. The light appeared to come from the hut. Her heart skipped. Had the rangers managed to get there after all? Her friends? Surely they would've come looking for her if that was the case? Or had they just got there? And if it wasn't the rangers or her friends, who could it be?

"I am not a fearful woman. I can be alone and do things. I am capable and I am brave," she whispered again as, choosing not use the torch to light the way, she carefully made her way down the hill.

But the calm Faye felt earlier had vanished. Even as she tried to convince herself that there was no reason to believe that anyone would want to harm her, she stepped slowly over the bridge, placing her boots on the wood as lightly as possible. As she crept low towards the cabin, she saw that the door was closed and that the light was shining from the small front window. She slipped her backpack from her shoulders and laid it on the path before stealing across the lawn to the lapa.

The room was a cavernous, black space. Faye planned to grab the iron fire prodder but, as she slunk up the stairs, she saw that she would be unable to locate the prodder in the dark. She peered towards the cabin. Once she was behind the walls of the lapa, she'd be able to switch on her torch undetected.

Two steps in, she pushed the button. As the bright light lit the stone walls, there was a loud flapping from above. Faye gasped and ducked as a bevy of bats flew from the room. She waited a moment, shaking with fear. After the noise died down and when there were no other sounds, she crept towards the wall where the prodder stood.

Grasping the metal rod at her side in her cold, clammy hands, she paused at the top of the stairs after she'd switched off the torch, and let her eyes adjust to the dark. She took a deep breath, descended the stairs and tiptoed towards the cabin. She inched along the wall towards the window and peeped in.

The room was exactly as she'd left it earlier. The beds were bare, the bags lined up in the centre of the room adjacent to the food supplies that she'd brought in after the visit by the baboons.

The light came from one of the cooler boxes, the flashy one with the battery, digital panel and inside light, which Michelle had bought and sent with Geoffrey and Clare. Somehow, the lid had popped open and the light had come on. Faye chuckled, her legs wobbly with relief, as she recalled the young baboon running her tongue across the lid with its buttons and knobs.

Thirty-Three

The sun's rays were touching the tops of the trees when Faye woke up the next morning. It had occurred to her as, washed and fed, she'd dragged a mattress onto the lawn the night before, that she'd wake up much later. Exhaustion had imbued every cell of her body and she'd slept deeply, dreamlessly. Even so, the lightening sky, cloudless today, and the calls of the birds roused her. She was, she thought, in tune with her surroundings and even some of the creatures she now knew existed there.

The short time she'd either been alone or with Clare in the wilderness had taught her that it was possible to unlock a part of herself and let the world in. The unlocking had also set some things free, and it was good. It was possible, she thought, that the nature within her was as beautiful as the nature around her.

Being with Clare had also shown her how pointless it was to compare herself to others. She wasn't Michelle or anyone else. She was Faye and the only person she should compare herself to was who she was before and how she might have changed since then. She'd taken so long to learn that. But still, it wasn't too late. Wiser Faye would be kind to herself, do her best and know that was enough. She knew life could be hard, but also that what she perceived it to be wasn't always the same as what it really was. She'd find a way to accept that the past was heavy, but that she didn't have to carry it with her for the rest of her life. She'd put it down and try to forgive herself for lugging it for so long.

She gazed at the cloudless sky and the trees, which today were motionless. The red breasted birds she'd spotted the morning she and Clare walked to the stream hopped about on the lawn. The hadedas were back too, but the baboons were nowhere to be seen or heard. Faye wondered if it would be possible to find somewhere to live beyond suburbia so she could wake to similar peace and see the world afresh every morning.

Showered and dressed, she drank coffee in the sun on the lapa stairs. On one hand, she wished that there was a way of finding out how Clare was. On the other, she was grateful that there wasn't; as long as she didn't know, she could continue to hope for the best.

"Be alive, Clare," she said. "For after all, life is all we have."

She heard the rumble of an engine and the sound of wheels struggling over the dongas. Faye stood near the cabin and watched as a Land Cruiser approached. A young man climbed out, and shaking her hand, introduced himself as Simon. He and his colleagues, he explained, had managed to pile sacks of sand over the river to create a temporary causeway safe enough to drive across.

"Do you have news of Clare? My friend who was helicoptered to hospital last night?" asked Faye.

"They were unable to operate last night. The doctors said they needed to stabilise her first," he said. "I left early this morning. My colleague said she'd radio as soon as they have news. Nothing yet."

Faye was quiet as Simon helped her load the bags and supplies into the vehicle.

"Geoffrey and Bruce drove to the hospital last night," he said. "The others are waiting at our offices for you."

She pushed the final bag into the cab without responding.

"Hopefully, when we get back to the office there'll be some good news," Simon continued.

Faye nodded and climbed into the vehicle.

⇥⇤

Diane, Bev and Helen were sitting on the bench when Simon pulled up. They jumped to their feet and hurried to the car, embracing Faye as she stood. There were tears and a few words. Simon beckoned Diane. The pair took several steps away from the group together, talking quietly. Diane returned and Simon went into the office.

"Our stuff will be brought to the cottage," said Diane. "Shall we go there? Are you hungry, Faye? Thirsty?"

"No. Thanks. Where's—"

"Faye, there's something I have to tell you—about Derek."

"I know," she said.

"What?" Diane glanced towards the office. "But—"

"He knew about the storm. The rangers warned Derek before we began the hike. They told him we shouldn't leave Heuningbos if there were any signs of bad weather."

Helen and Bev glanced at one another. Diane placed a hand on Faye's shoulder. "Yes. We know. They told us. But it's not that." She hesitated. "Faye, Derek is missing."

"Missing?" Faye leaned back against the car.

"After Geoffrey told us about Clare—Bruce and I were with Simon when we found him on the track on his way here—and Simon had radioed the office to organise the rescue, we went to Grootkloof to fetch him. But Derek wasn't there."

"But that was two days ago."

"Yes."

"And still—"

Diane shook her head. "Simon has gone to find out if there's any news."

"About Clare?"

"And Derek."

Faye stared at the bench beneath the tree where she'd seen Bev, Helen and Diane sitting when they'd driven into the yard. The sight of their faces had brought her comfort. For a moment, she'd forgotten that without Derek in her life, they might disappear.

"Do you want me to come with you?" asked Diane.

"Where?"

"Simon said he could take you to Grootkloof."

Faye looked down. "I don't know."

"Do you want to go? I'll come with you."

"Thank you. Yes. I guess so."

"They've also sent a party to start searching from Heuningbos," said Bev.

"Heuningbos? But I was just there."

"It's possible he's in the vicinity . . . that he crossed the river and was trying to get to you and Clare."

Faye nodded.

"That's where Bruce thinks he is. On his way to you," said Helen.

Faye gave a half shrug.

Diane bent forward, trying to catch her friend's eyes. "Where do you think he is?" she asked.

"When I last saw him, he was holding onto the rope. I told him to go back to the cabin."

"Holding onto the rope?" Diane raised her brows. "Where was Geoffrey at that point."

"He'd gone. Left to find help."

"But, are you sure?"

"Yes. Why? Does that seem odd?"

"Geoffrey told me you left before him. That he and Derek had . . . had talked after you went and only then did he leave."

Faye turned and looked into Diane's eyes. The other woman glanced away briefly. So, thought Faye, she knew. Diane knew what Derek had said to Geoffrey.

"I did leave," said Faye, holding Diane's gaze. "I walked away. Along the path past the reeds. And then I turned back. When I got to the river, Geoffrey had gone. I saw him turning onto the track towards the cabin. Derek was still at the river."

"Then he went to the rope?"

"Yes. He said he wanted to get across so that he could help Clare. I told him it was impossible and said he should go back to the cabin and wait."

"Did he?" whispered Diane.

"I don't know, Diane. The river was between us. I told him to go back and that I had to return to Clare. I left."

Diane nodded. "Why did . . . why did you turn back? Go back to the river after you left the first time?"

"I wanted to tell Derek that I—"

"Ahem. Excuse me." It was Simon.

The women turned to look at him.

"I'm sorry, but I have bad news."

Thirty-four

Faye watched Michelle walk to the bank opposite the rope. Although she'd never been there before, there was no doubt Michelle had heard the story often enough to picture the scene. Even so, it must've been unsettling for her to stand alongside the Bloukrans River and imagine her husband and friends taking it on in full flood. On the other hand, perhaps it was hard to imagine. There was nothing fierce about the river now. Gurgling and bouncing over the rocks, the water was clear and shallow. It was safe to cross at multiple points both up and downstream.

Geoffrey walked to his wife and placed an arm over her shoulder. She nestled against him.

Bev, Helen, Diane and Bruce ambled through the trees and stood with Faye where the track ended at the edge of the forest. It was exactly two years since the four of them, Geoffrey and Derek had clung to the rope and crossed the river with the rain bucketing down. Diane took Bruce's hand.

They were surprised when Faye emailed them and asked if they'd like to meet at Grootkloof Cabin and complete the hike as something of a commemoration. She'd been in touch with Simon and he'd confirmed that it would be possible. She'd make all the arrangements, she offered, fly to Port Elizabeth from Johannesburg and meet them at the rangers' offices.

None of them had expected Faye to move to Johannesburg. They'd imagined she'd want to stay near her friends. However, she wanted to be where Zach was and said she'd found a job in the city and looked forward to the change. They missed her, they said. Sounding surprised by the fact, she said she missed them too and that the hike would be a good opportunity to reconnect.

They gathered at the river with Michelle and Geoffrey. For a while, they were quiet as they watched a flit of Cape reed warblers dip and dive between the reeds surrounding a large pool above the rope. If it had been warmer and, thought Faye, a different occasion, she, Bev and Helen would almost certainly have stripped down for a swim in the clear, dark water. Maybe tomorrow.

The rhythmic crunch of running shoes on gravel made them turn towards the track. Clare smiled and waved as she ran towards them, her long plait bouncing against her back.

Geoffrey and Michelle had glanced at one another in surprise when Clare told them at Sunday lunch with Angus and Linda that she'd be taking leave from work so she could join them on the hike.

"I didn't know you and Faye were even in touch," said Michelle.

"Of course we are," said her daughter, helping herself to another potato.

Clare had emailed Faye as soon she could after she was discharged from hospital two years earlier. She wanted Faye to know that she was sorry about Derek, and to thank her again for taking care of her. The doctors agreed it would probably have been fatal for Clare to have walked any further than she did after her fall. Faye's decision that they stay in the forest had saved her life. But that wasn't all Clare wanted to say.

Faye's kindness and her sensitivity around Clare's anorexia and her advice, combined with a new urgency in Clare to live her life more fully, had changed the girl's thinking and plans.

While Clare was recovering at home with her parents, her father made it a habit to go to her room to chat to her after work every evening. For a while, they discussed how she was feeling and how his day had been. One evening though, Clare took another tack.

"Dad, are you okay if I ask you some questions about your therapist?"

"Therapist?"

"It's okay. Angus told me you went to someone years ago—because of me."

Geoffrey blinked and reddened. "He shouldn't have told you. Not like that."

"No, I'm glad he did. I'm sorry I put you through it."

He took her hand. "Thank you. But you don't have to apologise. It helped me understand myself and what you were going through."

"Would you recommend your therapist?"

"Yes. Why do you ask?"

"I'd like some help, Dad. To get better quicker. Even if she is not the right person, perhaps she could recommend someone."

Shortly after she began seeing the therapist, Clare phoned Mark. After an hour's conversation, she realised they didn't have to go running to talk. When, a few months later, he visited her however, they agreed that running and talking also still worked. Mark had applied for a transfer to Cape Town and was due to move in a few months.

Clare's initial email to Faye was the start of regular communication between the women. They spoke at least once a week and wrote frequently. Clare knew of Faye's plans to sell up and leave before her parents did and, when she was offered a job, she called Clare straight after she'd told Zach. When Faye found a new home in Johannesburg, Clare asked her about her plans for a dog.

"I'm on my way to SPCA this afternoon," said Faye.

A few days later, a picture of a terrier with a beard pinged into Clare's phone. "She's a schnoodle, I'm told. A schnauzer cross poodle. Her name is Murphy Brown," wrote Faye.

When Faye told her about her idea for completing the hike to commemorate Derek's death, Clare hadn't hesitated.

"Why don't you get Mark to join us?" asked Faye.

"No. Not this time. You'll meet him soon, but not this time."

Later that evening, when the others had walked to the cabin to get started on supper, Faye and Clare sat side by side with their legs dangling over the river bank. Faye's hair was longer and she'd had it cut in a bob. Her friends had admired the new look.

"But still the same Faye—embracing the grey, I see?" quipped Diane.

Clare was several kilograms heavier, but still as lean as a willow because of her running. She and Michelle regularly entered races together where, with their similar physiques and blonde hair, they were sometimes mistaken for sisters, which delighted Michelle.

The late sun cast an orange-pink glow on the mountain peaks. It was cool alongside the river. Clare pulled her sweater on.

"How does it feel, being here?" she asked.

"It seems unreal that only two years have passed. So much has changed in so short a time."

"That's for sure. But you're happy?"

Faye turned to her. "I am."

They were quiet for a moment.

"Mom and Dad worry that you're lonely. So far from your friends and without Derek. I mean, I know you have Zach and Murphy Brown there but—"

"I'm not lonely. It's true that I miss my friends, more than I thought I would. But in many ways, I feel more alive."

Clare smiled.

"Do you remember me telling you about my plans shortly before the helicopter arrived?" asked Faye.

"Yes. Of course."

"You are the only person who knows that I was planning to leave Derek. Did you know that?"

"No."

"The thing is, I'm sorry he died. But I would've been alone now even if he had lived. There was no doubt I would have left him."

Clare nodded.

Faye looked at her. "You never told anyone that I mentioned it?"

"Why would I? I told you things while we were in the forest I know you would never tell anyone else. It was an incredible time. I changed. I think you changed. But what we talked about had nothing to do with anyone else."

"I wondered though, if you ever thought about whether Derek knew I was going to leave him before he drowned. And whether that had anything to do with . . . well, anything. Did you?"

Clare was quiet. Faye looked at her.

"You did?"

"For a while. Yes."

"A while? But then?"

"When I was recovering at my parents' home, I overheard them talking about Derek. My father was pretty cut up about it. He said that he should have made sure that he—Derek, that is—went back to the cabin before he left. He said Derek was irrational. Stoned. Drunk. Saying crazy things."

"Like what?" Faye asked quietly.

"He didn't say. Mom asked but he said it didn't matter. The thing is my father felt terrible, guilty about leaving Derek at the river. Mom said—and this is why I stopped wondering whether you had told Derek that you were leaving him before he tried to cross the river—that Dad shouldn't blame himself. Derek, she said, would never do anything that didn't serve his own needs, regardless of his state of mind."

"She knew him better than anyone," murmured Faye.

"Better than you? You were married to him for more than twenty years."

Faye chuckled. "Oh yes. Much better than me."

Clare looked at her.

Faye went on. "If I'd known him as well as Michelle did, I wouldn't have married him. Or stayed with him. Or allowed him to manipulate me and turn me into someone I didn't know. Or like. Someone I was ashamed off."

"So you're glad he's gone?" asked Clare.

"As I said, I'm not glad he's dead. Even though I think he would have made it difficult for me to leave him, I'm sorry Zach doesn't have a father and I don't believe Derek deserved to die."

"But you're not ashamed of yourself anymore?"

"No. I'm not. Sometimes I feel a little cross for allowing myself to be duped and dominated for so long, but I am not ashamed. What about you? Has that changed for you too?"

Clare sighed. "Yes. You made me realise how stubborn I was being. How I was choking the life out of my life by not letting others in. By not accepting help. I saw that asking for help wasn't weak. It was sensible."

"And the help is helping?"

"What do you think?" Clare glanced down. "I won't pretend I'm one hundred percent fine. I have moments. But they're moments and I can talk about them, and I don't think about myself, my body and food all the time. Sometimes I think about running. Often I think about Mark."

They laughed quietly and Faye placed her arm around Clare's shoulders.

"Then we're both fine. I am so—"

"Shh!" whispered Clare, "Look. On the other side of the river."

Faye looked to where she was pointing. She saw movement between the reeds, the same reeds that she'd hurried past when she left the river two years ago, ignoring Derek's cries.

A leopard, sleek and wary, stepped into the open and onto the rocks. She looked around, her yellow eyes glancing briefly at them, walked to the water's edge, dipped her head and began drinking.

"She came to check on us," murmured Clare.

"And she found us well," said Faye. "Alive and fearless."

Acknowledgments

The idea of writing a story set in the Tsitsikamma came about during a hike there with several dear friends. After our first night in the mountains, one awoke with a debilitating migraine and was not up to hiking that day. She insisted we go on, saying she'd medicate and sleep it off, and hitch a ride to our next stop with the rangers. I was uneasy about leaving her in so remote a place without the ability to communicate with her or the rangers, but she was adamant and we went on without her.

As we walked, I imagined various scenarios, picturing what could go wrong. Nothing did. We were happily reunited that evening and, over the next several days, completed a wonderfully restorative and congenial hike. But the idea of what could have happened under different circumstances, to different people, took root and what grew was this story. As such, I thank my Tsitsikamma hiking friends, Dawie, Didi, Elouise, Lala, Michael, Philip, Rina and Rodney for accompanying me on a most memorable adventure, which, though no one suspected it might, became a book. Where shall we go next?

I am also deeply grateful to my smart, funny and supportive writing group friends, Gail, Justin, Paul and Peter, who encouraged me to keep going because of their enthusiasm and engagement with the story and characters.

Thank you too, to my running friend, Sue, who, while we were active half-marathoners listened, not only to me huffing and puffing alongside her, but also to lengthy literary monologues about who is who in my work-in-progress and what might happen to them—or not. And, to my unofficial business guru-friend, Karen for letting me prattle on about the business of writing and guiding me towards the right decisions, many thanks.

My gratitude too to the Köehler Books team for responding to a submission from an unknown African. To Hannah for seeing enough in the story to pass it to Greg, to Greg for championing it, and to John and Joe for taking it on, and, along with everyone else involved at Köehler Books, for turning it into this—thank you.

Finally, I am eternally grateful to Jan-Lucas, Sebastiaan and Claudia, who nod, smile and encourage me in everything I write— and never roll their eyes when I burst into the room, asking once again, "What do you think. . ."

CPSIA information can be obtained
at www.ICGtesting.com
Printed in the USA
BVHW081702220721
612636BV00008B/444

9 781646 634149